The Threlkeld Theory

The Threlkeld Theory

REBECCA TOPE

Allison & Busby Limited
11 Wardour Mews
London W1F 8AN
allisonandbusby.com

First published in Great Britain by Allison & Busby in 2022.
This paperback edition published by Allison & Busby in 2022.

A CIP catalogue record for this book is available
from the British Library.

10 9 8 7 6 5 4 3 2 1

ISBN 978-0-7490-2861-9

Typeset in 10.5/15.5 pt Sabon LT Pro by
Allison & Busby Ltd

Printed and bound by
CPI Group (UK) Ltd, Croydon, CR0 4YY

Another one for Esther

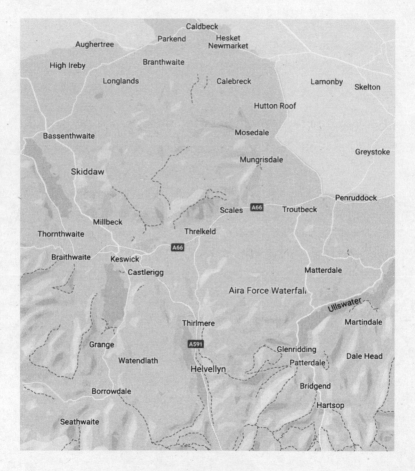

Author's Note

As with other titles in this series, the action is set in real villages. Threlkeld is generally pronounced as 'Threkkled' A few minor liberties have been taken with its layout, as they have with Hartsop.

Chapter One

It happened barely ten minutes before they were due to leave and Angie Straw blamed Russell for it entirely.

'Better have something to eat,' he said. 'It'll be a while before we get anything, otherwise.' So she bit down on a crunchy Hobnob and broke a tooth.

It was the small molar next to the eye tooth on the upper left-hand side. It had been mostly composed of filling and when she spat the debris into her hand, it was more black metal than white tooth. Half-chewed biscuit added more colour. She squealed and ran upstairs to the bathroom mirror. Unlike previous occasions, this time it looked worse than it felt. There was a jagged stump, dark brown in colour, the front wall of the tooth having disappeared completely. Even the smallest smile revealed it in all its horror.

'Does it hurt?' asked Russell when she went downstairs again.

She shook her head, unable to speak. If she made the attempt she feared she might cry. The day was already destined for high emotion – and now everything was condensed into this sudden calamity, which felt not far off the end of the world.

'Just keep your mouth shut and carry on,' her husband quipped, aware of an urgent need to defuse the situation. 'Nobody's going to look at us, are they?'

'Photos,' she mumbled, trying to speak through closed lips.

'It'll be fine. We'll phone the dentist in a quiet moment and get you seen to, probably tomorrow. Come on now, we mustn't be late. I'll drive,' he added heroically.

She found herself partially consoled, despite his culpability in giving her the fatal biscuit. Russell was solidly on her side at all times. After forty-four years, this was more true than it had ever been. Through sheer good fortune and with no special effort, they continued to like each other.

'All right,' she said thickly.

They were going to Keswick, twenty miles north of their home in Windermere, to witness the marriage of their daughter, Persimmon, to Christopher Henderson. It was late July, and the ceremony had been postponed from its original scheduled date in June. Robin, their baby, was now nearly four months old and the light of all their lives. The event had expanded, as such things did, and moved from one town to another as registry offices made difficulties and available bookings turned out to be in short supply.

Christopher had relatives in and around Penrith; he and Simmy lived in Hartsop, which was a lot closer to Keswick than Kendal, which was where they had originally proposed to get married. The Straws lived in Windermere, running a popular B&B business. Logistics and timings had mutated from basic and simple to convoluted and frustrating. All the original arrangements had been changed since April, when the decision to make themselves official had been cemented.

Now the post-wedding party was to be held in Threlkeld, a village close to Keswick, where Christopher's sister, Hannah, had ordained they assemble at the pub for a meal confusingly known (but with perfectly rational historical origins) as 'the wedding breakfast'. Nobody seriously challenged the choice of venue. Parking and navigating would both be easier than in the jumbled, tourist-thronged streets of Keswick and the place had a good garden. They could stay all afternoon. It was a Wednesday and none of the usual evening drunkenness was to be expected. Some people would fit the whole thing into a long lunch hour.

'It's only a tooth,' Angie insisted to herself repeatedly during the drive. It did not exactly hurt, although she was aware that every time she opened her mouth the stump reacted to the incoming air. Russell strove to distract her by pointing out various features along the road. Once they had passed Ambleside, the A591 ran unimpeded northwards all the way to Keswick. The unassuming little Thirlmere on Angie's side of the car was only sparsely dotted with visitors in the scanty parking areas that mostly had to be paid for. The day was dry with hazy cloud.

'Bicuspid,' she said suddenly.

'Excuse me?' This was a recent affectation on Russell's part, copied from an American B&B guest. He relished ridiculous idioms wherever he found them, and adopted them as his own in some cases.

'The tooth. It's a bicuspid. I've been trying to remember the word for the past seven miles.'

'I thought that was something to do with one's heart.'

'Oh. Is it? Now I'm confused.'

11

'We can ask Ben to google it,' said Russell, automatically.

'Don't let me smile,' she begged him. 'Can we arrange a signal for you to stop me?'

'I'll scratch my nose,' he said. 'Although I think you can risk a bit of a smirk, if not a fully-fledged grin.'

'As if a wedding on its own wasn't bad enough,' she grumbled. 'I'll be remembered forever as the crone at the feast. The wicked godmother at the christening party. There's one in every fairy tale.'

'Charlotte Rampling in *Melancholia*,' agreed Russell with a happy sigh. 'How I do love that film. It's so outrageously *true*.'

'Nobody remembers the groom,' said Angie randomly. 'I wonder if Christopher is feeling a bit left out.'

'It comes with the package – the groom being in the shadows, so to speak. But I've been wondering the same thing, now you mention it. Where did those boyish smiles go? I haven't seen him look really unworried for a while now.'

'It'll be the job. And the baby.'

'And getting married. He never was very good with responsibility. Not that I mean to criticise.'

The Straws had known Christopher Henderson from the day he was born. They remembered the little boy and the teenager he had been, before he took off on a prolonged spate of travelling, acquiring and discarding a wife along the way. Now he was back at the centre of their lives, they were enjoying getting to know him again. 'He might be worrying that he'll mess up this marriage like the first one,' mused Angie. 'Do you think?'

'I hope not. This time he's got our girl's happiness in his hands. He'd better get it right.'

Angie was watching the picture-book scenery and wishing the day was over already and her tooth fixed. 'I'd actually rather it would hurt more. Then I could demand a bit of sympathy. As it is, nobody's going to be remotely interested.'

'Nor should they be. This is not our day, old girl. Just remember that.'

Their daughter was wearing a garment that Angie thought of as a 'midi-dress'. It went a few inches below her knees and appeared a trifle heavy for high summer, but it made her look tall and slim and carefree. It was a shade of light brown that Angie could find no name for, with flashes of white here and there. Very short sleeves and a low neck gave Simmy a subtly virginal look, which Angie found disconcertingly moving. At forty, it was no longer correct to think of Simmy as a girl, but Angie and Russell were not even trying to shake the habit.

Christopher Henderson, the groom, was an inch taller than his bride, almost as slender and exactly the same age. The two had met on the day they were born. Nobody would dream of using the word 'incestuous' about their relationship, but it was undeniable that they had a great deal of background in common. He wore a pale grey suit and a pink tie, which made him stand out amongst the small crowd of guests who, on the whole, had not taken a lot of trouble over their clothes. His hair had been cut shorter than quite suited him, but the subtle flashes of auburn were still there.

Angie remembered her envy at the newborn baby's impressive quiff that glinted red in certain lights. Now here he was, waiting with the registrar for the business to begin. His gaze returned repeatedly to the window at the back of the room and the fells beyond, as if he needed to steady himself for a coming ordeal. Angie watched him closely, trying to assess his emotional state. Nervous, she concluded, and uncomfortable. As an auctioneer he was well used to being the centre of attention, so it couldn't be that. No – this was an anxiety about becoming a husband and a parent all at the same time. She sighed impatiently, remembering Christopher's father and how he had fallen short in so many ways. Was his eldest son doomed to follow the same road? Not if Angie Straw could help it, she decided, squaring her shoulders.

Everyone sat down, looking for Russell to bring his daughter into the room. *It's a parody*, Angie thought, to her own surprise. The ceremony struck her as a mangled mashup of the age-old church service with its careful symbolism that fitted so uncomfortably with modern life. The father giving his girl away; the pre-adolescent female children clustering uncomprehendingly around the skirts of the bride; the ribald remarks of the groomsman; the food and drink; the flowers and the music and the dancing. Simmy and Christopher had avoided the worst of it, but with nothing of equal gravitas to take its place, they were forced to comply with the basic pattern. They had selected much of the wording, consistent with the minimal requirements of the law, and let Bonnie go overboard on the flowers. Simmy carried a spectacular bouquet, and every man in sight wore a buttonhole.

The registrar gave a few introductory remarks, which included the word 'contract' more than once. He was a man of about thirty in a nondescript suit who smiled relentlessly. His nose was peeling as if he'd recently been outside a lot without suncream.

Angie explored her tooth with her tongue every few seconds.

'Stop it,' hissed Russell, when he came to sit beside her, having delivered Simmy as required by tradition. 'Leave it alone.'

Angie tried to distract herself by watching her grandson on the lap of his Auntie Hannah in a row full of Henderson relations. Robin was dressed in an outfit that looked vaguely Edwardian – a sailor suit, perhaps. Nobody had consulted Angie about what the infant ought to wear. He was placid by nature and more than happy to be passed from person to person, grabbing at hair or earrings as he went.

The next stage, which appeared to have no time limit to it, involved a lot of standing about in a courtyard while everybody took photos and chatted. Russell dutifully shook hands with everyone, posed for his picture and beamed indiscriminately at Christopher's four siblings whom he had known their whole lives. George Henderson looked unwell and mumbled about having to get home for something important. Eddie, the middle son, stood square and respectable, uttering vague phrases about the day being a long time coming. Hannah and Lynn, the two sisters, bustled and bossed and took almost all the photos.

It was Angie who said, 'Shouldn't we be getting on? The pub's going to wonder where we are.' Which worked rather well, and started a drift to the car park, followed by a procession through the eastern side of Keswick and on to Threlkeld where the Horse and Farrier pub awaited them.

Several people were already there, sitting around tables outside. A hasty welcoming committee was assembled, the couple cheered and more photos were taken. There was an almost indecent haste to get on with the planned proceedings. It was half past one and they had asked for food to be available from one o'clock.

'Sorry,' Angie heard Simmy saying to the man in charge. 'Everything took longer than we thought.'

Sandwiches, cold meat, salads and crisps were laid out on a long table under a gazebo and everybody got a free drink. Guests lined up and filled their plates. Angie had vetoed the making of speeches as one of her very few contributions to the event. But Christopher's brother, Eddie, would take no advice or admonition and stood up on a chair at the end of the buffet table, as people were milling about collecting the food, and spoke a few words. Red-faced and unoriginal, he uttered the usual platitudes and Angie groaned. Louder than intended, as it turned out, and also badly timed, coming at a pause in the speech, so that everyone heard her.

'Hush, woman!' hissed her husband.

Eddie glared and raised a beer glass in a toast.

Simmy went over to her parents. 'We should have had champagne,' she said with a sigh. 'Look at them!'

'It *is* rather informal,' said Russell carefully. 'But none the worse for that. It's lucky we chose this pub, with all this parking space.' He smiled vaguely at all the cars that had fitted themselves into the two areas on either side of the road. His attempt at cheering his daughter was unsuccessful. 'And the weather's just what we ordered,' he tried again.

'Mum thinks it's a shambles,' Simmy accused. 'Don't you?'

'I think no such thing,' Angie replied. 'But if the man had to make a speech, why couldn't he choose a better moment?'

'He meant well. He's got a good heart, as Granny used to say.'

'That's another thing. I'm the oldest woman here – and I don't like it. Everyone else is under fifty.'

'Nonsense. Corinne's nearly sixty, for a start. And Helen.'

'Helen's barely over fifty,' snapped Angie. 'She must have been well under forty when she had those twins.'

Simmy gave the special little frown she used when she wanted to imply that her mother was badly awry in her logic. 'What does that have to do with it?' she wondered.

'Take no notice, pet,' said Russell. 'Your mother broke a tooth. Show her,' he ordered Angie, who bared the stump.

Simmy peered into the mouth a few inches from her face. 'When? How? Have you phoned the dentist?'

'About two hours ago on a Hobnob. And no, there wasn't time to phone anybody. We were practically in the car when it happened. It would have made us late.'

'Does it hurt? Phone them now.'

'How can I? I don't go around with the dentist's phone number in my head.'

Simmy gave her a long look.

'She wants us to google it,' Russell explained. 'Like normal people.'

Angie heaved a sigh. 'Let's go and ask Ben to do it,' she said, having observed young Ben Harkness and his beloved Bonnie sitting together at a table under a tree. A sunbeam had found them, sneaking between two branches and picking them out as the golden couple, rather than the newlyweds. 'Look at them!' she breathed with a sudden fond smile. 'Like something out of *A Midsummer Night's Dream*.'

'Hardly,' said Russell. 'That play is pure cynicism from first to last. Especially the wedding scene.'

'Stop it,' said Simmy, turning back to look for her new husband. 'I'll see you later.' And she strode down a little brick pathway to where Christopher was talking to both his brothers.

Angie gave herself a shake and set about the task of circulating, taking Russell with her. All the Hendersons were there, and they knew the Straws well, thanks to many shared holidays when they were small. There were also several grandchildren, whose names Angie made no attempt to remember. Eddie had a son they always referred to as 'Jonty', she reminded herself, and George had a daughter of about ten whose hair was alarmingly ginger. Lynn and Hannah had three little ones between them, with expectations of one or two more yet to come.

'Auntie Angie!' beamed Lynn, the youngest and the only one who applied the technically inaccurate *Auntie* to Angie's name. 'Isn't this amazing. They've really done it. Don't you think it feels like *destiny*, somehow? Just such a shame Mum's not here to see it. You've got to be mother to both of them. And father,' she added, looking at Russell.

The faint suggestion of incest was not lost on Angie, chiming as it did with her own thoughts. Everybody was aware of it – the fact that Simmy and Christopher had been virtually siblings in their earliest years. When they developed romantic feelings for each other in their teens, both sets of parents had been concerned; in Angie's case because she felt strongly that her daughter should cast her net much wider. As it turned out, both youngsters cast unwisely as well as widely, with collapsed marriages behind them.

'We should have let them do it twenty years ago,' sighed Russell.

'Wrong,' Angie disagreed. 'They'd have been constantly wondering whether they'd missed something. And now it's the best of all worlds, with the baby and everything.' *Everything* included Simmy's florist shop, Christopher's responsible and lucrative work and a highly desirable house in the northern reaches of the Lake District. 'I don't want anyone to think I disapprove. I just hate weddings.' She sighed yet again, hearing its echo and resolving to stop doing it.

'Maybe two,' said Russell with incorrigible optimism.

'Two what?'

'Babies, of course.'

Angie allowed herself to relax into cosy reminiscences with Lynn about the vagaries of weather on the North Wales coast where the two families had spent their innumerable family holidays, recounting Christopher's valiant efforts to barbecue sausages for ten people when he was barely into his teens. But she was also eyeing the wedding guests, with persistent echoes of 'The Rime of the Ancient Mariner' running foolishly through her head. It occurred to Angie decades ago that her whole attitude towards weddings had been coloured by that poem. She found herself uneasily waiting to be collared by a stranger with a long tale to tell.

Afterwards she accused herself of making that very thing happen.

A man holding a full pint glass of beer approached her with a determined smile. 'Mrs Straw!' he proclaimed. 'Mother of the bride.'

'Guilty,' she admitted. 'A role I was never going to be suited for.'

He laughed excessively and sat down beside her, ignoring Lynn. 'No, no – I congratulate you on the informal tone. It's considerably better than any wedding I've been to. Not a photographer in sight. And the flowers are spectacular.'

'I can take no credit for it,' said Angie, waiting for him to introduce himself.

He got there eventually. 'Derek Smythe,' he said, patting himself on the chest. 'Newbie at the auction house. Learning the ropes. New start and so forth. A real stroke of luck, the way it's turned out.'

'Ah,' said Angie, who was dimly aware that a potential second auctioneer had been taken on to be trained up at the saleroom. 'Pleased to meet you.' She scrutinised him closely. Younger than she had first thought – probably only mid-thirties. Brash, loud, but essentially insecure, she decided. At least two stone heavier than was good for him, and going in very much the wrong direction as far as that was concerned. 'Are you married?' she asked, thinking the occasion of the wedding made the question relevant.

'Oh yes,' he said cheerfully. 'With a fine stepson for good measure.'

'Any other children?'

'Two little ones. The stepson is Bruno. He's best mates with Jonty and I believe he knows your husband.'

Angie frowned. 'Really? Is he here?'

'Seems not. He might feel he doesn't know you well enough; he only met Chris once, I think. He wouldn't regard that enough of an acquaintance to intrude. He's very shy. I've been trying to talk him into doing a bit of casual work for the saleroom, as it happens, but he says he wants space and freedom for a few weeks – whatever that means. I'm not in a position to force him, although we always need another pair of hands at weekends. Fetching and carrying. Gets on well with the clever lad, Ben. They've taken on a little house right here in Threlkeld for the rest of the summer, the three of them. It's all one big happy family around here, let me tell you. It's been a big relief to me, finding everyone at the auction house so friendly.' He smiled contentedly and waved towards Ben and Bonnie. 'You know Ben, of course. You probably know about the house, as well.'

'Of course I know Ben,' said Angie, who had mixed feelings about auctions, antiques and Ben Harkness's new job. 'But I hadn't heard he was moving house. He's supposed to be at university, not messing about with old pictures.'

'Ah,' said Derek Smythe cautiously. 'But he wouldn't be at uni now, would he? And he's getting great experience. I understood he was having a year out, or something of the sort.'

Angie had never properly mastered the art of discretion, and saw no reason to withhold her views about Ben and his career. 'His parents are very anxious for him to resume his studies,' she said pompously. 'This time last year he was destined for great things at Newcastle. Now he's thrown all that away – or will do if he's not careful.'

'He's young yet,' said the man, with a worried look. 'And with his feel for history, he's always going to have plenty of options. My stepson thinks he's a genius.'

'He is,' sighed Angie. 'That's most of the trouble.'

By four o'clock, the whole thing was almost over. Angie had a dental appointment for the coming Friday, thanks to Ben and his phone, and the newlyweds had departed with their baby for a token honeymoon night in a hotel in Carlisle.

'Why Carlisle?' Angie had demanded in bewilderment.

'No reason. We just fancied it. It seemed to tick all the right boxes,' said Simmy. 'We'll be back by supper time tomorrow, so Robin can go to bed as normal.'

Ben's mother and sister, Helen and Tanya Harkness, had taken themselves home some time before, leaving the young couple to make their own arrangements. Ben had been working in Keswick at Christopher's auction house for a month or so, and had found himself a temporary room in town. 'It's what used to be called "digs",' he told everyone. Bonnie still lived in Windermere with her foster mother, Corinne, and the logistics of meeting up with her beloved consumed much of her attention. Buses were generally involved, and lifts from willing people, whether friends or strangers.

The Straws were loitering.

'We ought to wait until everyone's gone,' worried Russell. 'Traditionally, we're responsible, aren't we?'

'There's nothing very traditional about all this,' muttered Angie. 'I don't know what the world's coming to.'

'I have a feeling it's come to something very much like what we wanted it to, back in the seventies. We wanted to throw out all those fusty Victorianisms – church, uniforms, hypocrisies of every sort. Remember?'

'We succeeded beyond our wildest dreams.'

Ben and Bonnie were listening. 'Didn't you like it, then?' asked Bonnie worriedly. 'I thought it was lovely.'

Angie gazed at her. 'Did you? Really? *Why*, for heaven's sake?'

'It was so *real*,' the girl said. 'They're such a perfect match, with the baby and everything. And they love each other like proper grown-ups, nothing mushy or pretend about it.'

'No hypocrisy,' summarised Ben with a look at Russell. 'It was what it was.'

'Hm,' said Angie, thinking again about Christopher. 'Well at least they were lucky with the weather, after all that rain. It's been perfect all day. Not too hot for comfort.'

'And Threlkeld's really sweet,' Bonnie went on. 'I've never been here before. It's the absolute right place for the wedding party. No touristy stuff, everything nice and simple. Just a mountain and nice, ordinary people with proper jobs.'

'Not so much as a lake,' said Russell with a laugh. 'It's like Coniston with all the embellishments removed.'

'How do you know about people's jobs?' wondered Angie.

Bonnie laughed. 'It's just a feeling, really. When we came here earlier on, we didn't see any signs of tourist stuff.'

'I have a theory,' said Ben, pausing to make sure they were all listening. 'I was thinking about it just now. It's something Bruno and I came up with. We don't think this place is nearly as simple and innocent as it looks. Nowhere could be. I just bet there's a whole alternate reality just below the surface. Nowhere with a name like Threlkeld could fail to have layers – dimensions.'

'He's been reading Philip Pullman,' Bonnie explained. 'It's made him go all whimsical.'

Everybody laughed.

'So, where is Bruno?' Russell wanted to know. 'I've been expecting him all afternoon. I wanted to talk to him about our man.'

Even Ben was bemused. 'Who's "our man"?'

'Come on. You've got to have heard him going on about the glorious EBL.' Russell gazed at the blank faces. 'Edward Bulwer-Lytton. Great man of the nineteenth century. Spent some months up here in his youth, married the impossible Rosina. Bruno's read all his novels. Or nearly all. I'm still revelling in *Alice*, which is a real joy.'

'Oh. Right,' said Ben. 'The "dark and stormy night" man.'

Russell grimaced. 'If you must, but it's galling to have him remembered for nothing else other than that. He was *great,* I tell you. He'll have his revival any minute now.'

Ben also grimaced. 'Bruno hasn't mentioned an interest in him to me.'

Russell shrugged. 'I get the impression that lad keeps his

interests in separate compartments, so to speak.'

Angie was still puzzling. 'When do you see Bruno?' she asked. 'Where does he live? Who *is* he?'

'You never pay proper attention,' Russell grumbled. 'Remember my little history group, and the course of talks we attended last winter? Well, Bruno did a paper, but he was too timid to read it. It was about Bulwer coming up here after his first girlfriend died. She's buried at Ullswater somewhere. He'd done very impressive research. I read the paper for him, and we got friendly.'

'He's that man's stepson,' Angie remembered. 'Smythe.'

'And he's Jonty's very good friend,' said Bonnie. 'The two of them are going to move into a house with Ben right here, next week. It's all happening,' she said with a slightly unhappy look.

'Without you, poor girl,' said Russell with excessive sympathy.

'She can come and see us any time,' said Ben, with a hint of irritation.

'How?' wondered Angie.

'Good question,' said Bonnie, making every effort to be stoical. 'Oh – and can you give me a lift home, please?' she added. 'Corinne isn't going to be able to take me. She's going to Penrith for some reason. She could drop me at the station, and I could get a train, but . . .'

'You don't wanna do that,' quipped Russell.

Chapter Two

Bonnie chattered incessantly from the back of the car on the drive back to Windermere. She had been comprehensively congratulated on the flowers that had not only adorned almost all the people at the marriage ceremony, but had also decorated parts of the Threlkeld pub. A table centrepiece, a summery garland draped over the main doorway and three large, free-standing vases outside all proclaimed her skill. 'So imaginative!' people had marvelled, and Bonnie had glowed. The pub agreed that everything could stay for a day or so, after which point Simmy or Christopher were expected to remove it all.

'I quite liked Eddie,' she burbled. 'He talked to me for a bit and said I should have been a bridesmaid and he was calling himself the best man, even if Christopher didn't want him to. He tried to be jokey about it, but I think his feelings were a bit hurt. Did you know his son was called Jonty? That's a good name, don't you think? Jonty's nearly nineteen – Eddie was only twenty when he was born, and they got married when he was three. And they've never had any more children.'

'We know all that,' said Angie. 'We've known the whole family since Christopher was born.'

'Oh, yes. So you have. I forgot. I mean – not exactly forgot, but nobody's ever mentioned Jonty as being one of the Hendersons, so he doesn't really feel like part of the family. When Ben got friendly with him last summer, he didn't seem connected to Christopher or Simmy at all. It was quite a big coincidence, when you think about it. If you see what I mean.'

'Sort of,' said Angie wearily. 'It's a coincidence I hadn't been aware of, to be honest. Ben knowing Jonty, I mean.'

Bonnie was in full flow, eager to explore every connection and observation that had arisen during the day, knowing she would get very little opportunity to speak to the main players again for some time. 'Did you go to Eddie and George's weddings, then? What about Hannah and Lynn? I talked to all of them a bit. But I'm still not sure which is which of the sisters.'

'Hannah's the one with the long, frizzy hair,' said Russell. 'And yes, we went to all but one of their weddings. We could hardly avoid it, once we'd moved up here. Kit and Frances would have been very upset with us if we hadn't shown up.'

'Isn't it sad that they're both dead? It seems to me that that's why this wedding was so small and quiet. Don't you think?'

Angie turned round, making a great effort to be patient. 'They've both been married before,' she pointed out. 'That makes an enormous difference, whatever people might pretend to themselves. And weddings are a terrible waste of money. I'm just thankful it's all over.'

'Take no notice,' said Russell. 'She's tired and she's got a broken tooth.'

'It's OK,' Bonnie assured him. 'I like hearing what people really think.' She smiled at Angie. 'Does the tooth hurt?'

'Not really – but it's *there*, if you know what I mean. It niggles me.'

'Robin was good, wasn't he? Fancy him having such an old cousin, though. Jonty, I mean. It was good that they all came – clever to leave it till the school holidays, so they'd be able to.'

'Bonnie . . .' said Angie tiredly. 'Do you think you could just sit quietly for a bit?'

'Oh! Sorry. Have you got a headache?'

'Sort of. It's more that I can't properly hear you in the back without turning round, and that gives me a sore neck. Your flowers were fabulous. The best part of the whole thing, by miles.'

'Thanks.' Bonnie subsided, and Angie caught Russell casting worried looks in the rear mirror, checking that she wasn't wounded. Angie had no such concern. The girl was irrepressible. Five minutes later, Bonnie was bobbing up again, her head hovering between the two front seats.

'I saw you talking to Mr Smythe,' she said to Angie. 'Ben's been telling me about him. I suppose that's another coincidence – I mean that Bruno's going to share the bungalow and his dad's working at the saleroom. I'm not sure what came first, if you see what I mean.'

'Bruno is Derek's stepson, is that right? I keep forgetting their names.' Angie's head really was beginning to throb.

'Yes, that's right. His mother's older than her husband,

28

and it's her son but not his. There are little ones as well. I can't remember how many. Bruno's almost nineteen and waiting for the results of his A-levels. They live in Penrith . . . and now Jonty's working at the auction house as well, Mr Smythe drives him there. Actually, I suppose it all connects rather neatly. Jonty and Bruno have been friends for ages, and Ben knows Jonty because of Christopher. So I expect that's how Mr Smythe got the job.'

'Bonnie, you have to stop,' Angie interrupted. 'You've said most of that already.'

'OK, but . . .'

'It's no good,' said Russell. 'It's all too much fun to just drop, I know. The coincidences are legion, with me knowing Bruno as well.'

'Did he tell you about the boys finding the house in Threlkeld?' asked Bonnie.

'No, he didn't,' said Russell. 'In fact I had no idea he was matey with Jonty until today. To be honest, it's been quite a while since I last saw him. Everything stopped for the holidays.'

'Please!' begged Angie. 'This is getting ridiculous. You sound like two old men in a pub reminiscing about everybody you've ever known. None of it *matters,* does it?'

There was no answer to that. They were entering the centre of Ambleside, which was the only actual town the route went through, and which could be slow and annoying. It was also interesting, because you quite often saw someone you knew on the pavement.

Not today, though. Angie leaned back and closed her eyes and Russell pulled faces at Bonnie in the rear-view mirror.

They were half a mile from Beck View when Bonnie started again, returning to the subject of the bungalow in Threlkeld. 'It's going to be great when they've got their own place. The rent's really low, so Ben's only paying a bit more than for the room he's got now. Jonty's earning money at the auction house and I think Bruno's got some that an old aunt left him when he was twelve. They've only signed up for two months. Apparently the owner might want to sell the house after that.'

'Sounds ideal,' said Russell heartily. 'Like in the olden days where groups of youngsters took over a house to squat in. Remember that?' he asked his wife.

'Vividly,' she said, and Bonnie laughed.

Then Angie, who was feeling better now she was nearly home, went on, 'But there's not much of the summer left now. Haven't they been a bit slow off the mark? Another month and they'll have to get back to school or whatever.'

'They've all left school. Bruno's got a place at Bristol, if his results are good enough. They will be – he's a bit of a prodigy, like Ben. Youngest in the year and all that.' Bonnie sighed wistfully, apparently thinking about her own inglorious academic career. 'Jonty only did two A-levels, and doesn't have a place anywhere. He might try for some sort of apprenticeship. His mum and dad don't seem in any hurry for him to leave home – or the area, anyway. Mr Smythe drives him to work every day, you know. I said that before, didn't I? He won't have to do that now, because he can easily cycle to Keswick from Threlkeld. And Bruno's got a car,' she finished irrelevantly.

'And there's you stuck in the shop and missing all

the fun,' said Russell with real sympathy. 'That must be frustrating for you.'

'It is a bit,' Bonnie agreed candidly. 'It's such a long way from here to Keswick. Even though Bruno's got a car, it's a lot to ask him to come and get me and then take me home again. And the buses take such a long time.'

'You'll work something out,' said Angie carelessly. 'After all, they're not even living there yet, are they? And I expect there's a lot to do in the shop, after all this wedding business. I don't imagine Persimmon's been much use to you these past few weeks.'

'She's coming in on Saturday to help us catch up.'

The girl's voice was flat; much of the exuberance dispersed by the prospect of going back to the old routines and seeing much less of her boyfriend than she would like. 'It feels like the day after Boxing Day,' she said. 'Nothing to look forward to for ages.'

'I know what you mean,' said Angie, suddenly confronted by visions of B&B guests with their demands and complaints and fussy requirements for breakfast. 'We should probably all go for a good holiday.'

'Now there's an idea,' said Russell.

In Threlkeld, Ben was still at the pub, sitting with Jonty Henderson and Derek Smythe, talking about the auction house and the recent changes there.

'Pity we can't persuade Bruno to work there as well,' said Jonty, who was as solidly built as the older man and who enjoyed a good game of rugby. His position as the boss's nephew had not given him any special privileges, much to his relief. Hefting crates of old books and rolling up precious Persian carpets were pleasantly mindless jobs that he was more than willing to perform.

Every time Ben saw Jonty and Bruno together, he was inescapably reminded of Don Quixote and Sancho Panza. Bruno was tall, thin and intelligent, his gaze fixed on some distant point, while his capable but unambitious friend ran round him smoothing his path. Which meant, on reflection, that where brains were concerned, the roles were somewhat reversed.

At work, Ben was shadowing a woman called Fiona who was the chief valuer for the business, as well as performing other roles. She advised vendors on where to pitch the reserve on their items, warned against inflated expectations and knew exactly where to look for expert confirmation of her estimates. She directed Ben to websites that would educate him about hallmarks and the scrawls on the bases of pieces of china. He was learning at his usual lightning pace and excitedly realising that a career in the antique business was not to be sniffed at. His parents, who clung to the hope that he would somehow, somewhere, acquire a first-class degree, were not happy.

Fiona had been at the post-wedding party, looking rather detached and friendless. Ben had resolved to go and talk to her, but as he approached he was overtaken by a man he didn't recognise. 'Who's he?' he asked Simmy, who was close by.

'That's George – you must have seen him before. He did say he wouldn't be here – just the ceremony itself. He's barely said a word to me. He looks rather ill, don't you think?'

Ben nodded and Simmy moved away. As he watched, Ben had the impression that George and Fiona were already acquainted, which struck him as surprising. George was the least sociable of the Hendersons. Ben remembered that he had seen George once before – at his father's funeral. The rest of the family habitually made disparaging remarks about him. But Ben had discovered that the auction business was a meeting point for all kinds of people from all over the region – and beyond. Well-dressed women with money to spare sat alongside unkempt dealers with sharp eyes and sharper wits. The most unlikely relationships would be formed over a mutual love of old cameras or Rosenthal porcelain. Competition could evolve into subtle deals and favours, nods and winks and a united front against the auctioneer.

Which left the auctioneer's employees caught in the middle. It was entirely permissible for them to bid for objects they might want, but it often sent a frisson through the room when that happened. Ben watched it all with fascination, at the same time as monitoring online bids and keeping track of buyer numbers. His quick mind had soon led to his being given much more responsibility than his youth might indicate.

Christopher had not even tried to hide his admiration. 'You could really make a career out of this,' he said, more than once.

'Tell that to my parents,' Ben would reply glumly. 'Without a degree I'm nothing, in their eyes.'

'In that case, they can't think much of me, either,' laughed Christopher. 'I went off on a gap year after school and didn't come back for a decade or so.'

They both knew that this was an oversimplification of the man's CV, but the point was made and Ben felt more conflicted than ever. 'I expect it'll work out somehow,' he said with a shrug.

Now, at his boss's wedding, he was determined not to think about his future. Bonnie had been his main focus, until the Straws had whisked her away – at her own request, he had to admit. With her magnificent flowers she had personally elevated the undeniably low-key event into something memorable. Colour, exuberance, scent and a sense of something special would all have been lacking without her contribution. The people running the pub had laughed and admired and only rolled their eyes at it all when they thought no one was looking.

Somehow, Ben had assumed the celebrations would last considerably longer, with more food as they lingered till sunset. But once the happy couple had disappeared much earlier than Ben had expected everything seemed to just fizzle out. Which was why he ended up with Smythe and Jonty, neither of whom seemed eager to leave.

'Where's Bruno now?' Ben asked. 'He could have come if he'd wanted, you know. It was open house, no proper invitations or anything.'

'He's never met Simmy and hardly knows Chris,' said Derek Smythe. 'It wouldn't seem right. The only people he does know are Jonty, you and me – and I don't count, being a mere stepdad. I couldn't have introduced him to anyone, either. They were mostly strangers to me, as well. I never even managed to talk to Jonty's Uncle George. He seemed to disappear quite early.'

'He's like that, apparently,' said Ben. 'You probably know that the last time the Hendersons all got together like this was when their parents died. Two funerals within a month or so of each other was pretty traumatic for them. I think George was the one who took it all the hardest. But he seems to know Fiona. Maybe he comes to the auctions now and then.'

Jonty spoke up, reminding Ben that he was related to the people they were discussing. 'Uncle George is OK when you get to know him. He takes a long time to trust people. My dad makes it worse, as I see it. Always teasing him, as if they were about ten. He misses Willow since the divorce. That makes him sad.' He raised his big head and gave Ben a look that felt like defiance. 'Divorce is pants. It should never be allowed. Not if there are kids, anyhow. I guess it's good that Uncle Chris is divorced, so he can marry Simmy.'

'Willow?' echoed Smythe, making a very obvious effort to keep track.

'My cousin. She's ten and she's got ginger hair. She's very shy. I used to play with her when she was about four. She worshipped me,' he added, with no false modesty.

'Where does she live?' asked Smythe.

Ben and Jonty exchanged a glance, unsure about the reasons for this interrogation. It felt like something more than idle chatter. Ben paid heed to his position as close friend of the boss's wife, which Smythe was perhaps trying to exploit in some way.

Jonty answered briefly. 'She lives with her mother, somewhere not far away. I think Uncle George sees her at weekends.'

'Willow.' Smythe nodded, as if committing the name to memory.

Jonty was folding a paper napkin with extreme care, tweaking and turning it one way and then another, until he produced a perfect little sailing boat, which he placed in front of Ben with a smile.

'Hey!' said Smythe admiringly. 'That's brilliant. I'd have thought the paper was too floppy for something like that.'

'Don't try sailing it,' said Jonty. 'The paper's too absorbent. It holds its shape, though.'

'Can you do anything else?'

Ben laughed. 'Only about a thousand things,' he said. 'It's his party piece. He's been doing it since he was about three, apparently.'

'Why don't we call Bruno and tell him we're still here,' Derek suggested. 'It's not too late.'

'I tried, actually,' said Jonty. 'He's not picking up his phone, which isn't unusual. The only person he seems to want to talk to is Patsy.'

'Who?' Ben frowned in puzzlement.

'You know – Patsy, his girlfriend. At least, I think that's what she *wants* to be. They do a lot of online gaming together. She's quite old, like twenty-four, and she's a social worker.'

'I've never even heard him say her name.' Ben was bemused. 'Not once.'

'Yeah, well, that's typical. I was surprised, actually, when he said it'd be OK for the three of us to share the house. He likes to deal with people one at a time.' Jonty looked at Derek. 'Isn't that right?'

Derek Smythe shrugged. 'Now you mention it, that sounds about right, yes. We've seen Patsy a time or two, but she doesn't say a lot. I'd guess it's putting it a bit strong to call her a girlfriend. She's just one of his clever friends. He knows Simmy's dad as well. I bet he never told you that, either.'

'Lord Lytton.' Ben nodded. 'He told us. Russell, I mean – not Bruno. It sounds interesting, actually. I didn't know there was a Lake District connection.'

Smythe and Jonty were both now looking as bewildered as Ben had just done.

Ben sighed. He was missing Bonnie, finding the all-male group rather heavy going. In a family with three sisters – not exactly mirroring the Hendersons, but close enough – he felt odd without a female in the mix. In the two terms he had spent at university, the only significant friends he had managed to make had been two girls. He liked Simmy enormously. Bonnie was a miraculous soulmate and at least one of his sisters was turning into excellent company as she grew up.

He looked from Derek to Jonty, wondering why he felt awkward. Perhaps, he told himself, it was simply that he was unsure about how they regarded Christopher and where the balance of power might lie. They all saw each other every day at work, but Smythe seldom chatted to the boys. The auction house had seen recent upheavals and a few fairly serious mistakes had been made since Ben had joined the workforce. One at least had been the fault of Derek Smythe, though the man had never fully admitted this; instead he had tried to shift the blame onto Ben. The sour feelings around that still hadn't gone away for Ben, although the older man seemed oblivious of any lurking resentment. There was something untrustworthy about him, which made Ben wonder about his relationship with Bruno. A stepfather was probably intrinsically unreliable anyway, but in Bruno's case, there was a major discrepancy in their intelligence levels, which had to be uncomfortable.

He realised he'd had enough of the wedding party and tried to weigh up whether or not he would feel better going back to his airless little room in a Keswick terrace, where he would have to provide his own evening meal and entertainment. He knew he had been rash in taking it on in such a hurry, as soon as he got the job with Christopher. The only upside to it was that it was a five minute walk from the saleroom, and that after Henderson had paid him, he could manage the modest room rental with plenty to spare. One of the many downsides was that he watched families enjoying their self-catering holidays in neighbouring houses, and the busy B&Bs offering large rooms with magnificent breakfasts, while he sweltered in a south-facing second-floor attic with only a microwave and a kettle to shield him from starvation.

His parents were sulking because of his shocking abandonment of his degree course. 'You're a dropout!' his father had exclaimed in horror. 'Of all people, I never thought that would be you.' As a result, they were in no mood to subsidise his current lifestyle. 'You're on your own,' said David Harkness, flatly.

At least the time in the Keswick digs was almost at an end, much to his relief; the suggestion from Bruno and

Jonty about a place in Threlkeld had come at just the right moment. The all-male aspect of the arrangement could be diluted with regular visits from Bonnie – and perhaps Simmy sometimes as well. She had reached the point where the days with a baby were growing tedious and regular outings essential.

'I can't go back to the shop yet,' she said. But she did call in once or twice a week to give Bonnie a chance to discuss any problems and relieve her feelings about Verity, the temporary assistant replacing Simmy. They all existed in a kind of bubble, knowing the current situation was sure to change before long, unable to make proper plans. 'The summer just makes it worse,' said Simmy. 'Everybody gets out of character by the time it reaches August – had you noticed? Even Christopher has gone a bit flat.'

Ben's thoughts were meandering back and forth along these lines, making him wonder whether the three glasses of white wine were responsible. His brief career as a student had at least taught him something about alcohol and its protocols. White wine was not the drink of choice for most of his contemporaries, but he had discovered a taste for it – especially chardonnay. True to form, he had investigated the many different varieties that came under that heading, recognising it instantly from the way it swirled in the glass, subtly oily and with its own unmistakable bouquet. He had spent an idle evening googling French wines, effortlessly memorising their names and regions. When he had revealed his knowledge to Christopher over some vintage Burgundy, he had been immediately dubbed the 'wine expert', with suitable jokes arising accordingly.

'I want tea,' he said suddenly and slightly too loudly. 'Can we have some tea?'

The three had been sitting in a corner of the pub garden, with empty glasses in front of them. Derek Smythe had the look of a drinker, but Ben had not seen him imbibing more than a couple of beers all afternoon. Jonty, rather endearingly, had stuck to Coke. It was approaching five o'clock and nobody else from the wedding remained in sight. The pub was trying to get itself back to normal, albeit festooned with flowers and tables in all the wrong places.

'Tea sounds perfect. Mind if I join you?' came the voice of a man Ben had spoken to only once over the course of the afternoon. He had arrived rather late and then gone missing.

Chapter Three

'Oh, hello,' said Ben weakly. He wanted to say *Hello, Mr Moxon* or *Good day, detective inspector*, but both sounded too flippant in his own ears. 'I thought everybody had gone.'

'They have,' Moxon nodded. 'All except us. I went for a little walk around the village, and came back just now for my car. I've never been here before, you know. I thought it would be a good chance to have a look. I went up by the beck to the top of Blease Road. Excellent views.'

'Never been here?' Ben repeated. 'Really?'

Moxon shook his head. 'No reason to. It's a quiet little place. I didn't catch the explanation for why they chose it for the wedding. You'll know, I suppose.'

'Easy parking,' said Derek Smythe. 'As a matter of fact, I think it must have been at my suggestion.'

Ben raised an eyebrow at that, having heard that it was Hannah's idea, but said nothing.

Moxon smiled and rubbed his hands together like somebody's slightly vague uncle. 'Well, I for one think it all went very nicely. Bonnie did a fine job with the flowers.'

Ben realised that he had a task to perform, and said to the detective, 'Do you know Mr Smythe, and Jonty – he's Christopher's nephew. And he's friendly with Mr Smythe's son Bruno. This is Detective Inspector Moxon from Windermere. He and Simmy are old friends.'

'Stepson,' Smythe corrected easily. 'Can't have people thinking I was a dad at fifteen, can we?' He was eyeing Moxon as if unable to credit the reality of him. 'Have we met?' he asked.

'It's possible,' said Moxon non-committally. 'I do get around.'

'Though never to Threlkeld,' said Jonty with more wit than usual.

'He probably knows all about you,' said Ben with a grin. 'Being in his line of work to keep a grip on what's what.'

Smythe attempted a matching grin, which Ben labelled as *cheesy*. 'Not guilty, Inspector,' he said. 'Innocent as driven snow.'

'I'm not sure that's the right metaphor, but you don't have to worry. I'm seriously off duty today. A day, I might add, that has made me very happy. I've seldom seen a better-matched couple.' He sighed contentedly. 'Your friend deserves every happiness,' he told Ben.

'She's OK,' said the youth awkwardly. 'Tougher than she looks.' Moxon in sentimental mode was embarrassing.

'Resilient,' nodded the detective. 'Like you.'

Moxon and Ben had a history encompassing a number of violent deaths, with one outstanding trauma in Hawkshead that had taught them both a lot. Nobody doubted how highly the man valued the boy and how far he would go to protect him. His tolerance of Ben's interference in murder investigations was itself tolerated by more senior officers, thanks to an impressive series of positive outcomes.

Tea was collected from the bar, and all four men sat around a large stainless-steel pot that would never have found favour in Christopher's auction rooms. Smythe made a production of pouring it out. They all drank quietly for a moment before Moxon spoke to Ben.

'What's the news about your studies, then?'

Ben had known the question was inevitable, just as he knew the answer would not be well received. He had been trying to avoid the man all day for this very reason. Moxon, every bit as much as Ben's parents, had rejoiced in his academic prowess and fully endorsed his choice of subject at Newcastle. He had confidently predicted a glorious career working in forensics and soon becoming a world-famous expert and consultant. Instead, Ben had rapidly discovered that he was much less suited to the course than everyone, himself included, had expected.

'I'm definitely not going back to Newcastle,' he said. 'But I think you knew that. I toyed with the idea of transferring to history somewhere, but everything got so complicated and uncertain that I decided it was too much of a risk. What if I didn't like that any better? The trouble is,' he said, his eyes on Moxon's, his expression disarmingly frank, 'I don't really suit the student life. I got the idea that you were left alone to pursue your own studies, with a bit of input from lectures and tutorials, but basically being treated like adults. And it just didn't feel like that. They kept banging on about schedules and reading lists and online seminars from places like Denver, until there wasn't any scope for individual research. I felt a lot more free when I was at school, which is crazy.'

'It would probably have got better after the first year,' said Moxon mildly. 'They've got to provide you with the groundwork, don't you think?'

Ben wriggled his shoulders. 'I don't know. I'm not explaining it properly. It's a cliché, but I felt exactly as if I was a square peg in a round hole. It was never *right* for me. I was either bored or confused practically the whole time.'

'Oh well. What's done is done,' said the man philosophically.

'Newcastle's loss is Henderson's gain,' put in Smythe fatuously. 'He's a real asset in the saleroom.'

Moxon nodded non-committally and changed the subject. 'It was interesting to see all the Hendersons gathered together. First time I've seen them en masse.'

'Jonty is Eddie's son,' said Ben quickly, elaborating on his earlier introduction and hoping Moxon wouldn't say anything embarrassing. 'Christopher's nephew.'

'And best mates with my stepson,' Smythe elaborated. 'Young Bruno.'

Moxon's head went up like an alert rabbit. 'Not Bruno Crowther?' he said.

'That's right.' Smythe's cheeks grew mottled as he stared at the older man. 'Why?'

'I saw him play, only a week or two ago. I was very impressed.'

Ben struggled to process this remark, as Smythe preened with obvious relief. Play what, Ben wondered. Cricket? The bassoon? Leading role in *Macbeth*? Never had the word held so many possibilities. 'What does he play?' he asked.

'Chess,' came the reply. 'He was in that international tournament they had a bit ago, up in Scotland. I watched the whole thing online. It was streamed,' said Moxon, as if streaming was somehow magical.

'I had no idea,' said Ben, feeling cheated. He turned to Jonty. 'You never said anything about that.'

Jonty shrugged his broad shoulders. 'Why would I?' he said.

'I play chess.' It sounded feeble and wrong as he said it. 'But I'm not very good. Everybody thinks I should be, but I'm too impatient. I don't like figuring out all that strategy.'

Nobody seemed very interested. 'We can't stay here any longer,' Smythe announced. 'They'll be sick of the sight of us.'

It was true that there was an atmosphere that suggested they might be surplus to requirements – especially if they were only going to drink tea.

'I'm quite hungry actually,' said Ben wistfully. 'I thought there'd be more food than there was.'

'I'm trying Bruno again,' said Jonty, tapping his phone. 'I can tell him he's got a fan.' He smiled at Moxon, who merely nodded. 'If he's not far away, maybe he can come and say hello.'

Ben sighed softly. A fifth male person joining the group would be too much. Something about groups repelled him – the difficulty in being heard; the tendency for conversation to sink to a painfully low level; the alliances that formed so carelessly and were then hard to break. Three people together was pretty much his limit. Even at home, he had been relieved when his older brother, Wilf, had gone to live elsewhere. His three young sisters formed their own little gang and had learned from infancy that the only way to manage Ben was one at a time.

But Moxon was already standing up. 'Sorry – I should go. It was good to see you.' He addressed Ben with a special look that Ben silently characterised as *avuncular*. 'And pleased to meet you two, as well,' he told the others. 'Perhaps I'll see you again.'

'Come to one of our auctions,' urged Smythe. 'Bring the missus.'

Ben waited for the qualification. *If there is such a person*, was surely a necessity these days? To his eyes, Moxon did not look like the married man he actually was, and only Simmy had met his wife. Why, he wondered now, had she not come to the wedding? Had he missed something and the couple had separated?

'I might just do that,' said Moxon, almost as if he meant it.

A yelp from Jonty drew threefold attention. 'What the—?' he spluttered. 'It's Patsy. A text saying she's looking for Bruno and saw on AA's Facebook that he's in hospital.' The young man looked from face to face. 'How can he be?'

Derek Smythe went rigid, his arms stretched across the slatted pub table, hands clasped tightly together. 'What?' he said. 'Not Bruno?'

'Facebook?' asked Ben incredulously. 'Who's AA?'

'Let me see,' said Moxon, plucking the phone from Jonty's hand. '"Where are you?"' he read aloud. '"Something's up with B. AA's FB says he's critical in hospital. WTF?"' He read the last three letters, and then muttered 'What the fuck' to himself.

Jonty gave him a bitter look. 'That's what I said.' Then he addressed Ben. 'AA must be Bruno's dad. His *real* dad,' he elaborated tactlessly. 'Anthony Ackroyd, he's called.'

'Critical,' muttered Smythe. He shook his head. 'What does that mean?'

'Phone Patsy and ask which hospital,' said Ben to Jonty. 'Why would anyone put it on Facebook?'

'His father's an idiot,' said Derek Smythe absently. 'He never makes a move without telling the world about it first.' His expression changed to one of anger. 'He's not fit to be anybody's father. Bruno says so himself.'

'He's no different from a million other people,' said Jonty. 'Putting things like this on Facebook can come in useful sometimes. Looks as if it did this time, actually.'

The boy was fumbling with the phone, his big fingers miraculously keying the instructions necessary for calling Patsy.

The call was answered in a shrill voice that could be heard by everyone at the table. 'I'm here in the hospital already, but they won't let me see him. Where's Derek? Where *is* everybody?'

'Chris Henderson's wedding, remember?' said Jonty. 'Derek's here. Mrs Smythe didn't come because she's working.'

'You mean Henderson the auctioneer?'

'Where I work,' said Jonty impatiently.

'Oh.' The voice grew shrill again. 'It sounds really bad, Jon. I think somebody attacked him.'

47

'What?'

'They found him by the beck in Threlkeld with his head all bashed. Some walkers. About an hour ago probably.'

Ben wanted to ask at least twenty questions, as Moxon obviously did too. But Jonty held onto the phone, his face very pale. 'But we're there as well. Why didn't we hear the ambulance? Why didn't somebody come and tell us?'

When Patsy made no reply, Ben flapped at Jonty to speak in his capacity as Bruno's closest friend and holder of the phone. Jonty took a deep breath and looked at Smythe. 'We can come right away. I don't understand how it could have happened.' He listened for a moment, turning away from the others. 'Not now, Pats. We'll explain it all when we see you. Penrith Hospital, right?' he said and then shut down the call.

Smythe and Jonty ran across the road to the former's car and were gone before Ben could assemble any meaningful thoughts. When he did, it was to worry about the plan for the three of them to move in together, if Bruno was badly hurt. Then he felt guilty at being so selfish. Moxon was frowning at the ground, his eyes flickering in thought.

'But I was just there,' he said. 'Did I hear her right? She said they found him beside the beck in Threlkeld, right?'

Ben nodded.

'But I was *right there*, less than an hour ago. It's about three minutes' walk from here.' The simplicity of the coincidence seemed to floor him.

'Could be another beck,' said Ben doubtfully. 'Or a different stretch of it. Did you go as far as the waterfalls?'

'Only as far as the car park. Where a big pipe empties into it. Quite a nice bit of engineering, actually. Very attractive and looks efficient. They had awful floods up here, of course, with paths washed away and landslips and all sorts.'

'Storm Desmond,' said Ben. 'Years ago now.'

'Twenty fifteen,' said Moxon. 'Still fresh in the memory.'

'What would Bruno be doing up there anyway? Where was he before that? Jonty's been trying to call him since about three o'clock. Who found him? It all sounds crazy.' Ben felt a sudden plunging misery. 'This is going to ruin everything.'

'It probably isn't as bad as that girl said. Listen, Ben – I really need to get off home. There's nothing to say this is anything for me to worry about. There are plenty of people based in Penrith, without me being involved.'

'But—' Ben stared at him. 'But you're a policeman,' he said childishly. 'And you might have seen who did it, without realising. They'll want you to make a report of who you saw, or if you heard anything. Why didn't we hear an ambulance coming?'

'We would have heard if there'd been a siren. It's my guess the whole thing was just a silly little accident and nothing like as serious as what's-her-name said. She sounds a bit of a hysterical type.'

'Yeah.' Ben nodded.

'The thing is, I'm off duty for the whole week. I'll be in very hot water if I get myself involved in all this for no good reason. We're going away tomorrow. Anglesey.'

Ben gave a weak smile. 'At Simmy's recommendation?'

'No, no, not at all. Why would it be?'

'Oh – she and Christopher spent all their summer holidays in North Wales until they were about sixteen.

49

Has she never told you? They go on about it all the time. Prestatyn, I think.'

'Oh. I did know that, I suppose.' Moxon jingled his car key in his pocket, and took a few steps. 'It's very strange, though,' he said, stopping to look up towards Blencathra. 'I was *right there.*'

Chapter Four

Ben was left as the very last survivor of the wedding party, his head in a spin and with no idea what to do next. There was a bus going to Keswick in a few minutes, which he supposed he ought to catch. But what would he do, once in Keswick? Was he going to sit in that sad little room by himself until somebody phoned with news of Bruno? Who was going to think of telling him anything, anyway? He was still rather peripheral to the friendship between Bruno and Jonty. There would be questions and gossip the next day at work, with both Derek and Jonty claiming the limelight as being closest to the injured Bruno.

But before that, there was a whole evening to get through by himself. The day had been fine up to that final shock. Simmy and Christopher were official, their status secure in the eyes of the world along with that of their little son. Bonnie had been comprehensively congratulated. Angie had a dental appointment, and Eddie Henderson had managed to deliver a speech that only he thought was called for. A funny little wedding, admittedly, but Ben agreed with Bonnie that it had carried none of the forced excess of the usual palaver.

His mother had not wanted to go to the wedding. Simmy was not exactly her friend, although they liked each other well enough – or used to. Ben was the link, and since he had behaved so bizarrely over his studies his mother had grown very cool towards the florist. Despite his repeated insistence that Simmy had had no part *whatsoever* in his decision, Helen remained suspicious.

'She has too much influence over you,' she claimed.

'If that was true, I'd never have dared drop out of the course,' he said. 'Simmy thought it was brilliant.'

'Huh,' said his mother. But she did briefly show up at the pub, being summoned as a chauffeur for her daughter Tanya, who, as assistant at Persimmon Petals, was a specially invited guest. Helen spent most of the time talking to Christopher's sisters. Bonnie was also in her bad books, being another person suspected of influencing Ben's infuriating decision about his future. Hannah and Lynn had been more than happy to keep her company.

So Ben caught the bus back to his digs, and let himself into the sad little room with no idea how to pass the evening. There were still a few hours of daylight left, and he had his bike tucked away in the shed behind the house. A good uphill ride might be just what he needed to blow some air through his cluttered mind.

I'll go up to Castlerigg, he decided, on a whim.

Russell Straw had mentioned it at one point during the day and Ben was reminded of a windy autumn weekend years ago when his mother had taken him and his brother there. He had not been since. He would be sure to take his phone, in the unlikely event that Jonty or even Derek Smythe might call him about Bruno.

* * *

As he cycled steadily up the final stretch of road, he found himself again anticipating the coming day at work, which was expected to be relatively quiet. It was over a week until the next auction, with the deliveries of items for sale already made. The staff would be numbering and listing it all, checking descriptions and putting everything onto the database for the catalogue. Unlike most of their fellow auction houses, this one did not give estimated values unless directly requested.

'It's too much like putting a price on things,' said Christopher. 'We're not a shop. Let it find its own level.'

Ben had watched many hours of antique-related TV programmes in the past months and was quick to query the practice. 'They *always* give a value range and usually a reserve as well,' he argued.

'Let them,' snapped Christopher. 'We'll do it in our own way.'

Ben was unconvinced, suspecting that more items went for below their value than would otherwise be the case.

When he got to the ancient stone circle he expected several other people to be wandering around the place as the sun glided down behind the fells, but there was only one woman with two large dogs and her mobile phone. A camper van was parked in the road outside, which he guessed might be hers. She was talking loudly in what was a natural amphitheatre.

Ben sighed. The place was infinitely more dramatic than he remembered. As a young teenager he had not appreciated landscape. He had an image only of low cloud, cold wind and shapeless old rocks from his previous visit. Now the sky was clear, darkening to a colour nobody could properly describe, and shadows patterned the ground like a very weird board game. The large dogs wagged at him from a respectful distance and he smiled back.

He read the information boards, assimilating the few facts about its age and purpose, then went to stand in the heart of the circle. On every side were crumpled fells, with occasional crags and sheer faces, sudden crevices and smooth, rounded heads. All on a massive, dwarfing scale that would give anybody a healthy sense of proportion. One board had suggested that it was a kind of commercial gathering place where people came to buy and sell, perhaps in a very important annual market. Or, Ben mused, it had been more of a political assembly, like the Thingvellir in Iceland. He had watched a film about it and thought that this Cumbrian version was decidedly superior in setting. He turned round in a complete circle three times, letting the scenery dominate him, shedding small human matters in this far greater and utterly timeless spot. How could anything matter up here?

But the woman was chattering about wallpaper on her phone, asking herself whether it would make her living room seem too small, as if it was something seriously worrying, and Ben knew that human trivialities would never go away. The uncaring mountains were, to this person, a mere backdrop, a place where the signal was good for a nice long chat while the dogs gave themselves a bit of exercise.

Slowly Ben's own small concerns came back to him. He was disappointed and worried that the plan to live in Threlkeld might be thwarted. He was concerned about

54

Bruno, who might have been wantonly attacked by some criminal on the slopes of Blencathra. He was – if he was honest – rather scared about his future. He knew he had been a trial to his parents in recent years and the corresponding relief when he had gone off to university in a blaze of glory had been sweet. To blow all that away because he couldn't bring himself to enjoy the life of an undergraduate was selfish, he supposed. But wasn't it his own life to do with as he wished? Was it fair or reasonable to demand three years of discomfort, knowing the course was wrong for him and fearing that the wasted time would never be recovered?

Bonnie understood, of course. Bonnie was faithful, adoring, trusting – but also clear sighted and well grounded. She knew what was important. She wanted him to pursue his undoubted talents, while rejecting avenues that only seemed right to people who never considered alternatives. The road less travelled, the risk, the adventure. University had looked like an adventure from a distance. When he got there it had turned out to be painfully conformist, risk averse and – astonishingly – quite often very stupid.

And the worst thing, which he knew sounded childish and pathetic, was that nobody at Newcastle had much liked him. The tutors were uneasy with the way he persisted in thinking for himself, and the other students just thought he was either dangerous or mad – or both. His huge and irreversible mistake had been to voice his doubts about the harm that climate change might wreak. 'I'm not sure that I understand quite why it matters so much,' he said, in the hearing of three or four fellow students, and from there on he was treated like the son of Satan.

'It was entirely my own fault,' he told Bonnie that evening on the phone.

'So much for freedom of speech,' she had sympathised. 'Not to mention logic.' Bonnie never had any difficulty in following Ben's reasoning, wherever it might lead. She saw no reason to hate him because he unearthed statistics and facts that at the very least constituted questions that ought to be answered by those suffering from climate hysteria.

'I should have known better,' he sighed. 'Heresy has always been a terribly dangerous business.'

'Well, it shouldn't be,' she said, which made him laugh.

He had not shared this aspect of university life with his parents, fearing that they would simply gaze at him in despair. They would confirm that it was all his own silly fault, while at the same time belittling the pain of ostracism that had resulted. 'Rise above it,' they would say.

Not only was that impossible, but he felt no desire to even give it a try.

So now he was on his own, in the northern reaches of Cumbria, learning everything he could about antiques.

It was dark by the time he'd cycled back down to the main road, but there was still a lot of traffic. With a healthy instinct for self-preservation, he crossed over into Threlkeld instead of risking three or four miles of A66. There was a cycle path that wound its way westwards into Keswick, following the line of the dismantled railway, which he had used a few times. In the dark it was almost as treacherous as the main road in its own way, but he went carefully, thankful that he had bought a new lamp before moving to Keswick. He and

Bonnie had endured some hair-raising night-time rides with glow-worm lamps that he shuddered to recall now.

Passing the Horse and Farrier again, his thoughts turned to Simmy, her parents and Christopher, in that order. Angie Straw was a puzzle to him, even after having known her for two years or more. She clearly thought of herself as a rebel, bravely voicing outrageous views, and yet Ben found her very much in the mainstream when it came down to the realities. She ran her B&B with utter efficiency, kept her promises, seldom got into a state – and was admirably healthy. Sadly, she compared favourably with his own mother in that respect. Helen was already being assailed by arthritis in most of her joints, suffering constant pain and losing mobility with appalling speed.

Up the little street to Blease Road, where he turned right to join the cycle track, he found himself thinking about Bruno and Jonty. The house they were due to move into in a few days' time was up here, set back off the road in the shadow of Blencathra. It was actually a bungalow, as many dwellings in the village were. They added to the atmosphere of sleepy normality which was Threlkeld's trademark, and which had given rise to Ben and Bruno's jokey theory about undercurrents of vice, or at least non-conformity.

Nowhere could be as bland and innocent as this, he insisted to himself. There were lighted windows on all sides, many of them uncurtained. What was going on in those rooms, he wondered. So many lives, with their struggles to survive, their loves and hates and guilty secrets.

And then, just beside the little school, he felt his phone buzzing in his shirt pocket.

It was Jonty, who said he had been expecting Ben to phone long before this to ask after Bruno.

'Sorry,' said Ben. 'I got distracted. How is he?'

'Not so bad, after all,' came the slightly anticlimactic news. 'I've been talking to Patsy. She says he was unconscious for about ten minutes, that's all. She's a bit embarrassed by the way she panicked. By the time they got him to the hospital he was talking. They said they should keep him in for observation, though. There might be a concussion to worry about. They're doing a whole lot of X-rays and tests and stuff.'

'Did he say what happened to him?'

'He thinks something fell on him or hit him somehow. A rock, most likely. He doesn't really remember properly.'

'Weird,' said Ben, thinking it was *more* than weird. 'How long do they think he was out before anybody found him? It might have been a lot longer than ten minutes.'

'Don't know,' said Jonty as if that hardly mattered. 'Not long, I guess. There are people doing that walk all the time.'

'Who actually found him?' Without noticing, Ben had slipped into his habitual mode of asking every question necessary to build a complete picture. 'And how did his father find out about it so quickly? Didn't Patsy say he'd put it on Facebook? That's pretty weird as well.'

'Don't know for sure,' said Jonty again. 'Most likely they – the people who found him – got into his phone and called his dad, to ask what to do. His name starts with an A, so he might come up first. Then he would have called the ambulance. I think it must have been different people who were there when the ambulance arrived.'

'Why do you think that?'

'Well, by the sound of it, the first one was a man, and then it was two women.'

'How do you *know*, though?' Ben's understanding was full of gaping holes.

'Patsy said. She spoke to Bruno's dad, and he must have told her it was a man who called him. And then Bruno was awake enough to remember it was women with him when the ambulance came.'

'But they might all have been together, part of the same group.'

'Yeah, they might. Does it matter?'

'It does if somebody hit him. Obviously.'

'The police can sort it out,' said Jonty easily. 'The main thing is, he's not too badly hurt. Not worth making a huge fuss about.'

'Yes, but—' All the things he should have asked hours ago in the pub with Moxon now flooded into his head. 'How did the ambulance get near him? *Where* exactly did all this happen? I'm not far from there now, actually. It's dark, though, so I can't do any exploring.'

It was plain that his friend was making no attempt to follow his jumbled thoughts. 'Why are you there?' Jonty said blankly. 'You can't get into the bungalow yet, you know. Are you mad or something?'

'No, I'm not mad. I went for a bike ride and now I'm going back to Keswick along the cycle path.'

'Makes no sense,' Jonty dismissed. 'But we can sort it out tomorrow. The point is, Bruno's fine – or will be soon. Nothing to worry about. Plan's unchanged. See you in the morning. Don't forget that huge table's got to be moved. You'll have to do it with me.'

One of the prime lots for the next week's auction was a large oak dining table, seventeenth century, with massive legs. It weighed something like two hundred kilos, and took four men to shift.

'Us and everyone else,' said Ben. 'Thanks for calling me, Jon. It was good of you.'

'Nobody else to talk to,' said his friend forlornly.

Ben got back to Keswick without mishap, but with the good cheer of the wedding long evaporated. Instead, he felt troubled. There was still a knot of guilt inside him despite the soothing influence of the stone circle. He had done nothing to help the day go well; he had been far too self-absorbed to care much about Bruno's damaged head and he felt little but resentment towards his parents. The only thing to do was to call Bonnie – which he would have done anyway, because they always ended the day together, if only linked by voice.

She was still fizzing with happy memories of the day. 'What have you been doing?' she asked. 'It seems *ages* since I saw you. I've been out with the dog, and made the supper and mucked about on Facebook. I had to put something about the wedding up, because nobody else seems to have done.'

'Is Corinne back yet?' He didn't like the thought of her alone in the house, despite the dog and the fact that Bonnie was quite capable of looking after herself. She had turned eighteen months ago.

'Half an hour ago. She had a good day as well. Somebody booked her for a gig next month in Scotland – something like that anyway.'

Corinne's activities were always slightly mysterious and impossible to keep abreast of. She sang at folk festivals, spent time with itinerant groups who would have been described as gypsies not long ago, and mucked in with rural tasks such as sheep shearing and litter picking. No two days were the same for Corinne.

'Bruno got hurt this afternoon,' Ben burst out, fully aware that he might be spoiling her mood. 'In Threlkeld.'

'Gosh – is it bad? What happened?'

'He was rushed to Penrith Hospital. He's still there, but they say he's not seriously hurt. His girlfriend phoned Jonty about it.'

'I didn't know he had a girlfriend.'

'Nor did I until this afternoon. She's called Patsy and she's a social worker. She seems to have been the first person at the hospital – she might even work there. There's a load of stuff I don't understand at all.'

'But I thought he and Jonty were each other's most important person. At least . . .'

'I know. But they're not exactly a couple, are they? Just very good mates. They never have a problem letting me be around. I mean, no jealousy issues or stuff like that – but Jonty was pretty upset. He went dashing off with Bruno's dad. Derek, that is, not the real dad. He's called Ackroyd – I did learn that much. Jonty phoned me a bit ago, wondering why I hadn't been onto him to ask how Bruno was. I forgot, to be honest. I went to Castlerigg and got distracted.' And he spent a minute extolling the wonders of the stone circle.

'Without me?' said Bonnie, in mock fury. 'How could you?'

'We'll do it again. Something special probably happens at the equinox. Like Stonehenge.'

'So Bruno's going to be OK to move to Threlkeld on Monday, then? I want to come and help, but I don't see how I can get there – unless Corinne takes me. It's such a long way,' she finished on a wail of frustration. 'I can't really ask her to give up a whole evening driving back and forth, can I?'

'If you get a move on with your driving, you'll be able to borrow her car,' he said, not for the first time.

Bonnie quite reasonably pointed out that she could not afford proper lessons and Corinne was never going to volunteer to teach her. 'She says that's the way to disaster. We might never speak to each other again.'

'Pity,' said Ben.

'And what about you? You're the driver now. If you save everything you earn at Christopher's, you can buy us a car yourself,' she flashed back. Ben had passed his driving test on the second attempt, but had no access to a vehicle.

'Neither of us can afford the insurance,' he reminded her.

'There's always a way around that,' she said airily.

Ben had no doubt that Corinne would blithely allow Bonnie to drive uninsured, once she mastered the necessary skills. He also had a strong hunch that Bonnie would turn out to be a much better driver than he was within a few weeks of passing her test.

'When I'm in the bungalow, you'll be able to stay over at weekends,' he consoled her. 'That'll be a lot better than when I was in Newcastle.'

'Mm,' she said, and changed the subject. 'Didn't Simmy look *young*! And wasn't Robin good? It was all so *sweet*. And Christopher in that suit – I hardly recognised him.'

'Lucky with the weather,' said Ben, which was all the enthusiasm he could muster. 'And the food was OK. Not enough of it, though.'

'They had no idea how many would show up. Being a weekday, they thought most people would be at work. Instead, they all took the day off.'

'Which was entirely predictable. Family and workmates were all obviously going to take the time off.'

'Plus about ten hangers-on, like Corinne.'

'Moxon came back,' Ben remembered. 'He went off for a walk about the same time as Simmy and Christopher left and then turned up again. He's taken a week or two off, apparently. They're going to North Wales for a holiday. Lucky Bruno wasn't murdered or he'd have had to cancel his plans.'

'So what actually did happen to him? Why would anybody want to hurt Bruno?'

'Nobody knows. Jonty doesn't seem to think it's important. Something hit him, was all Bruno said. He can't actually remember any details.'

'Where was he?'

'By the beck that runs through the village, from up the hill. Moxon was walking there more or less at the same time. He kept saying "I was *right there*." It was funny, in a way.'

'Funny peculiar anyway,' she agreed. 'Who else knows?'

'Nobody from the wedding. They'd all gone except me, Smythe, Jonty and Moxon. We were just getting up to go when Patsy called Jonty. And don't ask me any more, because I don't know. As Jonty says, it probably doesn't really matter if he's not seriously hurt.'

'Hm,' said Bonnie.

Chapter Five

But by the end of the next day, it all started to matter rather a lot. Bruno was collected from the hospital and taken home by his stepfather at eight-thirty on Thursday morning. Derek Smythe then showed up at the Keswick auction house fifteen minutes late, having left his wife in charge of the invalid and collected Jonty from his home a little way south of Penrith. Bruno insisted he was in no way an invalid. His vision was clear, his blood pressure normal, his thoughts reasonably lucid. 'He still can't remember what hit him, though,' Derek told Ben.

Jonty joined them, looking more like the victim of an assault than his friend apparently did. Red-eyed and grey-skinned, his hair unbrushed and wearing odd socks, he was the picture of distress.

'I didn't sleep a wink all night,' he claimed. 'I was so *worried*. I kept thinking of what might have happened and how upset his little sisters would be, and what about the bungalow – it went round and round my head all night.'

'How's Patsy?' Ben asked, unable to resist. It was mischief and he knew it.

'What? Don't ask me. How would *I* know?'

'At least you knew she existed. I had never once heard her mentioned.'

'Right. Well, there isn't much to say about her, I s'pose. She works most of the time, and gets horribly stressed about everything. Bruno has known her for years. They're not *dating* exactly, but they are pretty good friends. She does online gaming with him. I have no idea how she knew about his accident yesterday so quickly, when she should have been at work.'

'Accident?' Ben repeated. 'Is that what we think it was?'

'Must be,' said Jonty with a frown. 'What else? Nobody's going to bash him on the head and run off in broad daylight, are they?'

'It wouldn't be the first time,' said Ben ruefully. 'Does Patsy know Bruno's father?'

'What?' Jonty blinked.

'She was looking at his Facebook page yesterday, wasn't she? So she must know him.'

Jonty scowled. 'So why ask me if you already know the answer?'

'Sorry. I suppose I meant – do you know him?'

'I've seen him a few times. He's tall like Bruno, with black hair. They live somewhere this side of Carlisle. He's got another wife now – and more kids. Actually, I don't think he was ever married to Mrs Smythe because Bruno's got her name from before she was married. His dad's called Ackroyd.'

'Yes, I knew that,' said Ben. 'I'm just trying to get the whole picture.'

'You're pissed off because Bruno never told you about Patsy,' Jonty realised. 'So now you're wondering what else you've missed.'

'Got it in one,' said Ben with a laugh. 'But if Bruno's OK now, we can try and forget the whole thing. Can't we?'

Jonty was fiddling with some brown wrapping paper that had contained an item for sale. Within seconds he produced a small unicorn, almost without noticing what his own fingers had been doing. 'Somebody hit him,' he muttered. 'And then just left him there. He might have died, for all they knew.'

'It could be that the same person phoned Ackroyd,' Ben pointed out. 'And then ran off because they didn't want any trouble.'

'I know. But why hit him in the first place?'

'Good question.' Ben watched his friend with concern. Jonty was clearly not his usual self. A sleepless night was not enough to explain his condition. 'What's bugging you most?' he asked.

'I haven't been able to *see* him,' the boy burst out. 'I don't know what to believe. Derek came for me this morning, same as always, and he seems to think everything'll be OK. And Patsy texted again saying she's going to pop over there before lunch. What about *me*? I'm his best friend.'

'You are,' Ben agreed generously. 'But you're here now, so you'll have to stay all day. Then maybe Derek'll take you back there after work. Just ask him.'

Jonty shook his head. 'I can't. I'm going to see if Patsy can come and get me this morning and we'll visit together. Uncle Chris isn't here to stop me. Besides, I'm bound to drop something, the state I'm in.'

'Good idea,' said Ben insincerely. 'Bruno's going to be glad to see you.' Privately he wondered how often this other threesome had got together, excluding him. Now Patsy's existence had been revealed, she seemed to be taking centre stage.

Jonty got busy on his phone, while Ben concentrated on a collection of old postcards, having been informed by Fiona that the presence of several Victorian nudes would hugely inflate their value. As far as Ben could see, the naked ladies were impossibly lardy and hairless, and not remotely erotic.

Details from the previous day darted through his mind at random. Speculation about Bruno's injury made little headway, but he did construct a neat scenario where the original person on the scene would hesitate to call an ambulance and instead find Bruno's phone and approach the first person on the contact list for advice. The puzzle was how the news had affected Ackroyd, father of the injured party. Had *he* called the ambulance, or merely instructed the nameless stranger to do so? The latter would make more sense, since he would know the exact location and be able to describe the condition of the patient.

Was that the person who had hit Bruno? If so, it seemed obvious that he had not intended to kill him, so what was all the fuss about? If there was a fuss. If Jonty could be believed, nobody was particularly bothered after the initial upset.

The morning passed slowly, with Fiona bossing everyone about and making a big issue of a spelling mistake in the catalogue, which was still in its very early stages. Ben tried to keep clear of her, as he always did.

She had been unwise – or insecure – enough to take alarm at his unconcealed intelligence. When he mispronounced Prinknash she was loud in her glee as she corrected him.

'Thanks for putting me straight,' he had said calmly. 'I would never have guessed.'

He did not mention that she herself had got 'Rosenthal' wrong, by pronouncing the *h*. The sort of low-level resentment she felt towards him was all too familiar from school. The world did not much like clever people, it seemed. Although at university there had been others just as bright as him, if not more so, it turned out that clever people did not much like each other, either.

Derek Smythe, to nobody's surprise, mispronounced almost everything and would not take correction. Christopher was training him up as assistant auctioneer, giving him the job of selling the pictures and books at the end of each Saturday sale.

'Nobody cares whether he gets an obscure painter's name wrong,' sighed the boss.

The day felt odd without Christopher's guiding hand. He had been the overall director and proprietor for only a few months, but a natural flair for leadership had made his elevation comparatively easy, although Ben thought there were occasional signs of stress. The staff knew and respected him without exception and did their best to keep everything running properly. Fiona had risen to the challenge of her own sudden promotion and the engagement of Smythe as Christopher's replacement was sometimes irritating but seldom disastrous. He was good with customers in a hearty, bucolic sort of way and capable of bluffing through the myriad pitfalls connected with valuations and provenances.

'He'll learn,' said Christopher at least once a day.

Privately, Fiona expressed some doubts. Ben had heard her questioning Christopher's judgement in tolerating the man when he obviously had many limitations.

'I don't think Christopher's altogether comfortable being in charge,' one of the other workers had replied. It was Denise, who had worked at the saleroom for years on a part-time basis. Now in her late fifties, she had gone full-time and become quietly indispensable. Ben often asked her for information and advice. Her insight into the boss should probably be heeded, even though Fiona dismissed it. 'He's a brilliant boss,' she said.

There were people arriving with entries for the following week's auction and everyone was kept fully occupied. It was half past eleven when Ben noticed that Jonty had disappeared. Presumably he had prevailed on Patsy to do as he wanted and she had come to take him over to the Smythe house in Penrith.

Ben phoned Bonnie in the early afternoon, when things were generally quiet at both their workplaces. She was still basking in the afterglow of the wedding and all the accolades for her flowers.

'Funny little honeymoon, though,' she said with regret. 'Last year they went to Lanzarote for a week. They should have done something like that again.'

'Too much hassle with a baby,' said Ben, as if he knew all about it.

'It's not, though,' Bonnie corrected him. 'I remember when Corinne took four of us to Skegness for ten days.

And a dog. There was a baby, a toddler, an eight-year-old and me. It was heavenly. We just ran about on the beach all day.'

Corinne had been a dedicated foster mother for much of her adult life and the accounts of her intrepid activities were legendary.

'Not relevant,' said Ben heartlessly. 'You can't hold Corinne up as a model for anybody. She's a one-off.'

Bonnie laughed and told him to hold on while she served a customer. It took her three long minutes and Ben heard most of the transaction.

'You sounded like a proper professional,' he told her when she came back to him.

'I've been doing it for long enough,' she said, sounding a trifle wistful. 'It gets automatic after a while.'

'You need a holiday,' he said, surprising himself at least as much as her. 'It's annoying seeing all these visitors lounging about while we have to work.'

'Most of them are yomping up and down the fells,' she pointed out. 'And good luck to them.'

'Not where you are. They're going on the lake cruise and spending all afternoon in pub gardens.'

'Oh well,' she said vaguely. 'Simmy says I can have Saturday off, which is great. And you haven't got an auction, so we've got the whole weekend.'

'Assuming we can actually manage to get together,' he reminded her. 'I'm no closer to figuring out how it's going to work. Without a car, it's a logistical nightmare. We really ought to go away somewhere. The landlady here isn't going to let you stay overnight.'

As often happened, the same thought hit them both at the same moment.

'Hey—' Bonnie was the first to voice it. 'If Bruno's out of action, do you think he'd let you borrow his car on Saturday?'

'He might. But he could be better by then. They let him out of hospital this morning and everyone seems to think there's no lasting damage. He'll probably be driving again by Saturday.'

'Knickers,' said Bonnie. 'Is it very wicked to hope he has just a little bit of a relapse?'

'Definitely,' said Ben.

Less than two hours later, Bonnie's hope was fulfilled to excess. Derek Smythe received a hysterical phone call from his wife, to say that Bruno had settled down for a nap after his visitors had gone. At half past two she had gone to check on him and found him lifeless. The ambulance people came quickly and confirmed that he was no longer breathing. 'I can't believe it,' she sobbed down the phone. 'He was *fine* this morning. Laughing with Jonty, happy to see his dad.'

Smythe repeated all this to anyone who would listen and then raced off, his face ashen. Ben was left in a state of stunned self-reproach. What had he and Bonnie done with their careless joke about a relapse?

Facebook played a much-reduced part in the second and more terrible chapter in the unfolding events surrounding Bruno Crowther. Instead, Detective Inspector Nolan Moxon was directly informed of Bruno's death by an efficient woman in the admin department of Penrith Hospital. Moxon had, rather to his wife's irritation, left a clear request the previous day that any developments in the case should be reported to him in person.

'But why?' asked Mrs Moxon.

'Because I've got a bad feeling,' was all he could reply. 'I just want to be kept informed, that's all.' The fact that nobody had told him that Bruno had been discharged that morning was forgiven. That had been good news, and therefore not really news at all.

The helpful hospital woman soon brought him up to date, adding, 'He must have been a lot more injured than we realised. Oh – and don't quote me on that, will you?'

Already it was beginning to look as if somebody there had been negligent. Moxon had reached that conclusion within about five seconds.

When he heard the lad was dead, he knew his role in solving it could not be left until his holiday was over. The couple had not yet set off for their Anglesey break; there was nothing to stop the detective from driving northwards, well outside his usual area of responsibility, to talk to his colleagues at Penrith.

'After all,' he insisted, 'I was *right there* yesterday.'

'I warn you,' said his wife, 'I'm going, with or without you.'

'I would expect nothing else,' he said and gave her a hug.

To be fair, she had to admit that this was only the second time in their entire marriage that he had failed her in this way. The usual clichés so beloved of stories about police investigations – of cancelled leaves, late nights and missed birthdays – had almost completely passed them by.

'The newlyweds will be coming back any time now,' he mused. 'I might just go and have a word with her people. They might not hear about it otherwise.'

Angie Straw stared at him for several seconds before letting the detective into the hallway of her large guesthouse. 'What?' she said.

He explained as simply as he could, but still had to say it all twice.

'Persimmon will be back soon,' she said. 'Back to Hartsop, that is. Why tell me about it?' She called to her husband, who was in the kitchen. 'Come and hear this. That boy – one of those boys – who's going to live with Ben in Threlkeld – the one whose father works with Christopher – he's dead.'

Russell was only present for the final few words. The rest had been delivered in a raised voice through the kitchen door.

'What?' said Russell. 'Not Eddie's lad?'

'No, you fool. I *said* – the Smythe one. Bruno, he's called.'

Russell was still being slow. 'He wasn't at the wedding, was he?'

Angie closed her eyes, trying to visualise every guest. 'No.' She turned to Moxon. 'We've never met him. I don't imagine Persimmon has, either. Wouldn't you be better going down to tell Helen Harkness about it?' She paused. 'And even that would be odd.'

'Was he murdered?' asked Russell. 'Are we suspects? Where did all this happen?'

'After you left yesterday, he was found in Threlkeld, beside the beck that runs through the village. He had head injuries, but they weren't thought to be serious, so he was discharged this morning. He went home and . . . died.'

'Happens all the time,' said Russell. 'Where did they take him?'

'Penrith.'

'Ah – there you have it. They won't have done much in the way of diagnosis – not like those American TV hospitals where they run everybody through the scanner thing for a broken fingernail. They'll have missed a fractured skull. Did somebody hit him? It wasn't me, I promise you.'

'Stop it,' his wife ordered him. 'That Smythe man's going to be distraught. It'll rebound on us eventually, through Christopher and Persimmon.'

Moxon was regretting his decision to deliver the news to this couple who were inconveniently remote from the main players. 'Well,' he said. 'I'll have to go and talk to the people in Penrith.'

Russell gave him a searching look. 'You feel involved because you were at the wedding,' he said astutely. 'And there's nobody else you can talk to like this, who was there as well.'

Moxon sighed. 'That's right. But it's worse than that. I went for a walk round Threlkeld yesterday, about the time you came home, and I must have gone right by the spot where the boy was hurt. I can't help wondering . . .'

'If you walked right past him?' said Russell.

'Exactly,' groaned Moxon.

Chapter Six

Simmy and Christopher remained in their bubble of ignorance until Friday morning. 'Married!' they kept saying to each other, and 'Do you feel any different yet?' Their baby seemed to have leaped several weeks in one day, thanks to all the excitement. The hotel staff in Carlisle had made a great fuss of him and the comprehensive walk around town the day after the wedding had given him a great deal to process. 'He's never been to a proper town before,' said Simmy. 'Only Keswick and Windermere.'

Now they were back in Hartsop, where their converted barn was at last more like a house than its original incarnation. There had been builders in and out for the past six months, but they had departed for good the week before and their bill had been paid. New walls, stairs, windows, floors and a full complement of bathroom and kitchen fittings all proclaimed that here was a building for people to live in.

The plan had been for Christopher to drop into the auction house for a few hours on Friday morning, more with the purpose of rounding off the aftermath of the wedding than doing any real work. 'Though I should check that it's all running smoothly,' he said.

Then Simmy would drive down to Windermere the next day and spend a whole morning in the shop while her parents took charge of baby Robin. Bonnie would have her weekend off, while Ben's sister, Tanya, deputised for her.

But instead, at the ominous hour of seven-thirty on Friday morning, Simmy noticed a text on her phone. *Can I call you? There's news*, it said.

'Uh-oh,' she muttered. Christopher was still in bed, but Simmy and Robin were at their usual place on the chair by the window, enjoying the morning feed. Over the spring and summer the timing had gradually slipped from about four in the morning to a far more civilised seven or later. Still entirely milk-fed, Robin was plump and placid and the source of overwhelming pride for both his parents.

'What?' said Christopher.

'Ben. He says there's news. What could possibly have happened in less than two days?'

'Knowing him, it could be anything. Why are you looking at your phone anyway?' They had made it a rule to keep phones out of the bedroom and neither of them ever felt tempted to break it.

'I left it on the window sill last night by mistake. It buzzed at me so I had a look. My bad, as they say.'

'Much to your father's disgust.'

Russell Straw persistently waged war on bad grammar and general misuse of the language. He had a long list of usages that angered him, which included *my bad*.

'I think I'll call him back now, before we get busy. You'll be going down for some tea any minute now, I expect.'

'I expect I will,' sighed Christopher and rolled out of bed.

Ben wasted no time in conveying the salient facts when Simmy phoned him. It left her with surprisingly few questions. All she could think of was, 'But surely it must have been some sort of accident?'

'Might have been. They'll be doing a post-mortem today, I imagine, although it must seem pretty obvious from the X-rays and so forth that they did on Wednesday.'

'Poor Derek. Poor Jonty.'

'I know. Anyway, you can warn Christopher to expect long faces at work. Is he going in today?'

'That was the plan. Just for a few hours. What about you?'

'Oh yes, I'll be there.'

'Well, thanks for telling me.' Already she was wondering what it had to do with her and what she ought to be feeling about it. She had never met Bruno, barely knew his stepfather, and was not under the impression that Ben was unduly upset. 'Were you very fond of him?' she asked, just to be sure.

'Well . . . I was, in a way,' came the thoughtful reply. 'We were going to live together, remember. In a bungalow in Threlkeld. I was really looking forward to it. Bruno was easy to get along with. Clever. It's all wrong that he should be dead.'

It hit her then. Of course it was completely wrong that a promising young man in good health and in possession of an impressive brain should die so abruptly. 'He's got little siblings, hasn't he?'

'Right. Two small sisters. They adored him, according to Jonty.'

'It's awful, Ben. Absolutely awful. Right out of the blue like that.'

'On a fine summer's day,' he said, as if ironically quoting from somewhere. 'And Moxon was *right there*, as he keeps saying.'

'Pardon?'

'Oh – I forgot that part. He was walking up by the beck at pretty much the same time as it must have happened. He's supposed to be going on holiday, but I doubt if he'll go now. He's going to be involved, one way or another.'

'Well, I'll tell Christopher,' she said. 'I've got to go now.'

'OK.'

'I'll see you,' she finished vaguely.

Robin was on her shoulder – a position he had begun to dislike as he grew bigger – and was banging his head against hers in protest. 'OK, you,' said his mother. 'You can lie on your rug for a bit.' She was discovering that four months was a frustrating age where physical matters were concerned. Liking to be propped up, but not restrained, the infant was disconcertingly unstable when upright. He would topple sideways unless wedged between cushions, so she mostly laid him flat on the floor, on a warm shaggy rug, and left him to play or to practise rolling over. A colourful contraption had been donated by Angie, from which dangled an array of plastic objects that jingled or spun when swiped by a determined little fist. Placed underneath it, he would play for several minutes.

'What was Ben's news then?' asked Christopher before Simmy could begin to tell him.

'Brace yourself,' she said. 'There's trouble at t'works.'

'Not *my* works, surely? Why tell *you* about it, if that's what it is?'

'Good question. It's Bruno – Derek Smythe's stepson. He died.'

'What? When? How?' Christopher was slow to register any implications for himself, but when he did, his eyes grew wide and his jaw very rigid.

Simmy repeated everything she could remember. 'And Moxon's involved, because apparently he walked past the very spot at more or less the time it probably happened. So he might be a witness or something.'

'And I'm right in the middle of it.' He groaned and rubbed his cheek. 'So two of my staff, at least, are going to be prostrated with grief for the foreseeable future. Three, if you count Ben. Were they very matey?'

'Quite, I think. Jonty's the link between Ben and Bruno. He's close to them both, but really he and Bruno were the main pair. Ben not so much. But it'll wreck their plans for living in Threlkeld. I don't suppose all the implications have dawned on people yet. It only happened yesterday.'

'Wednesday, actually,' he corrected her.

'He only *died* yesterday. They thought he was all right before then.'

'He wasn't deliberately attacked, was he? Couldn't he just have slipped into the beck and hit his head on a stone?'

'Let's hope so,' said Simmy, wholeheartedly. 'Anything else would be unthinkable.'

'And yet we're both thinking it,' Christopher said. 'Don't you wonder whether there's ever any real *peace* in life?'

She looked at him. 'What's the matter?'

'Just that. What I just said. Every time I think it's all settling down and we can breathe easily with no worries, something like this happens.'

'It hasn't happened to *us*. And I have a feeling peace can be overrated. We're OK, and that's what really matters.'

He pulled her into his arms and pressed his face into her hair. 'Let's hope so,' he said, his voice muffled.

Jane Moxon had an annoying big sister who always knew best. She knew that Jane lived a nightmarish life with her detective husband, because all the police procedure novels she read insisted this was so. Nolan might outwardly appear to be perfectly easy to live with, remembering birthdays and anniversaries, showing no sign whatever of stress or moral anguish or addiction to whisky – but Diana knew better.

When Nolan said softly and miserably, 'I'm not sure I can go to Anglesey after all,' Jane's first thought was that her sister would crow unbearably. Diana was also going to North Wales, along with her daughters Laura and Catherine, who were both students and both failing to make best use of their summer vacation. In fact, the holiday had been Diana's idea. She had booked a large self-catering house for two weeks, and insisted that the Moxons join her. 'Just for a few days, then,' Jane had said. 'And don't let it rain.' They both half-believed that Diana had power over the weather, along with everything else.

'But why?' Jane wailed now to her husband. 'What is it that's so important?' She followed the news, and knew quite well that no local murders had taken place that week.

'That boy, Crowther, up in Threlkeld. After the wedding. I told you.'

In fact, he had told her almost nothing. Jane thought she understood his feelings towards Simmy, and saw no reason to worry about them. His strong protective instincts needed an outlet, and in the absence of any daughter of his own he hovered over the accident-prone florist in a role that gave body to the word 'avuncular'. He never knew what to call her, which Jane found endearing. Usually it was 'Mrs Brown', but once she had taken up with Christopher Henderson, that seemed wrong. Never had Jane heard him utter the name 'Simmy', but once or twice he had said 'Persimmon'. It amused her, if anything. The two women had met two or three times, and Jane had been surprised to find her husband's protégée to be barely five years younger than herself. From Nolan's remarks, she had expected someone in her twenties.

'Persimmon Brown's wedding,' she said, wanting to be clear. 'That's the one you mean?'

'How many weddings have I been to this year? Or in the past *ten* years. Obviously that's what I'm talking about.'

'Has she asked you to help?'

He reached out and took both her hands, shaking them gently. 'Jane, Jane, listen. I spoke to her parents yesterday. Then I went up to the Penrith station and explained why I feel involved. I was *right there,* in the place where the boy was hurt. Attacked, probably. I know the people he knows. Ben Harkness, for a start. And his father works for Christopher. I was sitting with him when the news first came that Bruno was hurt. I might have seen who did it, without realising. It's the height of the season – the place is swarming with hikers. And dogs and bikes and all that. The results of the PM will be through any minute now, I shouldn't wonder, and I need to know what killed him. I can't just swan off to the seaside without knowing what happened.'

'All right. I'm not going to argue with you – even though it seems to me you could still have the holiday and deal with it by phone, if you must.'

'If it turns out it was obviously an accident, then I'll come – of course I will. I was looking forward to it. I like those girls. Your sister's done a good job on them, considering.'

'No, she hasn't. She's made them into spineless idiots. I'll never understand how they got into university.'

Moxon winced. University was still a painful topic for him, thanks to Ben Harkness's incomprehensible behaviour. There was another person he regarded as being in need of his oversight, if not direct protection. He was as proud of Ben as any uncle might be. And now the boy had thrown it all away for the glitter of useless old antiques. Moxon would have liked to blame Christopher Henderson, but he couldn't make that work. Ben had almost forced himself into the job at the saleroom, very much against Christopher's inclinations.

'It wasn't an accident,' he said, reverting to the main issue. 'Not unless he was doing something really stupid.'

'Which is not impossible. Climbing a tree after a red squirrel? Walking along the beck itself, for some reason. Is there any water in it at the moment?'

'Quite a lot actually. It runs off the fells all the year round.'

'Maybe he was rescuing a sheep. There are all sorts of possible explanations. Dodging a bike. Pushed in by a big dog.'

'Stop!' he begged her. 'You're as bad as Ben. He'll have come up with some sort of theory by now. Maybe I should go and talk to him,' he added speculatively. 'He's always got something useful to say.'

'Just let me know what to tell Diana,' said Jane resignedly.

Before any further information came through, Moxon was putting in an appearance at Persimmon Petals – the Windermere flower shop where Bonnie Lawson was in charge, assisted by an irritating woman called Verity. For months now the two had been struggling to establish a working relationship that exploited their respective talents, with moderate success.

Verity talked too much about trivial topics, took offence easily and was a walking disaster if allowed near the computer. But she could drive, knew every nook of the area and was efficient and pleasant when making deliveries. She could also construct acceptable displays for weddings and other events, and was always eager to do the daily run to the undertaker with funeral flowers.

Bonnie handled orders, advised on the qualities of various plants, kept the window display in perfect condition and dealt with customers in the shop. She had become adept at dodging opportunities for conversation – at least enough to stave off the damaging levels of frustration and impatience that ensued if she listened to Verity's babble for more than five minutes. Ben's daily phonecalls were crucial to her sanity, or so she assured him.

All of which made the detective's arrival a cause for rejoicing. 'Hey!' she said, with a beaming smile. He half expected her to throw herself into his arms for a fatherly hug. Bonnie had been short of fatherly hugs all her life, and had yet to find a reliable substitute. David Harkness was not in the running, even if he did have three daughters of his own. 'Fancy seeing you.'

That was what Simmy often said to him, and they both laughed. 'Are they back, then?' he asked her.

'I suppose so, but she hasn't called me. She's meant to be in here tomorrow with Tanya, while I go up to Ben's.' Her smile faded. 'But now he might not be able to move to Threlkeld after all, and he's already told the Keswick woman he's leaving, so he'll be in a pickle.'

'You know Bruno died,' said Moxon, with no attempt at any soft sentiment or prevarication.

'Oh, yes. The hospital must have missed the cracked skull. Embarrassing for them.'

'It might not be as simple as that. A slow bleed would be very difficult to detect, for example. Don't go casting aspersions. It's a perfectly good hospital most of the time.'

'Ben thinks he must have been attacked. I mean – it wasn't just some sort of accident. Don't you think so? Pity Bruno couldn't remember anything – wouldn't that have made it all nice and simple.'

'He only said something must have hit him, apparently. My wife just came up with about eight possible explanations for why it could have been an accident. She wants me to go to North Wales with her this afternoon.'

'And you can't if it's murder?'

'Well – I probably could. It won't be my case, all the way up there. But I feel involved.'

'Of course you do,' she said kindly. 'Like the rest of us. Even Simmy will have to show an interest.'

'You reckon? She's got every reason not to.'

'She always does in the end, though, doesn't she? Being just married isn't going to make much difference.'

Moxon's phone gave an imperious summon. He took it out of his pocket and checked the screen. 'Results of the PM, probably,' he muttered to Bonnie, before giving it a swipe. 'Though I didn't expect a call about it. Hello?' he said into the phone.

He listened for a few seconds, spoke a few words and ended the call. He had no hesitation in conveying the basics to Bonnie, which might have caused a degree of disapproval if not outright horror in some of his colleagues. 'They've done a preliminary external examination and found a contusion – which they already X-rayed on Wednesday. They've got to assume there are suspicious circumstances,' he reported. 'Bruising and damage incompatible with any natural hazards.' He looked up at a point on the ceiling and sighed. 'Nice of them to tell me. Not that it paints a very clear picture.'

'You mean he didn't just fall over and hit his head on a stone.'

'Seems not. Nor did he fall out of a tree or skid out of the way of a bike. Though a bike could perhaps have hit him.' Moxon went thoughtful again. 'I did see a cyclist or two going along the path,' he remembered. 'Which they really shouldn't.'

'I've never been up there,' she said. 'So I don't know what it's like.'

'It's pretty. You have to cross two footbridges over the beck, because the path changes sides. It's a bit rough, but easy enough to walk. I wouldn't want to push a wheelchair up there, but a baby buggy would manage it all right.'

'As well as bikes.'

'Right.'

'Does it lead anywhere?'

'It ends in a car park, and then you can walk up Blencathra. I came back down a road, Blease or something, past a little school, and then I went all the way out to the main road at the top end. It's a nice village. I don't think I saw a single B&B sign the whole way.'

'Unspoilt,' Bonnie agreed. 'It was a good place for the wedding party. Timeless, if you ignore the main road. Simmy thinks it's lovely.' She leaned closer, as if not wanting to be overheard, even though they were alone in the shop. 'If you ask me, she rather wishes they'd found a house there instead of Hartsop.'

'That's a pity,' said Moxon, with real concern.

Before Bonnie could say more, the door pinged open and Verity came in. 'That's the funerals done,' she gasped. 'I was only just in time for the one this morning.'

'Where's the van?' Bonnie asked her. 'Haven't you taken it round the back?' Verity coming in through the front implied that the vehicle was not in its usual place.

'Bonnie – have you forgotten it was booked for its MOT today? That's why I'm so out of breath – I've walked all the way from the garage. I've got to go back for it at half past eleven. There might be deliveries this afternoon.'

'Let's hope it passes,' said Bonnie fervently. 'We couldn't possibly manage without it.'

'Fingers crossed,' said Verity, still breathing fast. 'I've had enough rushing about for one week.' Belatedly she turned her focus on the detective. 'Hello,' she said uncertainly.

Bonnie was unsure as to whether she should introduce him. He was in plain clothes, which she always assumed meant he wanted to avoid recognition as a police officer. Surely that was the whole point. But more than half the local population were fully aware of his role, so it seemed pointless to try to hide it. 'This is Detective Inspector Moxon,' she said formally. 'He's friendly with Simmy.'

'Oh, I've heard of you,' Verity gushed with a wide smile. 'Funny we've never met, really, but then I've never had any reason to get involved with the forces of the law, as they say. Nothing like that in my family.' She gave Bonnie a superior look which plainly said *not like some people I could mention.*

Bonnie ignored the implication, and was again saved by the shop door pinging.

'I should go,' said Moxon. 'Good luck with the MOT.'

Verity gave a subdued squawk and announced that she had to have a coffee before going out again. The new customer approached warily, unsure who to address.

'Can I help you?' smiled Bonnie, and everybody got back to business.

Chapter Seven

Ben found himself in the midst of another all-male conclave that morning at the auction house. Christopher, Jonty and Moxon all gathered in the small office, with Ben included. Jonty was an even greater mess than the previous day: a bewildered, scared little boy, reverting to a child in the face of something he couldn't begin to understand. The others instinctively formed a protective circle around him. In the absence of Derek Smythe, it fell to Christopher and Ben to keep Bruno's friend going. Ben had been surprised when Jonty showed up for work, and Jonty had been surprised to learn that there was any other course of action.

'But how did you get here, without Derek?' he wondered.

'My dad drove me in. He said it would do me good.'

Moxon's own role was confusing. 'I'm not really here as a detective,' he admitted. 'I just wanted to try and get a better picture. I never met Bruno. Tell me about him.'

Christopher spoke first. 'He was another Ben in some ways. Clever, anyway. I would have been happy to find a place for him here, but he said he wanted some time off after the stress of the A-levels. Isn't that right, Jonty?' He tilted his head at his nephew, encouraging him to speak.

'Yeah,' Jonty muttered. 'We'd fixed up to share a house in Threlkeld with Ben.' He shook his head miserably. 'It took ages to persuade his mum it would be OK. It would have worked out easily. And he's got a car, so we'd be able to stop asking for lifts all the time.' He looked to Ben for rescue.

'That's right,' Ben confirmed. 'Things were getting a bit crowded in the Smythe house, so it made a lot of sense.'

'How did you meet him?' Moxon asked Jonty.

'I've known him since we were about three. We all lived in Clifton then. His mum and dad were still together. My dad was doing a big building job near there, a bunch of new houses going up. We went to the same primary school and our mothers got friendly.'

'Clifton . . .' said Moxon. 'On the A6, right? I'm a bit hazy about places up here. It's a long way from Windermere,' he said, as if quoting a film title.

'Tell me about it,' said Ben with feeling.

'It's just a few miles south of Penrith,' said Christopher. 'Site of the last battle on English soil, according to the village sign. Seventeen-something.'

'You know Bruno's real dad then,' said Ben to his friend, ignoring Christopher's irrelevant comment. 'You know way more about his family than I do. I never thought to ask about his real dad.'

Jonty nodded. 'He keeps in touch, even though he married again. He's got two girls, same as his mum. Bruno's mum, I mean. He used to joke about it, having four little half-sisters.' He sniffed at the need to use the past tense, which was never going to change back to the present again. The others watched as the awareness etched itself on his face.

'Happens a lot,' murmured Moxon inconsequentially. 'They'll all be badly affected by what's happened, poor things.'

'Ghastly,' said Christopher, making Ben wonder how deeply the man really felt anything. Simmy's new husband had known loss, with both his parents dying in their sixties, and at least one close colleague being murdered, but it seemed to roll off him without leaving much evidence of damage. Or perhaps he was just very well defended, because his own losses were still uncomfortably raw. Ben was inclined to give the man the benefit of the doubt, which he might not have done a year earlier. Now that Simmy was married to him, Christopher had to be taken on board, warts and all.

Moxon was looking indecisive, glancing at Jonty and chewing his lip. Ben peered through the glass panel into the reception area. 'Looks as if there's somebody wanting help,' he said.

Everybody turned to watch a man trying to manoeuvre a large picture from outside through the door, which kept trying to close on him. 'Go and give him a hand, will you, Jonty?' said Christopher. 'He's going to damage it if he's not careful. Oh – and Jonty . . .' Christopher called him back at the last moment. 'After that, you should go home, don't you think? We'll be closing up early today anyway, and next week's going to be busy. Long days. You know how it goes. Get some time off while you can.'

'He can't, though, can he?' said Ben. 'Derek's not here to drive him.'

'I'll take him myself. I don't intend to stay here all day anyway.' Christopher adopted a manly pose, as if shouldering all the complex logistics by himself.

Jonty acquired a rebellious look, clearly in no hurry to go home.

Ben interceded. 'Will anyone be there?' he asked.

Jonty let out a long, defeated breath. 'My dad said he'd be home early. He's just finishing off a job.'

'Good old Eddie,' said Christopher who seemed to think a comment was expected. 'He'll be worrying about you.'

When the boy had gone, Moxon exhaled much as Jonty had done and said, 'We've had the preliminary results back. Just an external examination, which seems fairly conclusive. It's hard to believe it was an accident. Skull damage consistent with a blow. Even if he slipped into the beck and hit himself on stones it wouldn't be easy to account for the way he was hurt. It was behind his ear, apparently. Not a good place to be struck.'

'Somebody hit him?' said Christopher slowly. 'Surely not?'

Ben's mind was working quickly. 'Well, you and I are both in the clear,' he said. 'And Jonty and Derek Smythe. We all have plenty of people to say where we were all afternoon.'

Moxon grunted in a mixture of protest and admiration. 'Steady on, son,' he said. 'It hasn't come to that.'

'I expect it has, though,' said Ben. 'If Bruno was murdered, you're already way behind the curve. There won't be any usable forensics at the scene after two days. You'll have to concentrate on motives and opportunities – which means family and friends. Or else some random lunatic who didn't like the look on his face.'

Christopher made a choking sound. 'On a summer's day in the middle of a village – how is that possible?'

'Threlkeld's not exactly heaving with tourists, though, is it?' argued Ben. 'Walkers and cyclists are about it. Blencathra's popular, but there must have been plenty of quiet moments on that path. You were there,' he reminded Moxon. 'How many other people did you see?'

'A few,' said the detective. 'But mostly they park at the top and then go walking up the fell. The beck walk isn't of any interest to serious hikers. It's only short.'

'I wonder why Bruno was there to start with,' said Ben. 'Maybe somebody was with him and suggested it, deliberately trying to find a quiet spot to kill him.'

Christopher emitted a high-pitched syllable of horror. 'Stop it,' he pleaded. 'This is horrible.'

Ben eyed him with interest. Here at last was some genuine feeling, if only of revulsion. Squeamish was the diagnosis. Ben's assessment of Christopher Henderson had already been threaded with a hint of contempt. To his mind, the man lacked backbone. Pleasant, competent, nice enough as a husband and father, but not much good in a crisis.

'He's right, though,' said Moxon heavily. He gave Christopher much the same sort of scrutiny as Ben was doing. 'And the fact that your wedding was going on a couple of hundred yards away, is looking more and more significant.'

'How?' demanded Christopher.

'Most of the people present knew Bruno – or knew who he was. Jonty was trying to phone him, to see if he wanted to join in. It's all part of the picture.'

'But plenty of people who knew him *weren't* there,' Christopher blustered.

'True – and the wedding might have been used as a smokescreen,' Moxon suggested.

Ben interrupted him. 'Even then, the wedding is still relevant,' he pointed out. 'Smokescreen is exactly right, though.' He beamed approvingly at the detective. 'I hadn't thought of that.'

'Gold star to me, then,' said Moxon with a wink at Christopher, who failed to respond.

'So you need to interview the Patsy person, and Bruno's father, for a start. Who else is there – uncles or anything? We have to think about motive.' Ben was in full flow.

'Steady on,' Moxon cautioned for a second time. As he spoke, Jonty came back into the room, looking from face to face. 'All right?' Moxon asked him, eyeing the phone in his hand.

'My dad called me. He wants to speak to Uncle Chris.' He proffered the phone towards Christopher, who took it with a puzzled look.

'Eddie? What can I do for you?'

There followed what must have been a stream of unanswerable questions. 'I don't know . . . What makes you think that? . . . It's far too soon to say, but I'm sure you've got it wrong . . . You'll need to ask Patsy about that . . .' It went on for two long minutes before Christopher firmly ended the call on a promise to keep in touch. He blew out his cheeks and looked ruefully at Ben. 'He's in a right old state,' he said.

'Why?' asked Ben. 'What's his problem?'

'He seems to think Bruno must have been involved with dodgy people of some sort, implying that Jonty must know them as well, probably through all the riff-raff – his word, not mine – that comes to our auctions.'

'Well, it's a theory,' said Ben unwisely, with a smirk at Jonty. The boy did not respond.

Christopher glared at him and Moxon sucked his lip. 'You don't have to take any notice of Eddie,' said Christopher, aiming for a light tone that was obviously never going to convince. 'He thinks the worst of everybody.'

Jonty was hovering. 'What do you want me to do now?' he asked his uncle.

Christopher reached out a friendly hand and patted the boy's shoulder. 'You need to go home, old chap. Your father wants you where he can see you. I'm not sure he's going to want you working here any more, the way he's talking.'

Ben was alarmed. 'Is he going to try to stop us having the house as well?'

'He didn't say – but that's going to be off now anyway, surely? You can't afford it without Bruno, can you?'

Jonty said nothing. Again, the reality hit him and his eyes became shiny.

'Give it a few days,' advised Moxon, including Christopher in his address. 'No need to decide anything now.'

'We'll have to tell Mrs Padgett something,' Ben realised. 'She thinks we're moving in on Monday.'

'I'll drive you there some time over the weekend,' offered Christopher. 'If you think it's necessary.'

Nice of him, Ben thought, despite the contradiction inherent in his promises. Hadn't Christopher just said he was going to take Jonty home as well? Then he remembered that the boss was only intending to stay a short time at work, and could easily spend part of the afternoon driving his young employees around the Northern Lakes.

Moxon went from Keswick to Penrith, unsure of his role in what must now be a murder investigation. Nobody else seemed too sure, either. Based in Windermere, he rarely associated with colleagues in the north of the region, but they knew him by reputation. 'That soft DI who lets a teenage boy do his thinking for him,' was one end of the spectrum. More charitably, some insisted that he got results by inventive and unconventional means, and good luck to him. Now he was a potential witness, not merely close to the individuals concerned, but physically at the scene at much the same moment the crime had been committed.

'You didn't kill him, I hope,' said the senior investigating officer with a laugh, when Moxon presented himself in his office. The laugh had come through thin lips and was altogether mirthless. Murder committed by police officers was the least funny subject anyone in the force could imagine.

'I did not,' said Moxon firmly.

'Well, there's a few more snippets from the pathology chaps. They've gone over him with a magnifying glass. Broken toenail, undeveloped testicle. Amazing what you can find out about a person after they're dead. None of it much help, it has to be said.'

Moxon experienced a sudden wave of sadness that almost knocked him off his feet. Bruno Crowther had sprung into a fully three-dimensional human being without warning. Moxon thought it might have been the broken toenail that did it.

The SIO failed to notice, and carried on in the same unfeeling voice, 'You need to sit down with the whole team and go through everything again. That wedding – how they all link up to the deceased and to each other, and where we might sniff out a motive. Plenty of opportunity, by the look of it. Too much, you might say.'

'Yes, sir,' said Moxon hopelessly. There was nobody from the wedding he wished to see convicted of murder. He had liked them all. 'But I don't think—'

'Too early for thinking,' snapped the senior man. 'Just gather up the facts for now.'

Moxon sighed quietly. He had already come to the conclusion that this man had a poor opinion of him, seeing him as soft and possibly lazy. There was a geographical aspect to it, as well. Those in the northern reaches of Cumbria regarded the Windermere end as having life much too easy. They got half the snow, floods, gales and landslides that they did up around Keswick, Cockermouth and Penrith. They lost barely a handful of brainless hikers on their tame little fells, compared to the constant rescue parties called out onto the stern slopes of Helvellyn and Blencathra.

'I'm to be part of the team, then, am I?' he asked.

'Wouldn't hurt,' said the SIO grudgingly.

* * *

Another detective inspector interviewed Moxon, drawing out of him his precise movements on Wednesday afternoon. It was not an entirely unpleasant experience, surprisingly. *Now I know how other witnesses feel,* he thought. There was a sense of being useful, along with a high quality of attention that was in itself gratifying. He did his best to recall every detail.

'I set out at roughly a quarter to four and strolled up the path beside the beck. When I got to the top, I went a little way further, towards the mountain, before turning back and going down Blease Road. I stopped a few times to look at the view and just enjoy being there. I sat on a rock above the car park for a few minutes as well. There were a few people, mostly hikers, going the opposite way to me. I wouldn't recognise any of them again. I stopped for a look at the school, and again to read the names on the war memorial in the main street. I went all the way to the end, then turned back and went past the bottom of Blease Road to the pub. Again, I went slowly, and read the dates on the houses I passed, and just . . . as I said before, it was all very relaxed and peaceful. I could hear children playing at one point, and a lawnmower going, but it was mostly very quiet. I should think hardly more than three cars passed the whole time I was in the street. I was really not concentrating at all, thinking my own thoughts and wondering a bit about the history of the village. I got back to the pub about an hour later. I'd been away longer than I realised, and there was hardly anyone left from the wedding. I had some tea with Ben Harkness, Derek Smythe and Jonty Henderson. Jonty got a call about Bruno just after five, it must have been.'

'So the attack must have taken place between four and around four-fifteen? That's when Mr Ackroyd got the first call. The same person dialled 999 at four-eighteen, according to their log.'

Moxon nodded. 'I must have been in Blease Road then, I suppose. It's only about thirty or forty yards from the beck, but there are houses between it and the road. I couldn't have seen anything from where I was.'

The interviewing officer had already laid out a map of Threlkeld and was following Moxon's account with his finger. He nodded. 'Right,' he said. 'And there's a school playground as well.'

The interview had been taped, and at this point the machine was switched off. 'That's fine,' said the man. 'Very comprehensive. Ironic, really – you being at the scene, very nearly. But short of a very complicated conspiracy, I can't see that there's any reason to think you were involved.'

'Thank God for that,' said Moxon. 'But I still can't figure out what Bruno was *doing* up there in the first place.'

They went on to a more informal chat and Moxon gleaned that there had been interviews with Bruno's girlfriend, father and stepfather thus far. There were reports of each conversation, details of whereabouts on Wednesday and a few items concerning Bruno's life. He had left school and was awaiting his A-level results, due in a few days. A place was waiting for him at Bristol university, where he intended to study history. He played chess to a high standard and was extremely keen on films, especially those made in Japan. 'I get the impression he was rather a misfit, trying to find his place in the world. But nobody had a word to say against him.'

'Sounds a bit lost,' said Moxon.

'You think? I thought he just seemed a bit of a geek. Friendly with that Harkness boy in Bowness, I gather?'

'Right,' said Moxon, feeling sad all over again. 'Did you see the girlfriend? Did you do that interview?'

'For my sins. She's a right weirdo. Thin as a stick, hardly any hair, big clunky boots, even in the height of summer. You don't half meet some people in this job. Lord knows what her clients think of her. She must scare them half to death.'

'Why? What does she do?'

'She's some sort of social worker. Mental health, I think. Or something to do with the homeless. Spends half her time at the hospital supporting clients in the psych ward. Funny that – the way you can't always distinguish the client from the therapist, or whatever she calls herself.'

'Is she very upset?'

'What? Oh – fairly, I s'pose. Stunned, if anything. Kept saying what a huge loss to the world it was, and how he'd got a great future in front of him, and it was a massive tragedy. She's a fair bit older than him.'

'You think they met online?'

'No, but they do a lot of that sort of thing. Some kind of forum, with conventions and all that. Harmless stuff. Something they call LARPing, re-enacting battles.'

'But nobody was waving toy swords about on Wednesday,' said Moxon, still trying to construct a feasible storyline.

'Nope – just bashing heads with a rock,' said the detective inspector.

* * *

Eddie Henderson was in a state. Combative by nature, the middle one of three boys born to Frances and Kit, life never seemed to settle down for him. He had made that speech at the wedding despite everybody insisting there was no need. Jonty had visibly squirmed as he spoke, and several people had gone on talking, ignoring him. Angie Straw had sneered and Christopher clearly thought him a fool. But *somebody* had to mark the occasion properly. It wouldn't be a real wedding otherwise. As it was, it had been a dreadful disorganised mess, as anyone would admit. When Jonty got married, the whole thing would be done a lot more decently.

And people had wondered where Eliza was, of course. Sister-in-law to the groom, still officially married to the groom's brother, she should have been there. But his wife was her own mistress, doing whatever she liked, regardless of anybody else. Still nominally living together, they barely spoke, and slept in separate rooms, whilst making dwindling efforts to remain civilised. That's why Jonty was so keen to move out, of course. The atmosphere was not much short of toxic at times.

Eddie worshipped his only child, but was well aware that the feeling was not mutual. Eliza had seen to that, always belittling him in front of the boy, putting him to bed before his father got home, when he was small. Eddie had trained as a builder, learning all the relevant trades, but in recent times had specialised in roofs. He was good at it – quick and accurate in placing the tiles, whereas he was prone to blunders in other areas of the work. On top of a house he felt free and in perfect control. The world shrank to manageable proportions from up there. He felt at one with the pikes that thronged the region, king of all he surveyed. He had mellowed as a result, letting his wife's barbs bounce off him and finding his own amusements.

But now Jonty's best friend had been killed and there were sure to be all kinds of consequences. Eddie had not heard about the attack until Wednesday evening and assumed instantly that it had been no accident. That would be bad enough, but in Eddie's experience, things were usually worse than just 'bad enough'. He knew Eliza was worried that the friendship was more intense than was comfortable even while marvelling that her son could attract such a brainy person as a friend. She did not want her son to be gay – it always reflected badly on the mother, as far as she could see – but she was careful not to say anything to that effect. Whatever the precise nature of the relationship, Jonty was going to be deeply hurt and lost without his clever mate. Bruno had been distant with Jonty's parents, but they admired him none the less for that.

Eddie knew Threlkeld very well – what there was of it. He had replaced a couple of roofs there, watching the slow daily lives going on in the sleepy little place. He knew almost all the villages and towns in Cumbria and entertained himself by making comparisons and inventing histories for them. Threlkeld was a bit like Coniston, with similar geographical associations. It had its own mountain looming over it protectively, but Blencathra had none of the charisma of the Old Man of Coniston. It was just a big plain lump, to be hiked up because of its height and the fabulous views to be had, but it rarely featured in paintings

101

or stories or legends. The only interesting thing, really, was that it had been known as the Saddleback for ages, until the Wainwright man rechristened it. Nothing very romantic about a saddleback, thought Eddie.

But the village had a strong appeal for him for that very reason. In the fugue state imposed by the hypnotic rhythm of hammering roof slates into place, he found himself identifying with it. It chimed with his own lack of ambition – or charisma. Nothing ever happened in Threlkeld, apart from a cluster of uninspiring new houses, designated for the elderly and tucked away down a slope close to the main road. Many of the buildings had their dates displayed on their walls. The first decade of the last century had evidently seen a bit of a boom. Since then it had quietly slumbered under its unremarkable mountain. Until now. Now, Threlkeld had a murder to its name.

On Friday afternoon, Eddie finished work early. It had been a disrupted week anyway, what with his brother's wedding. As August approached, the job often became quite busy, with people realising their roof wouldn't survive another hard winter with the penetrating wind and rain, and shouting for urgent attention. But this year was slower for some reason, and there were only a couple of jobs in the diary. He could finish up and leave everything until Monday. His son would be needing him, whether he knew it or not. Eddie was determined to be there for him, despite Eliza's efforts to keep the boy to herself. Jonty had to be protected, because there were obviously evil forces at work out there.

The family lived in a characterful old house quite near the centre of the village, which was strung unexcitingly along both sides of the A6. Eddie had always made good money and Eliza had more than pulled her weight financially, once Jonty started school and she could devote her considerable energy to freelance work as a tour guide. She took busloads of tourists to beauty spots across the region, making people walk for miles before depositing them in a pub garden for a rest. Mostly they were Americans, free with their cash and loud in their appreciation. Many of them were extra happy when it rained. They had been told to expect rain and they looked forward to it – especially those from Arizona or Texas.

This was her busiest season and Eddie did not expect to find her at home. In fact, he was relying on her absence because he wanted to talk to his son in peace.

Jonty was in the garden lying flat on the grass, one arm over his face.

'Got off early, then?' said Eddie. 'I thought you might. But how did you get here?'

'Uncle Chris brought me. Sorry you wasted your time driving me there this morning. I wasn't fit to work, really. I can't stop thinking about Bruno.'

'It's good you saw him yesterday, don't you think? One last time, and all that.'

'Not really,' mumbled the boy. 'We didn't say much.'

With no conscious effort on either one's part, and no real acknowledgement that it existed, there was often a degree of telepathy between father and son. They would bump into each other in town, arrive home at the same moment, start saying the same thing, with no advance intention. It was as if their lives ran on parallel rails from the start, regardless of how detached they both believed themselves to be.

Eliza ignored it, finding it uncomfortable to be forced onto the furthest point of the triangle. She had grabbed the child as her own exclusive possession and found the persistent presence of his father quite an irritation. Nature, or instinct, or sheer infuriating fate, had seemed to work against her from the outset and continued to do so now. The two men in her life liked each other more than they liked her, and there was no denying that unhappy fact.

'What's it like at work, then?' Eddie asked, trying to shift the focus.

Jonty sighed, but did manage a reply. 'A detective was there. He knows Uncle Chris. Mr Smythe didn't show – not surprising, I guess. It's so *awful*, Dad.'

'I know. It's bloody horrible for you. What did the detective chap say?'

'Not much. They sent me out, so I s'pose they were talking about post-mortems and stuff they thought would upset me. Ben was there. He's only a bit older than me, and he was Bruno's friend as well, but they let him stay.'

'Not the same sort of friend as you, though. And Ben Harkness has been around murders and suchlike before. Plus he was doing that course at Newcastle all about bodies and maggots and blood splashes and I don't know what.'

'I s'pose. I didn't know you'd taken that much notice.'

'I didn't, not on purpose. But he's been around ever since Grandpa died, so I've just picked it up. Your aunt Hannah talks about him all the time.'

'Right,' said Jonty, obviously barely listening.

'We'll just have a quiet weekend, eh? Your mother's got a load of Texans doing stone circles and old ruins. I doubt we'll see much of her.'

'Is that someone at the door?' Jonty cocked his head. 'I heard a knock.'

Eddie got up and went to see, coming back a minute later with a woman he barely knew and already disliked. 'It's Patsy,' he said, unnecessarily.

'Pats,' Jonty acknowledged. 'How're you doing?'

Eddie watched the pair of them, trying to work out what they thought and felt about each other. Patsy was mid-twenties to his son's eighteen. It seemed like a big gap. Bruno had obviously been far too young for her, making more people than Eddie wonder what she was thinking of.

'I'm in pieces,' she said flatly. 'You must be as well.'

'Yeah. Sort of. None of it seems real.' He glanced at his father, as though wishing he'd take himself out of earshot somewhere. Eddie stayed where he was.

Patsy sat down close to Jonty and patted his leg. 'What have they told you? All they did with me was ask a whole lot of questions about him. Made me miss two appointments, and then I got sent home on compassionate grounds. They didn't even ask me – just said it was procedure.'

'Bummer,' said Jonty.

'Upsetting for your clients, if you're emotional,' offered Eddie, curious to know more about her work. All he really knew was that she was employed by the council and mainly dealt with individuals adrift from society and suffering mentally. Homeless, jobless, witless – he could dredge up little sympathy for the people she called her clients.

'Worse to have them left to themselves, when they're so dependent on me,' she argued. 'Means they've got to spend even more time in limbo. There was nobody else to stand in for me.' The implication was that she alone could conjure up accommodation, or hospital beds or practical advice, leaving the pathetic 'clients' to huddle in a doorway somewhere until she came to the rescue. For all Eddie knew, this was exactly the situation.

The garden was washed with the full blaze of the lowering sun, with no trees to cast any shade. Patsy shied away from it like a vampire, while Jonty unconsciously spread himself out to get the full benefit. He had the olive skin of his maternal grandmother, and instinctively sought the sun at every opportunity. Eddie thought of Eliza and her Americans up at Castlerigg or some equally exposed spot and gave a small rueful smile. If the visitors came from the southern states, they would much prefer cloud and rain.

'They didn't talk to me much,' said Jonty, answering her question. 'But Ben says they obviously think it was murder. Someone killed Bruno on purpose.' His face went pinched and pale, and his father flinched at the pain he could do nothing to assuage. 'And we saw him just before he died. You, me and his dad – we were all there. I still can't believe it.'

'It might not be murder,' said Patsy. 'And I don't think they have done a proper post-mortem. I've got friends at the hospital, and I phoned one of them last night to check. No need, probably. They already know what killed him.'

'Yeah,' said Jonty with a frown. 'But don't you think it might have been an accident?'

Patsy shook her head. 'Seems unlikely. Though whoever attacked him must have been pretty useless, just hitting him like that and then leaving him. If they'd wanted it to look like an accident – which they probably did – they should have pushed him off the top of a pike, not into a beck with hardly any water in it.'

Eddie flinched again at the tone. *Bitter*, he diagnosed. The woman was bitter. But Jonty seemed almost reassured by it. 'Yeah,' he said. 'But who?' He stared from his father to Patsy and back again. 'Who could possibly want to kill Bruno?'

Chapter Eight

Angie quite liked her dentist and felt no fear of drills or needles or antiseptic smells. The broken tooth was deemed just sturdy enough to take a crown.

'At least for a few more years,' said the woman heartlessly. 'It's a case of fire-fighting at this stage. Just keep everything going for as long as we can.'

'Thanks,' said Angie grimly.

'I'll put a temporary one on now, after taking a few X-rays and impressions, so they can make the permanent one. I've got an hour, which should be enough.'

'Good,' said Angie. There were two sets of B&B guests due at around six – she'd be back in plenty of time for them.

She relinquished all control to the pleasant forty-year-old dentist, and thought about her little grandson. She would have to put a baby seat in the car, for when Persimmon allowed her to drive him around. And she would buy a stack of books to read to him. The time when her daughter would get back to working regularly in the shop was fast approaching, and Angie would have custody of the baby for several hours a week.

It would be a mixed pleasure, she admitted to herself. A curtailment of a freedom she had not made the best use of in recent years. Now she was losing it, she regretted not getting about a lot more. But on the other hand she could take Robin out to a whole variety of places – with Russell sure to want to go with them. A change to their routine would be welcome.

'All done,' said the dentist, sooner than expected.

Angie barely waited for the adjustable seat to return to a position from which she could easily rise. But seconds after she was on her feet, she was gripped with a wholly unexpected cramp, all down the inner thigh of her right leg. She gasped and sat back on the dentist's chair. It was agony. She couldn't breathe.

'Cramp!' she said. 'Oooh!'

'Oh, Lord,' said the dentist unhelpfully. 'That happened to another woman last week. Something about the change of position.'

'Never mind that,' panted Angie. 'Do something!'

From behind the dentist, a young nurse pushed forward. 'Let me,' she said, and started to knead the rigid muscles, having unceremoniously grabbed Angie's leg inside the light summer trousers.

'Ow!' shrieked Angie. 'That's making it worse.' She was drowning in the pain, her whole body tensing in sympathy.

'You need to try to relax,' said the girl. 'It'll go completely in a minute.'

'Relax!' shouted Angie. 'You're joking.' Her body was betraying her, behaving entirely outside her control. It hurt prodigiously, lavishly, making her want to roll on the ground and cry. It frightened her and made her think of death. Was this what old people had to endure? People with cancer or angina? Regular violent assaults, wracking and beyond remedy? How was it to be borne?

'Haven't you had it before?' asked the dentist.

'Not there. The back of my leg, lower down, sometimes in the night. This is much worse. It's unbearable.'

'And yet you're bearing it,' the nurse pointed out.

Angie looked at her. 'Am I?'

'Take deep slow breaths. Don't fight it. It'll be gone in another minute. I can feel it getting softer. Can't you?'

'Yes, but it might come back.' Angie was going to live in dread of it coming back, for the rest of her life, she was sure.

'It won't. You'll forget all about it by tomorrow. Like childbirth.'

'I hope so.' She looked again at the girl. 'You're very good at this.'

'I teach antenatal classes,' came the surprising reply. 'I'm trained for this sort of thing.'

'Well, you can give me as a reference any time,' said Angie, and cautiously got to her feet. 'You're right. It's gone. I feel all soft and wimbly now.'

'You'll be back to normal in no time,' the girl promised.

'I won't, though,' Angie realised. 'I felt as if Death was stroking me, with a horrible smile on his face. I won't forget that – ever.' She shuddered. 'I really saw it for a second.'

The kind nurse had nothing to say to that and neither did the dentist. Angie had stepped quite a way over a line and could expect no comforting response. Nobody was going to accompany her down that road if they could help it. She was escorted to the reception desk and left to make the next appointment for her permanent crown. *How will I feel about coming back here?* she wondered. At least they'd make sure she got out of the chair with all due care.

'People quite often die at the dentist,' said Russell unsympathetically, when his wife tried to tell him what had happened. 'But not of cramp.'

'"Men have died from time to time and worms have eaten them, but not for love",' said Angie. 'Is that what you're trying to say?'

'Oh, such glorious cynicism,' sighed Russell. 'We'll have to teach it to Robin.'

'If we live long enough,' said Angie glumly.

'Our daughter telephoned,' he remembered to tell her. 'Events are developing in Threlkeld and she assumes young Ben will have a theory about it any time now.'

'Didn't he have one already? Something about nowhere being as calm and innocent and bland as it looked on the surface?'

'He did, and all of a sudden he's proved right. He tempted the gods, silly fellow.'

Angie tried to think. 'What if the killer was listening and wanted to make his point for him?'

'Impossible. Nobody would be as insane as that. Even fictitious serial killers have a better motive than that.'

'And the timing doesn't work,' said Angie, striving to think like a detective. She'd tried it before, and it never worked out successfully. The truth was, she had no idea about the timing of the latest murder. All she knew was that nothing untoward had happened by the time she and Russell had left the wedding party with Bonnie.

'Simmy thinks it must have happened some time after four. So if a person was listening to Ben at about three, it would work perfectly well,' Russell corrected her. 'Christopher had a talk with Moxon today, and caught up with some of the story. Moxon went for a walk up by the beck some time after three o'clock and there was no dying youth there then.'

'Yes, we knew that. Except he seems to think he might have walked right past without noticing. I imagine him with his head in the air, probably composing poetry, or at least quoting Wordsworth to himself. He's an awful sentimentalist at heart, you know.'

'I think we can safely discard any idea that he writes poems, all the same. He's no Adam Dalgliesh, for heaven's sake.'

'He might be,' Angie insisted. 'It wouldn't surprise me at all.'

'Oh well. I agree with you insofar as he was probably lost in thought – most likely about Simmy – and wouldn't have noticed a murder going on a few yards away.'

'"Insofar",' she murmured. 'That's a new one.'

'Good, though, don't you think?' he twinkled at her.

Angie wouldn't think any more about dying, she promised herself. It did no good, and if she forced her husband to listen to musings about mortality it would only depress him. It would happen eventually of its own accord, after all, whether she contemplated it or not.

'Don't forget we've got Robin all morning tomorrow,' she said needlessly. Russell had been accumulating items for the baby's amusement for days. 'I hope the guests don't linger over breakfast.'

As if conjured by magic, the doorbell rang and a family of four flowed into the hall. Angie went into autopilot, reciting the details of keys, local eateries, location of various rooms, while Russell disappeared into the kitchen with his dog.

Another two guests turned up an hour later, filling the house to capacity. Much of the evening was going to be spent preparing for the next day's breakfast, everything laid out with military precision, the sausages pre-cooked for rapid warming, fruit already in bowls, everything to hand for maximum speed and efficiency.

'This is a mug's game,' Angie muttered to herself as she worked. She had never been a natural or enthusiastic cook, and the financial return for all this attention to food often seemed ludicrously inadequate, especially on a summer evening when she might be sitting out beside a lake somewhere.

But Russell liked the people, and it gave their lives a focus. And the money was actually far from derisory. Over the years they had accumulated an impressive amount of savings, joking about a world cruise or a hideaway on Malta or Fuerteventura for their old age. But now they had a grandchild and there was no question of leaving the area because they couldn't miss a moment of his growing up.

Simmy was berating herself for a surprising level of anxiety about the prospect of spending a whole morning in the shop.

She had always been vague about when she would return full time – if she ever did. Now it seemed to have rushed at her before she was ready. Robin was only four months old; it felt wrong, almost violent. But she assured herself that he would be perfectly happy with her parents and the shop would benefit from her attention. Bonnie was brilliant at the surface stuff – the window display and the friendly greetings she gave the customer – but she let dust accumulate in the corners and forgot to order boring things like cellophane for wrapping and new light bulbs. Verity was even worse, not seeing any of that as her responsibility. Simmy was going to be kept busy making lists and putting in orders.

'You'll love it when you get there,' Christopher told her, noticing her agitation.

It had been a shock when, a week or two earlier, he had said he wouldn't be able to promise to mind the baby while he was still so small. In fact, she had not believed him at first. When she chose a Saturday morning at the end of July, she made sure it would be a day when there was no auction. She had simply assumed he would do his bit as a parent when it came to the point. She began to explain about the bottle of expressed milk when he stopped her.

'I told you before, I think it would be much better if he went to your parents,' he said. 'That's who's going to have him when you go back to work properly, so you may as well get him used to it now.'

'That's true, but this is just a trial run. It seems excessive to bother them when I can just leave Robin with you for a morning.'

'I disagree,' he insisted.

She might have understood if he'd used the death of Bruno as his reason, but he had told her long before that happened that he could not be relied on. 'But *why*?' she had demanded.

'I need to be free to go out at short notice,' he had said.

'What for?' It had been so unexpected, she could hardly speak. 'I hope you're not trying to tell me you're never going to have him, in case he cramps your style. This is madness.'

'When he's a bit bigger,' said Christopher weakly. 'But now . . . it's just . . .'

'So where do you think you might have to rush off to?' Hadn't they discussed this, when she was pregnant? She tried to recall an actual commitment from the child's father, in vain. 'You *knew* I'd want to leave him with you sometimes.'

'Not really. I always assumed you'd leave him with your mother when you were at the shop.' There had been a hunted look on his face that scared her. Her heart had thumped with an irrational panic. They were newly married and were hoping for a second child. They had a new house and were even planning to acquire a dog. What had gone wrong at this very last moment? She stared at him. 'Am I taking this too seriously?' she wondered. 'Is it something I need to worry about?'

'It's only while he's so little,' Christopher tried again. 'What if he cries and won't stop? And I don't understand bottles. Give me a bit longer, OK? Don't get worked up about it.'

Gradually, she accepted that he was genuinely frightened of being left alone with an infant whose mother was twenty miles away. Even his own familiar son, who trusted and loved him unreservedly, was frightening. It seemed mad, in the context of twenty-first-century fatherhood, but it would have been unremarkable a century earlier. Perhaps it was her own fault, not standing back enough to let Christopher learn and practise every aspect of baby care. Well, she could easily change that without making an issue of it.

'OK, I'll leave him with Mum and Dad, then. They'll be delighted,' she had added in a confused attempt to make Christopher feel bad.

It had not actually been a difficult decision, and nothing was lost by it – except for a spoonful of trust and respect she had automatically accorded Christopher. That had gone, and she felt a burning need to talk it over with someone. The fact that nobody came to mind as a reliable confidante worried her. She should have more friends, she concluded. Somebody her own age who understood these things.

There were two possible candidates – Helen Harkness and Corinne. Both in their fifties, with a lot of life experience. And both too closely linked to Ben and Bonnie to be trusted with something so intimate. It was all too close, too incestuous. That word occurred much too often as it was, with Simmy and Christopher so nearly siblings.

'New blood,' she muttered to herself. 'We need new blood.'

There was a woman in Glenridding, only a mile away, with a baby the same age as Robin who had come for coffee a few times. The woman at the Patterdale pub had introduced them. But it had not developed into a genuine friendship. Abby was too risk-averse, too concerned about germs and sterilising everything to ever become a soulmate to the daughter of Angie Straw. Even the babies did not like each other much.

On this late Friday afternoon, it was apparent that Christopher could think of little else but the killing of Bruno Crowther. The childcare arrangements for the following day were all settled in his mind, and needed no more consideration. Instead, he made Simmy listen while he went over everything Moxon, Ben and Jonty had said that morning, with special reference to any implications there might be for the auction house.

'Don't be silly,' said Simmy. 'How could it reflect on you, in any way at all?'

'It was my wedding going on when it happened. I know all the people involved. And there's a *history*,' he finished miserably. 'It only takes the slightest hint for everyone to start thinking the worst again.'

'Nobody's thinking anything yet,' she pointed out. '"Young man dead in Threlkeld, police investigating" is about as far as it goes. It's summer – everybody's either away or going mad trying to cope with all the tourists.'

'That's true,' Christopher reluctantly agreed. 'Jonty says his mother's working about fifteen hours a day with her Americans.'

Jonty's mother was Simmy's sister-in-law – *or was it in-law-in-law*, she wondered. Anyway, they were married to brothers, which made them family.

'I quite like Eliza,' she said inconsequentially.

'She's a bully. Nobody likes her,' Christopher argued. 'Not even Eddie.'

Simmy gave a doubtful laugh and changed the subject. 'Has anybody seen the Smythes since Thursday? They must be in a dreadful state.'

'Derek was at work on Thursday morning, when he thought Bruno was going to be OK. He rushed home when Eliza phoned in the afternoon. Haven't I told you that already?'

'Probably. What about yesterday? Did he phone or anything?'

'No – I wouldn't expect him to. Do you think I ought to go and see how they are?' He looked worried.

'I don't know about *ought*, but it would be a nice gesture. You could go tomorrow, to justify your failure as a babyminder.' She had not intended to say that, and the way it popped out startled her as much as it did Christopher.

'You're never going to let that go, are you?' he reproached.

'I thought I had. It must run deeper than I realised.'

He opened his mouth to reply, and then closed it again. They both knew that there was nothing he could say to change the situation.

Simmy pressed on with the main topic. 'Actually, it is quite a nice idea to go and see Derek and his wife. Have you met her? What's her name?'

'Once. He brought her in to show her around when he first started. It's a funny name. Let me think . . . Tilda. That's it. Derek mostly calls her Tilly when he's talking about her.'

'Short for *Ma*tilda, presumably. What's funny about that?'

'Nothing when you explain it to me. That never occurred to me.'

'You're hopeless,' she told him, with less affection or tolerance than he might have expected.

'I remember the names of her other children. Harriet and Lucy. Nice and straightforward. Plus they've got the same initials as Hannah and Lynn, which helps. Derek's always going on about them.'

'How old are they?'

'Small. Barely started school.'

'Imagine trying to explain what's happened to them,' Simmy agonised. 'Where would you even begin?'

'Bruno was much older than them, remember. Kids get over things more quickly than we think. And they don't have to tell the girls everything all at once. Just break it to them a bit at a time, somehow.' He tailed away feebly and sighed. 'Ignore me. I'm talking rubbish.'

'I don't think you are. You've had a lot more experience of children than I have – with Hannah and Lynn,' she said.

'I guess that's right,' he said slowly, as if struck by a sudden thought. 'Although I don't recall very much detail. I was at school by the time they turned up. It was all rather confusing at the time. They weren't babies, remember. They came fully formed, like something in a Greek legend.'

Simmy laughed. 'None of which has much to do with anything,' she said carelessly.

Christopher shrugged and walked away, leaving her faintly aware of having missed something by laughing at the wrong moment, or letting go of the main subject just as Christopher wanted to share something important. Life was like that, she supposed. It kept getting in the way. Or were they both just tired and emotional after a very busy and life-changing week?

Her thoughts drifted to Ben, all alone in his poky little Keswick room, stranded because he had no transport except for the bike. He would be phoning Bonnie, no doubt, and trying to find a way they could be together. But the last Simmy had heard, Bonnie was being whisked off on a shopping trip by an implacable Corinne. 'She says I can't go on with these same clothes,' the girl had told Simmy. 'And she's taking me to Kendal. I can't get out of it.'

Which left Ben on his own, at least for the Saturday. Perhaps he would amuse himself by drawing up one of his flowcharts in an attempt to analyse Bruno's murder – but he was still by himself, when he shouldn't be. She and Christopher should have thought to invite him to stay with them for the weekend, once they realised Bonnie would not be with him. There were two spare rooms in their newly-converted barn, all finished and pristine.

The buses in the north of the area ran from east to west, Penrith to Workington, via Keswick and Cockermouth. It was possible to get to Patterdale without too much difficulty, which was within walking distance of Hartsop, home of Simmy and Christopher. Perhaps she should call Ben and suggest it. Or perhaps he would cheerfully cover the ten miles or so on his bike. The point was, she reminded herself, that she was a great deal closer to Keswick than Bonnie or Ben's parents were. And it was due to her that the boy was in Keswick in the first place, since he had started working for Christopher.

There was a theme developing – young male persons in need of care. Bruno had been allowed to get himself killed; Jonty had an air of vulnerability, and Robin's own father was scared of being left in charge of him.

I've only been married for three days and here I am feeling resentful and anxious, she thought, trying not to blame Christopher for how she was feeling. Her mother had often insisted that a person was responsible for her own feelings, and nobody could *make* anybody feel anything. It was a bracing theory, but Simmy knew it to be wrong. The feelings were direct reactions to the behaviour of other people. Without those people, the feelings would not exist. *Plain logic*, she thought defiantly. Cause and effect. Just as her baby made her feel warm and strong and protective and proud.

It was still only five o'clock. The day was far from over. The weekend stretched ahead, with the shop and her parents, and Bonnie and Ben to think about, in addition to the fact that she was now Mrs Henderson, which produced a considerable quantity of paperwork to be updated. Again there was a flicker of resentment, as she realised that it was the female partner who had to make the changes. All her husband had to do was give some attention to life insurance and the fate of his pension if he died. And there was no urgency for that.

In a transparent effort to redeem himself, Christopher drove out to Patterdale where he had ordered a takeaway meal from the hotel there. It was not something they did regularly, but public demand had prompted the hotel to offer Friday night specials during the summer, which were proving very popular. Christopher came back with fish, pasta and pudding enough to last them all weekend, but before they had finished their meal, DI Moxon was at the door.

Chapter Nine

Simmy had not seen him since Wednesday, which already seemed a long time ago. She stared at him, trying to recall why it felt wrong to have him there now. Finally it came to her. 'Aren't you supposed to be on holiday?' she said.

'Anglesey,' he agreed. 'I might get off tomorrow for a day or two, but I didn't feel I could leave today. Everything's so up in the air. And Ben . . .'

'Yes! Ben. I've just been worrying about him. He's over there in Keswick all by himself. Bonnie is otherwise engaged tomorrow, which is going to be frustrating for them. And Bruno was his *friend*. He's bound to be upset.'

Christopher was on the sofa with Robin, looking as if this visitation was a long way from agreeable to him. 'Ben's fine,' he said irritably. 'What d'you think'll happen to him?'

For the first time, Simmy felt a flash of fear that whoever had killed Bruno might decide to slaughter Ben Harkness as well. It had not occurred to her until then. To judge from Moxon's expression, he was equally startled by this new idea.

'He shouldn't be on his own,' said Simmy in a small voice. 'That's all.'

They both looked at Christopher accusingly. 'What?' he demanded. 'You think we should have him here, I suppose.'

'Just for the weekend,' Simmy said quickly. 'Until things are a bit clearer.'

'That would put everybody's mind at rest,' said Moxon.

'He's got a perfectly good family,' Christopher pointed out. 'If it's that important, why can't they come and fetch him?'

'Because it wouldn't occur to them, unless he asked them – and he won't do that,' said Simmy. 'For all we know, they haven't even heard about Bruno.'

'Of course they have,' scoffed Christopher. 'It's all over the news by now.'

'Except it isn't,' Moxon corrected him. 'A small piece, giving no names, was on last night. The headlines are all focused on the home secretary's latest blunder. I'm not sure Ben would have told his parents – would he?' He looked to Simmy for an answer.

'Probably not. They're not on very good terms just now.'

Moxon shrugged as if this was too much for him to take on board. He looked at Robin on his father's lap, and by an obvious association of ideas, smiled as if here at least was a family in total harmony. Simmy resisted the temptation to put him straight. She offered him the chance of doing a bit of dandling, which he politely declined. But every now and then she caught him eyeing the child and pulling faces to amuse him.

'Are there any suspects?' she said suddenly. 'Anybody who might benefit from Bruno being dead?'

Moxon sucked his lip for a second, adjusting to the very direct question. 'Not that I'm aware of,' he said carefully.

'Young man with a good brain, trying to decide what to do with himself after leaving school with good results . . .'

'The results aren't through yet,' said Simmy. 'But it sounds as if he'd have done well.' It hit her afresh that Bruno was never going to know how he'd done, and his parents would have to bear that additional blow when the pointless results finally arrived. That sort of thing made grief and loss all the more terrible. 'Isn't that awful!'

'It is.'

'Maybe he had a rival at school who couldn't take being beaten by Bruno getting better A-levels,' said Christopher lightly. 'I imagine people have killed for lesser reasons than that, from time to time.'

'I doubt it,' said Moxon, with a ponderousness designed to warn Christopher against undue flippancy. 'People tend to kill for gain, revenge, security, uncontrolled rage – but not so much envy or resentment.'

'Security?' Simmy echoed. 'What does that mean?'

'Well – self-defence, I suppose. Ridding themselves of a perceived threat. Get him before he gets you, kind of thing. Not very common, I admit.'

'Are you actually part of the investigating team?' Christopher asked him. 'I don't think we went into that this morning, did we?'

'I think you could say I'm in the loop,' Moxon told him. 'But I'm not doing any of the interviews or background checks. If I can be of use, I will do all I can. It's understood that I have a personal connection.'

'And you were in the very spot where it happened, at almost the very same time,' Christopher reminded him with a little smirk.

'Don't be nasty,' Simmy told him crossly.

Christopher blinked and looked down at his little son. 'You're right – that was a bit uncalled-for,' he admitted. 'It's all getting on top of me, if I'm honest. It's selfish I know, but I keep worrying about what it means for the saleroom – Smythe and Jonty both being knocked sideways, not to mention Ben.'

'Fair enough,' said Moxon, with a fatherly glance at Simmy. Here, she suddenly realised, was the friend she had been yearning for, right under her very nose. She came close to leaning her head on his chest and letting him deal with her whole unsettled life. Then she saw sense and hoped he hadn't noticed before she pulled back and started fiddling with a thread at the hem of her shirt.

It seemed she had acted in time, as Moxon went on speaking to Christopher. 'You've nailed it precisely,' he said with a sigh. 'The bit about me being at the scene without realising it. And a very uncomfortable fact it is, I can tell you.'

'You were off duty, a guest at a wedding, just going for a little walk,' said Simmy. 'The last thing you were expecting was anything criminal going on. I rather wish I'd gone with you. I still haven't seen much of Threlkeld.'

'You were just about to leave. It felt as if the main event was over. I should probably have gone straight home.'

'Yes – why didn't you?' asked Christopher. 'According to Ben, you stayed another hour or more.'

The detective showed no sign of rising to this mild provocation. 'It seemed like a good opportunity to explore,' he answered peaceably. 'The sun was shining, and my wife was out all day. I'd warned her not to expect me until past five. I don't get many chances just to wander about like that. I gave a full report of my movements earlier today, to my colleagues at Penrith.'

'It's a shame,' said Simmy. 'The whole thing's a terrible shame. It's clouded the wedding, in retrospect. It's selfish, I know, but I'm rather glad I never met Bruno. It's bad enough as it is.'

Christopher gave a noisy sigh. 'Have we got to the main point yet? The actual reason why you're here, miles out of your normal area? Haven't you and I seen enough of each other already today?' He smiled as he spoke, but the question was genuine.

Simmy spoke for the detective. 'Come on,' she reproached her husband. 'You must see how crucial it is to explore every little detail. You know most of the people involved – and it's because of you and me that Ben's up here by himself, if you think about it.'

Christopher kinked the side of his mouth in a grimace of compliance. 'True,' he murmured. 'If a bit irritating.'

'That's it, really,' said Moxon, still perfectly calm. 'The people involved. There appear to be quite a number of them. Bruno's father, for one. And his mother, stepfather, friend, friend's parents, girlfriend.'

'That's another thing,' Christopher interrupted. 'That girlfriend, who nobody even knew existed. And the father sounds pretty weird, with all that Facebook stuff. Those two should be the focus of your attention, if you ask me.'

Moxon nodded. 'I agree it's peculiar. We've pieced most of it together, but there are some gaps. We're not sure exactly who found Bruno first. Somebody – a man – called 999 but wouldn't leave a name. Apparently that same person scrolled through Bruno's phone and called his father. His biological father, by the name of Ackroyd. When the ambulance got there, the couple with him said they'd only come on the scene a few minutes before and they'd also called 999, to be told there was already an ambulance on its way. And of course, because Bruno didn't seem all that badly injured, there was very little investigation of the scene until late the next day. Yesterday, that was.'

'Right.' Simmy nodded, as if reminding herself. 'Of course. No wonder there wasn't anything much on the news. It wasn't a very dramatic death, was it? Not from a news angle.'

'He's still just as dead,' said Christopher, sighing again.

Robin finally detected an atmosphere and began to grizzle.

Simmy stood up. 'Bedtime,' she said. 'Is there anything else you wanted to say?' she asked the detective.

'Probably, but I think it can wait.'

'Until the smoke clears?' said Christopher. 'Looks to me as if this one's going to end up in the "Pending" tray for the foreseeable future. Or do they call it the "Unsolved Crimes" file?'

'Something like that,' said Moxon.

'But what about *Ben*?' Simmy persisted. 'Do we think he'll be all right?'

'Listen,' said her husband. 'I'll go over and fetch him now. Phone him and make sure he's there first. Tell him we can have him all weekend. I can see you'll be awake all night stressing about him otherwise.' He gave her a wide, open smile, and she remembered why she'd loved him for so much of her life.

'Thanks,' she said. 'I'll call him now.'

She did, and Ben was surprised and slightly confused. 'I'm perfectly all right,' he told her. 'I was going to go up Blencathra tomorrow, actually. And do a bit of cycling on Sunday, if Bonnie can't get here. I am quite sad about that, actually,' he admitted. 'We've both got the whole weekend off and we can't work out how to be together. It's pathetic. I've hardly seen her since I came up here. It's as bad as being at university.'

'You can climb Hartsop Dodd instead, if you come here. We just thought everybody would be happier if you were with someone. And we're closest.'

'I'll come on the bike then. Give me an hour or so. But aren't you at the shop tomorrow? Is Christopher minding the baby?'

'Yes and no. I am at the shop, with your sister, and my mother's having Robin. It's all a bit experimental at this stage.' She deliberately avoided looking at Christopher. Moxon was standing by the front door, on the verge of leaving.

'I could maybe go and see Jonty, then. Clifton isn't too far from you.'

'It is, Ben. It must be nearly twenty miles. Uphill for much of the way, as well.'

'Downhill on the way back,' the boy pointed out. 'And actually, most of it's fairly level. Twenty miles is nothing on a good bike. You should try it.'

'I don't think so.'

'Actually, it's twenty miles from here to you, as well. Isn't that nice and symmetrical?'

'Exhausting,' said Simmy. 'See you in a bit, anyway,' and she ended the call.

Christopher spent a pedantic two minutes establishing that both journeys were under twenty miles, when she reported the conversation. Moxon rolled his eyes and took his leave.

Robin claimed a handsome repayment of all the attention he had missed over the past forty minutes. Before they knew it, Ben Harkness was at the door.

'I called Bonnie,' he burst out excitedly, almost before he was inside. 'She can get here more easily than she can to Keswick, if she gets the train to Penrith. Although she has to go down to Oxenholme and back up again on the direct line. That's why we never considered it for getting to my digs. It'd take much too long.'

Simmy shook her head to indicate a lack of interest in the complexities of public transport. Her father favoured buses, and sometimes embarked on the convoluted route from Windermere to Patterdale. He did it mainly to make a point, although he insisted he enjoyed it. 'You're telling me she's going to show up here as well, are you? When?'

'Well – would tomorrow afternoon be OK? Corinne might drop her at Oxenholme after they've been shopping.'

'And how will she get here from Penrith?'

'Bus!' he declared. 'There's one that comes almost to the door. It's brilliant.'

Simmy refrained from asking what would happen after that. She could well imagine herself doing a prolonged round trip, via Keswick and Ambleside, taking both youngsters home for Sunday night. Depending on her mood, she inwardly resolved that she might well ask them for petrol money.

It dawned on her through the evening that the talk of buses and trains had been largely employed as a distraction from the business of Bruno's death. This was highly unusual for Ben, who had previously dived into murder investigations with unseemly enthusiasm. But he knew the victim this time and the death had direct personal implications for him. More than that, he seemed stunned by Bruno's sudden disappearance, as a young child might be.

Gradually he began to talk about it. 'I keep looking for him,' he said. 'I want to *talk* to him. It was going to be so great living together. He had so much to say – he was always thinking about big subjects, and quoting Socrates and Heidegger and Nietszche and really getting into it. His head was absolutely *full* of it. Where did all that *go*?' he cried, throwing his hands out as if trying to catch Bruno's lost thoughts.

Christopher was back on his favourite sofa. Ben and Simmy were on one of the two window seats that had been cleverly constructed by Humphrey, the builder. Shaped and cushioned for maximum comfort, they quickly became the place of choice for Simmy and most of their visitors, especially on a summer evening. Facing west, they caught the last rays of the sun.

Humphrey had erected a handsome stone wall incorporating a new chimney and fireplace to divide the

130

living room from the big kitchen, as well as a staircase to an upper floor now containing four bedrooms and a bathroom. Everything was of the best quality, paid for by the sale of Simmy's cottage in Troutbeck. The original barn had become a faint memory for a handful of local residents, little remaining but the basic shape and the wide doorway which had become a feature in its own right. Everything had been discussed, with the council building inspector calling in from time to time. He had disapproved of the fireplace, but could cite no actual law against it.

'I ought to go to Threlkeld again,' worried Ben. 'There've got to be clues somewhere. I still want to live there, you know – with Jonty, if his people will let him. There's something about the atmosphere that gets to me.' He looked from Simmy to Christopher. 'Hartsop's a bit the same, actually, but you've got more tourists here. That chalet park, I suppose.'

'Threlkeld's so close to the big road,' Simmy reminded him. 'That spoils it a bit.'

'It's very easy to ignore it,' Ben argued. 'And it means there's no traffic through the village. I went to Castlerigg yesterday,' he said, abruptly. 'Have you been there?'

'Um . . . no, I don't think so,' said Simmy. Christopher shook his head. 'Why the sudden change of subject?'

Ben frowned. 'I don't know. It feels connected. A link somehow. Makes no sense. I just went up there on my bike for no reason, and it was mind-blowing. The stones are like ghosts. They *are* ghosts, in a way. Their original shapes have disappeared, and these are just the stubs and stumps that are left. You feel as if people don't matter at all when you're up there.'

'Was it just you?'

'And a woman on a phone. She was a nuisance. Oh – and I found a typo on one of the information boards. That really brought me back to earth.'

'Trust you,' grunted Christopher. 'You should write to the National Trust or whoever owns it.'

'I could put it on Twitter,' said Ben with a grin. 'I bet nobody but me has ever noticed it. It's quite subtle.'

'Don't flatter yourself,' said Christopher.

'He's probably right, though,' Simmy defended. 'Ben's usually right.'

'Well, we'll never know, will we?' said Christopher.

Ben was allotted one of the spare rooms and left to his own devices. Simmy heard him talking and assumed it was yet another call to Bonnie. She hoped the room wouldn't be too hot, and then found herself wondering if she and Christopher should have provided themselves with a second bathroom. In America, there'd be one for each bedroom, as Humphrey had pointed out. 'At least let me put a shower in that corner,' he'd pleaded. 'You won't regret it.' But Simmy and Christopher had shrugged and said they couldn't see the point. Neither of them really liked showers.

'And it might tempt us to start doing B&B,' laughed Christopher. 'Which would be perfectly dreadful.'

Ben was the first overnight guest they had had, and he was unlikely to resent the absence of his own personal shower.

It wasn't Bonnie on the phone, but Jonty. He called Ben just after ten and they were still talking an hour later. The subject of the conversation was predictable, but Ben was surprised at how focused and urgent his friend was in what he had to say.

'We *have* to find who did it,' Jonty kept repeating. 'We owe it to Bruno. It's not just a crime – it's far worse than that. There isn't even a word for it.'

'Right,' said Ben, glimpsing the truth of this. It was like trying to look into the sun – facing the full, terrible horror of a deliberate killing. He understood, with a sense of shame, that this had never got through to him before. He had treated murder as a puzzle, had observed how upset people could get, and backed away from all the extreme emotions. He hoped – and believed, most of the time – that his detached contributions had actually helped with police investigations. DI Moxon had seemed to think so, and perhaps, the boy now realised, had actually approved of the detachment, even seeing it as a healthy sign, if the alternative was distress, anxiety or despair.

All of the above made dealing with Jonty quite tricky. His friend was vulnerable, and Ben did not think he himself had ever been. Jonty was slower, lacking in comprehension of other people's processes, and often impossibly stubborn. He was like an angry young bull, bashing his head against a sturdy gate, when there was a much easier pathway at the other end of the field if he would just search for it. He even looked a bit like a bull. He was loyal, good-natured, patient and plodding.

Finding and befriending Bruno had been the making of Jonty. Bruno had been naturally impatient, to the point of disdaining most people he encountered as hopelessly dim. But he had seen something in Jonty and fostered it.

An easy friendship was born, where each one had found the confidence to explore and express their own essential nature. Bruno had laughed at Jonty, but never mocked, and Jonty had quickly learned that his new friend had many blind spots when it came to simple daily matters involving other people. He was shy of public speaking and painfully self-conscious with anybody new. They had both embraced Ben as an unthreatening addition to their lives.

All three of them had grown up as misfits, in their various ways. None of them had trusted the overt brainwashing that went on at school, which had been the original connection between them. Bruno and Ben had been too clever by half, and Jonty demanded cast-iron proof for every statement, often to the fury of his teachers. In the final years they had become aware of each other's existence with relief.

Ben, who attended the Windermere comprehensive, had joined a wide-ranging gaming club, which had developed into live-action role-playing and entailed regular visits to other schools. Bruno had instantly stood out as someone to get to know. They had walked the fells together, the previous summer, utilising the same frustrating and capricious bus and train services that now beset Ben and Bonnie with difficulties. But Bruno had somehow passed his driving test at the first attempt, aged seventeen and two months, and at Christmas had been given a car. Without really thinking about it, Ben had understood that there was money to spare in the Ackroyd household, some of which came Bruno's way. The car was the most precious thing imaginable for a little while – but Ben missed out on most of that, as he struggled through his second term at Newcastle, abandoning the attempt to mould himself into the life of a student, shortly before Easter. Since his relocation to Keswick he had bonded powerfully with the other two boys.

He and Jonty rekindled some of the past few months in their protracted phone conversation. It was therapeutic for them both, finally ending with a pact to solve the mystery of who could possibly have wanted Bruno dead, and how exactly they had accomplished it.

'Of course,' Ben cautioned, 'it might have been a mistake. Wrong person, or careless accident. Someone could have been chucking stones and hit him by accident. You have to keep an open mind, especially when there's hardly any evidence.'

'We should build a shrine to him,' Jonty said, out of the blue. 'Right there where it happened. So he'll never been forgotten.'

'Mm,' said Ben slowly. 'You think Threlkeld's the right place for that, do you?'

'Where else? He *loved* that place, Ben. You heard him. He thought it was the best little village in the world. Remember? It was all going to be so *great*.'

'I know,' said Ben. 'I was thinking the same thing. Maybe it was always going to be too good to be true. One of us might have backed out or changed our minds at any moment.'

Jonty made an odd sound, a groan or a sob, or a syllable of disagreement. 'Not me,' he said. 'Never.'

Ben had developed his own affection for the settlement, so ordinary and unassuming, and yet so rooted and ancient. He had wanted to delve below the surface and find something special. Only now did it strike him that Bruno had been the impetus for that feeling. Bruno had declared an intention of living there forever once he'd got his degree from Bristol, perhaps writing or painting, or if necessary commuting to work in a nearby town. 'Whatever it is I end up doing, I'm going to do it here,' he had announced. And his two friends had been happy to do it with him, at least for a while.

'Yeah, actually,' Ben agreed. 'A shrine would be good.'

Chapter Ten

'Was that Bonnie you were talking to?' Simmy asked Ben next morning. He had been up early and gone out for a walk by himself without saying anything. Breakfast consisted of some toast and fruit. 'Not very organised, I'm afraid,' she apologised. 'Christopher is meant to be in charge of the catering, but he's lapsed a bit lately.' There was no sign of the men of the house. 'I've left them both in bed,' said Simmy. It was half past eight, and she was trying to motivate herself to gather up the baby for the drive down to Windermere. Tanya Harkness would be waiting on the doorstep for her at this rate.

'You look smart,' said Ben, before answering her question. 'Actually, it was Jonty. On the phone.'

'Oh. I'm doing the shop today. Didn't I tell you?'

'Yes, you did. Sorry. Robin's not staying here, is he?'

'No. I told you that as well. My mum and dad are having him. Then I'll be close by if he plays up.'

'Right. Makes sense. You can leave Tanya in charge if you have to dash over to Beck View.'

He was saying the right things, but she could tell his attention was somewhere else entirely. He looked awkward and out of place in her kitchen, an obstacle to be worked around. Something was seriously out of kilter, but she didn't have time to get to the root of it.

'Have you sorted out what Bonnie's doing? I don't know why we haven't arranged for me to bring her back with me this afternoon. Wouldn't that be the simplest thing?'

He nodded with a startling indifference. 'Assuming she could stay here tonight, I guess. Then she can take her time going back on the train tomorrow.'

'Ben – is everything all right between you two? I mean, something seems different.'

He looked at her properly then. 'Does it? I don't know why really. Except that things change whether you want them to or not, don't they? She's not the same as she was last summer. She seems a lot older.'

'Well, she *is* older, I suppose. She's taken on a lot of responsibility at the shop. Listen – tell her to call me and fix a time for bringing her back here this afternoon. It'd be daft not to, surely?' Then she looked at the clock on the wall. 'Gosh – I really have to go. Sorry. I should be back before three.' She sighed. 'This is how it's going to be from here on. Rushing off to work, and fitting the baby in around my commitments. Not the ideal way to live, let's face it.'

Before he could respond, she was running up the stairs to collect her infant, coming back with him within two minutes. Ben watched as if it was a vaguely interesting TV documentary.

'Everybody does it, though, don't they?' he said, evidently not wanting to let her go, following her to the door. 'The kids seem to survive it well enough.'

'What? Oh – yes, I hope they do. He'll be happy to see Granny and Gramps.' Taking a deep breath, she made herself stand still and listen to Ben. Nothing was so urgent that she needed to dash off and leave him in mid-sentence. Some visceral fear reminded her that you never knew when you might be having your last words with someone. Even Ben – *especially* Ben – was vulnerable to disaster.

He showed little sign of understanding any of this. He folded his arms and spoke slowly. 'Bruno talked about extended families, the oddness of blood relationships, childhood influences. It was one of his things. He was interested in what happened to Bonnie.'

'Ben – I do have to go now. Tell me about it later.' She was almost out of the door. 'See you later,' she called, to Christopher upstairs, who did not reply.

Ben went on with an internal conversation that had been sparked by his latest memory of Bruno. So much had been discussed between the three boys in recent months, whilst walking, sitting about in pub gardens, or playing chess while Jonty made his origami figures. The working hours at the auction house had been a distraction from the intense evening gatherings. And – he realised with a painful jolt – Bonnie Lawson had come close to being a distraction, too.

Working at the saleroom had taught him a lot, and he absorbed information with little conscious effort. Hallmarks, porcelain factories, textiles, paintings – he inhaled it all because he was interested and wanted to convey his new knowledge to his friends. Jonty's presence made that even easier. Neither one wanted Bruno to feel excluded by the fact that he did not share their working days, so they regaled him with endless accounts of vendors, fakes, breakages and arguments. They told him about Fiona and Jack and others they worked with. Ben described the databases and Jonty laughed about the woman who had dropped a big planter onto a whole box of glass light fittings.

Bonnie had missed out on all that, despite their regular phone calls. June and July had passed in a muddle of complex travel arrangements, cadging lifts and meeting in places that were mutually accessible. Bruno had been the driver a few times.

But now Ben was musing over the accounts he had heard of Bruno's early life. His parents had seldom been in harmony, and then when he was twelve, his mother took up with Derek Smythe. Three years later, the Smythes and the Ackroyds had both produced little half-sisters, which the boy had found deeply unsettling.

Only when Christopher finally came downstairs did Ben shake himself out of his reverie.

'Sleep well?' asked his employer.

'Fine, thanks,' he lied. He had in fact lain awake for much of the night.

'So, what's the plan?'

'Pardon?'

'Aren't you doing your usual detective work? Spreadsheets or whatever it is you do? Lists of suspects and so forth?' It wasn't said nastily, but neither was it particularly friendly.

'Not much to go on yet,' Ben said.

'Oh – I don't know. Bruno's life was pretty complicated. I'd imagine it would be quite helpful to draw it all out. That girlfriend, for a start. What's her name? What's she like?'

'I've never met her. I don't think she was really his girlfriend at all. He never once mentioned her to me.'

'You're saying you didn't know she existed?' They stared at each other, the unlikeliness of this striking them both at the same moment. 'But you were such close friends,' Christopher protested. 'How is that possible?'

'Good question. Although we hadn't spent very much time together lately, when you think about it. When we did, we talked about other things – abstract, I suppose it was. Bruno turned everything into a theory – trying to make sense of life and morality and pain and stuff like that. And he liked history. Things like girlfriends didn't really arise – though he was interested in Bonnie's life.' He sighed.

'Did Jonty know about her?'

'Oh yes. He and Bruno had been friends forever. I suppose that made it different.'

'Still seems weird.'

'It probably isn't really,' said Ben. 'People keep saying how Bruno kept everything in separate compartments. The people in his life never mixed, except me and Jonty. He even knew Simmy's dad but I had no idea about that, either.'

'I'm going to ask Jonty all about Patsy,' Christopher asserted, apparently seeking Ben's approval. 'I wonder if the police have questioned her.'

'They have, I think.' Ben closed his eyes, recalling all that Moxon had said. 'Yes, obviously, they must have done because she was with him in hospital more or less from the start on Wednesday. And she visited him on Thursday as well. She came and got Jonty from Keswick and they went together.'

'Complicated,' said Christopher. 'What about his father – what's his name?'

'Ackroyd. I think he went on Thursday as well. He's the one who put it on Facebook, five minutes after hearing about it on Wednesday. That still seems barmy to me.'

'I guess he just thought it was important news, even if at that point it was just a mysterious accident, and everyone must have assumed Bruno would get over it.'

Ben frowned at this, detecting a logical glitch. 'Patsy said he was critically ill when she texted Jonty at the pub. She was practically hysterical. And the only person who could have told her that is Ackroyd.' He tapped his front teeth with a finger. 'That's interesting, don't you think?'

'Is it?' Christopher was thoroughly out of his depth. 'Why?'

'It implies a relationship.'

'Well don't ask me. The only person I know in all this is Derek – and Jonty, of course. But he's really been more of a messenger than an active participant, if I've got it right.'

'More or less,' said Ben, still drawing imaginary lines between the various individuals.

'Anyway – if you and Derek and Jonty were all sitting together when it happened, then you make excellent alibis for each other, don't you? No wicked stepfather bumping off his annoying stepson.' said Christopher with a hint of self-satisfaction. *See how well I've paid attention*, was the subtext.

Ben couldn't decide how to take this remark. He suspected that Christopher did not really like his new employee as much as he had expected to. Smythe was conscientious and eager to please, but he was slow to grasp the subtleties of the job; things that were awkward to spell out in plain language, but which were crucial to the success of the business. Things that Ben had understood within moments, such as the bidders who worked together to keep prices low; the deliberate 'dressing down' that some of the women buyers went in for, so as to conceal their affluence; the vendors who expected special treatment and did not deserve it, and the ones who really did have to be kept sweet. It was all one big game, with enormous scope for individual quirks and complex deceits. Smythe was never going to grasp it all and was, as a result, much less of an asset than Christopher had hoped for. When Ben and Jonty had repeated some of this to Bruno, Derek Smythe's stepson had laughed.

'My dad's got fifty times the brainpower of poor old Derek,' he confirmed. 'But don't let my mum know I said so. She says men are like dogs and there's a lot to be said for the dim ones.'

'If she thinks that, it won't matter if she hears you saying it – will it?' frowned Jonty.

Bruno had patted his friend's cheek, and said, 'She'd rather not have to hear it spoken out loud. Most of what goes on between people is never actually uttered, you know. It's all in the facial expressions and body language. We're much more like animals than we like to admit.'

'Alibi,' Ben repeated to Christopher now. 'That's true. But I could never imagine Derek committing a murder anyway. Could you?'

'I might,' mused Christopher. 'Everything we see might just be a clever act.'

Ben blinked. 'You're stealing my lines. Trust no one. Follow the evidence. Take nothing for granted.'

'You've taught us all well.' Christopher smiled. 'Don't go soft on us now.'

'No need – as you say, Derek's got a cast-iron alibi. So has Jonty. They were both at the pub the entire afternoon. So was I. So were you, until you and Simmy left together.'

'And nobody else we knew was in Threlkeld that day – we'd have seen them.'

Ben shook his head scornfully. Sometimes this man said the silliest things. 'Not if they drove through, parked up at the top of Blease Road and walked down beside the beck from there. Anyone at all could have done that. After all, Bruno was there without us knowing.'

'Risky, if they came past the pub.'

'But they wouldn't have to do that – they'd come off the main road at the other end of the village. Then they'd turn up Blease Road without going near the pub.'

'Oh,' said Christopher. 'I didn't know that. I wasn't taking much notice, to be honest, and I've never been to Threlkeld before.'

'Hm,' said Ben, distracted by a fresh thought, which he was not ready to share. 'Can I make myself some coffee?'

'Of course. Help yourself. Did you have breakfast?'

'Toast. An apple.'

'Good. Tell you what – I'll make some proper coffee and we can go and sit outside with it. I think I'm supposed to be marking out some new beds for flowers and things. Potatoes,' he added vaguely. 'Sim wants to grow our own vegetables. I could get started on that. You can advise.'

'Right,' said Ben, without enthusiasm.

'Or do you want to call Bonnie or something? She must be feeling pretty much left out these days. When do you actually *see* her?'

'Sundays mostly. She's coming back here today, probably staying the night. I need to check that with her, actually. Didn't Simmy tell you?'

Christopher shook his head. 'She's very welcome,' he said. 'The more the merrier. We ought to cook something, then. Can't have takeaway two nights running. I'll see what's in the freezer while the coffee's brewing.'

Ben remembered Simmy's comment about Christopher slacking off in his catering responsibilities. Robin was four months old – which perhaps seemed long enough for the new mother to get back to a bigger domestic role. There were hints that Christopher was a trifle old-fashioned in his views about gender roles, which Ben had not missed.

He reviewed what he knew about the man and his origins. Son of a carpet fitter, never went to university, roamed around the world for years, pausing briefly to get married, working here and there as the need arose until finally coming back to home territory, minus the wife, just in time to witness the deaths of both parents and rekindle his boyhood relationship with Persimmon Straw, now Brown. Bright enough in his way, charming and apparently contented, he fitted somewhere between Bruno and Jonty where brains were concerned. Ben tended to categorise everybody by their IQ, and secretly downgraded Christopher for being only marginally above average. But he was undeniably impressive at work. His experience of life and people was considerable and he used it to brilliant effect in the antique business. He was observant, confident and engaging. Everybody liked him and a lot of people trusted him. But as a husband, Ben had a worrying feeling that Christopher was falling just a little bit short.

'Thanks,' he said. 'Where do you do your shopping? There's not much locally, is there?'

Christopher replied in snatches as he prepared the coffee. 'Well, there's a shop in Glenridding that's not bad, but apart from that there's almost nothing . . . A few farm shops dotted around, but for good old-fashioned supermarket shopping, it's a pretty hefty round trip. The daft thing is, neither of us gave that a thought when we came to live here. I think we must have expected everything to grow on trees.'

'You can get deliveries though?'

'Oh yes, but somehow we never got into that. I was in and out of the Glenridding shop every day for the first month or two and that seemed to keep us going. And now we've got a handsome new freezer, all very organised. I could get a leg of pork out for tomorrow, come to think of it. And probably some sort of stew for tonight. Simmy had a big cooking session last week. I think she thought that's what a married woman ought to do. Except she wasn't actually married a week ago, was she?' He chuckled. Then the coffee was deemed ready and he poured it out.

Ben laughed uneasily. The fact of Simmy being married was still difficult to compute. He couldn't work out how much it mattered, and whether it changed anything. And the wedding itself would be forever tainted by the death of poor Bruno.

There did not seem to be very much more to talk about. The coffee was good, he supposed, but it was still not a drink he really liked. He sipped at it, wondering whether the whole morning was going to carry on like this. There was nothing worth mentioning going on at work, and Ben had a suspicion that his boss would not welcome any auction-related chat. It would feel like taking advantage, sort of a teacher's pet, earning special attention or even advancement at the expense of other employees.

Fiona had already shown herself to be wary of Ben's obvious talents. Twice in the last week she had asked him whether he was going back to university soon, despite it being clear to everyone that it was not going to happen. 'Such a waste,' she had murmured. 'You're going to regret not having a degree, you know. Everybody needs one these days.' She herself had a BA in Fine Arts from Leicester, and never let anyone forget it.

'I'm still deciding,' he had told her.

'You seem a bit flat,' Christopher observed. 'Missing Bonnie?'

The remark seemed deeply tactless to Ben. His friend had just died – wouldn't that make anyone 'flat'? He simply shook his head helplessly and got up from the table.

'Got any plans for the morning?' Christopher went on. 'I suppose we could wander up to Patterdale and have a bit of lunch at the pub.'

Is food the only thing the man ever thinks about, Ben wondered savagely. 'What about the gardening?' he said.

'Oh – right. I forgot. Well, I'll give it an hour or so, and then we'll be off. It takes a while to get there on foot. I thought we could go along the path that comes out at Crookabeck. Simmy and I really love it there and it's a nice walk.'

Again, Ben was conscious of a lack of tact. Hadn't Bruno been on *a nice walk* just before being coshed and killed? Was Christopher doing it on purpose? Or had the whole business of Bruno just slipped his mind? The man's mind did seem to have a tendency to let things slide out of it. Not at all like Bruno's, which had held tenaciously to every fresh thought; linking, expanding, theorising all the time. Ben almost wept, then. Something began to rush and flow at the back of his nose and his eyes were stinging. This was awful. He hadn't cried since he was fifteen. He turned away and blundered towards the stairs. 'OK,' he blurted thickly. 'Call me when you want to go.'

'Right,' came the uncertain reply. 'About half eleven should be OK. There'll be swarms of tourists, of course, but we might beat the rush.'

'OK,' said Ben again.

He sat on the bed in Simmy's spare room and let black thoughts overwhelm him. Stray images from years ago pushed themselves into his mind. The loneliness of school where nobody quite knew what to do with him; the awfulness of Bonnie's early life; the ocean of fear and pain and cruelty that was essentially the history of the world in a nutshell. Every individual death was a horror, a rip in the fabric of existence. He wallowed in it, remembering how Bruno had revealed his own despairing nihilism when confronting these realities. And how Jonty had taken on the task of maintaining a balance, with his essential good cheer and simple contentment. 'It's really not so bad,' he would say with a laugh.

And what about Threlkeld? Ben's thoughts were slowly coalescing into more concrete details. Threlkeld, with its impossible name and unassuming attributes. A place to just *be*. Threlkeld was undemanding. There were no malign influences there. 'This is where I want to live, for always,' Bruno had said. 'I think we might have discovered the true and actual Garden of Eden, right here.'

Ben had gone along with it, while suggesting that it could all be a delusion. 'There might be hidden layers of wickedness,' he said. 'In the back rooms, where nobody can see, there could be witchery and evil plots. If it can be the Garden of Eden, it can just as easily be the control room for a conspiracy to take over the world. Who would ever think to look here? The conspirators operate by a system of sending postcards around the world, and using carrier pigeons. They signal from the washing lines, and whether there's a pink or white geranium in the window.'

It turned into the potential for a game that all three might play. In the space of a few minutes, Threlkeld became as complex and multi-layered as any fantasy land imagined by George R.R. Martin. It would be a continuation, in some ways, of similar games Ben had played with Bonnie in previous summers. In Hawkshead they had re-enacted Wordsworth's early life, with maps and made-up anecdotes. But now, in Threlkeld, Bonnie was going to be excluded, not just by geographical logistics, but by a sense that she would no longer fit. She just might think they were all too old for such amusements. And anyway, it was never going to happen without Bruno.

Ben believed it would have become intensely serious, underneath the play-acting. He mourned its loss, while trying to persuade himself that these plans and dreams had been completely irrelevant to what had happened to Bruno. There could be no connection at all.

Christopher called up the stairs to him in what felt like barely ten minutes after they'd gone their separate ways. It turned out to be nearly half past eleven. Christopher was washing his hands when Ben joined him in the kitchen.

'Made good progress, have you?' Ben asked.

'I hope so. I have been guilty of digging up the wrong things in the past, and making elementary errors out there, so I just hope I've got it right this time. Gardening has never featured amongst my activities until now.'

Ben laughed. 'I suppose it comes to us all eventually.' But not his own father, he reflected. David Harkness was a teacher, gradually and reluctantly approaching retirement and expressing no intention of taking up horticulture. Quite what he *would* do remained a mystery. Marking exam papers seemed to be one of the few openings for retired teachers.

The first stages of their walk took them along a small road running northwards towards Patterdale, and leading to a fairly new chalet park. At that point it ceased to be a road and became a narrow path with stiles, gates and occasional steep sections. On their left a stream ran between them and the main road, and on their right fells rose gently towards Hartsop Dodd. There were sheep and wild flowers and mossy stones. It carried on like that for over a mile, passing a farm or two, and emerging into the relative busyness of Crookabeck. In summer there were two or three sets of tourists using the self-catering accommodation, bringing dogs that caused great anxiety to the sheep.

Christopher and Ben met five walkers in total, four of them male. The fifth was a middle-aged woman with a dog. They all carried the requisite kit of rucksack and stick, with sturdy footwear and protective socks. None paused to do more than nod and mutter 'Hi!' or 'Morning!'

'Is this part of a long walk or something?' Ben asked his companion.

'No idea. Maybe it's the approved route from Ullswater to Haweswater. I've never thought to find out, to be honest. Simmy's dad would know.'

'That would work,' Ben mused. 'They look as if they've been walking for a while, but there's still a lot of day to go. I'll check it out. Might be something I can do with Bonnie.'

For some reason, mention of Bonnie darkened the mood. He knew he had neglected her for quite some time now, and that the prospect of seeing her later in the day was nothing like as agreeable as it once would have been. Something had gone stale, and he was sure it was entirely his fault. The whole world had gone fairly stale on him, for some reason. Bruno had felt much the same, but had dignified it with philosophical labels and intellectual rigour. 'There is life beyond Sartre and Nietszche,' he had said. 'But we haven't got there yet.'

And now he was never going to get there, thought Ben miserably.

Christopher was apparently making an effort to stay aware of his young friend's moods. 'You and Bonnie OK then, are you?' he asked lightly, reverting to an earlier topic. 'Not seeing so much of each other these days.'

'It's the distance mainly. We didn't it through properly when I asked if I could come and work for you. I suppose

151

it seemed closer than Newcastle, and that'd make it an improvement. When it comes to it, this isn't much better.'

'You need a car. Why don't you ask Derek if you can have Bruno's? It might be available for free, you never know.'

'I'd still have to tax and insure it. Insurance costs a fortune.'

'There's always a way around that. Nobody pays the full rate,' said Christopher in a very similar airy tone to the one that Bonnie had used some months earlier.

Ben snorted. 'Don't let my dad hear you say that. He's told us all he's definitely not going to get involved in any underhand insurance fiddles.'

'That's a bit harsh. Mind you, he'd never manage it with five of you. What does your brother do?'

'Wilf? He's got a motorbike. Doesn't use it much. He's in Leeds now and never seems to go anywhere.'

'Well, don't be defeatist about it. There's always some kind of wangle. We might even put it on the auction house books. Something like that. You could use it for house clearances once in a while, if you want to stay legit.'

'It's only small. No space for old ladies' wardrobes or carpets. But it's a nice idea – thanks.'

'You soon learn in my line of work that nothing's impossible. There's always a way around if you look for it.'

'Hm,' said Ben. 'Probably not for much longer. Wait until they do away with cash and make everybody register before they even step inside your door.'

'That'll never happen,' said Christopher with total confidence. 'There's a vast gulf between what the rules say and what real people actually do in their daily lives. It's like two different worlds.'

'That's what Bruno said as well,' Ben remarked.

'Good for him. He's going to be a very sad loss to the world.'

'Yes.' *But was there something about him thinking like that that got him killed?*

Chapter Eleven

Angie was experiencing mixed feelings about having sole care of her baby grandson. Despite the presence of Russell, all the actual work was down to her. A new nappy had been needed barely twenty minutes after Simmy had left, which proved idiotically challenging. The male infant's nappy area turned out to be considerably more complex than the female one she barely remembered.

'It's gone *everywhere*,' she howled at her husband. 'I don't know where to start. Can you keep him still for me? Entertain him or something.'

Russell's efforts were tentative and the child was unnerved. These incompetent grandparents were not inspiring any confidence, and he protested. The nappy was recalcitrant and the sticky tabs wouldn't stick. 'Didn't there used to be safety pins?' said Russell. 'Great big things with a sort of safety catch at the end?'

'Obsolete,' sighed Angie, still struggling. 'That'll have to do. Sorry, baby.' She picked him up, hands under his armpits and stared into his face. 'Silly old Granny, eh? Let's go and see what's in the garden, shall we?'

Robin was persuaded to give her the benefit of the doubt and took a polite interest in the first buds on the dahlias and the flamboyant roses that Russell had managed to produce. B&B guests were not allowed into the garden, after early experiments had shown what havoc they and their dogs could wreak. In summer it was a sanctuary every bit as precious as the big kitchen.

'It's still only ten o'clock,' said Russell, walking at her side. 'It feels as if we've had him for hours already.'

'I know. And we've signed up for at least three more years of this. I doubt if she'll let him go to a nursery full time much before that.'

'And they might have another one by then.'

'They do say that two are easier than one. They entertain each other.'

'He's not so much *difficult* as all-consuming,' said Russell. 'We can't just carry him around all morning. How about trying that bouncy chair thing?'

The Straws had availed themselves of Freecycle over the past month, acquiring an assortment of equipment that now occupied a corner of the kitchen. Simmy had carefully inspected everything for hazard and passed it as acceptable, after a good clean. The bouncy chair had evidently been bounced quite a lot already by quite a hefty child, but Robin liked it.

At least, he liked it for almost ten minutes. After that he got bored, or tired, or hungry, or wet. Whatever it was, it made him cry loudly. Simmy had guaranteed that he would not be hungry until at least eleven-thirty. She had left a new bottle containing expressed breastmilk, admitting that the child had never in his life encountered an artificial breast and would find it startling. 'He'll take it if he's hungry enough,' she had said with confidence. 'Another month and he can have mashed banana or something. This is all very temporary.'

Russell and Angie warmed the bottle, before offering it to the unhappy infant. All three had by then descended into moods of rage, panic and despair. None of them came out of it well.

Russell backed away, having decided that he was only making things worse. 'Take him for a walk in the buggy,' he suggested.

'I will,' snarled Angie. 'I'll take him to the shop and dump him on his mother. This is ridiculous. I always was a hopeless babysitter. They made me do it for the kid next door to us, a few times, and it always ended in disaster. I just don't have the patience.'

'We've got out of sync, somehow. It's all new to him and us. We need to take a deep breath.' The fact that he had to shout these words over the yells of his grandson rather diminished their effect.

'He's been here fifty times already. It's not new to him at all.'

'The bottle is. And his mother not being here. And us being such ditherers. Try to see it from his point of view.'

'It's too late for wise words. Look at him! He'll burst a blood vessel if he goes on like that.' Robin was deep red in the face and his mouth opened as wide as any screaming brat in a cartoon.

Russell asserted himself. 'Give him to me. We need to go back to basics.' He cuddled the child to his chest and swayed rhythmically, crooning meaningless syllables. Gradually it took effect as they walked up and down the passageway that ran through the house. Robin's head slumped on his grandfather's shoulder, and the cries turned to whimpers.

'Is he asleep?' Russell whispered to Angie after two more minutes.

She went around her husband and peered at the little face. 'Almost. But you'll never be able to put him down.'

'So be it. I'll hunker down on the sofa with a magazine for a bit and you can get on with something.'

'He didn't take a drop of milk. He'll be hungry in an hour or so. Are we allowed to warm it up again, do you think? What are the rules about that?'

'Don't ask me. It won't hurt him to have it cold, I suppose.'

'Oh well.' She sighed. 'I haven't felt this incompetent, since . . . I don't know when. I thought it was going to be *fun*.'

'It will be, later on. It's just a bit too soon for him. He'll get used to being here. We can't let Simmy down, can we? We've got to get the hang of it.'

Angie sighed again. 'And there was me thinking it was such a nice idea, having a little boy here a day or two a week, brightening the place up.' She stared at the man and child. 'It would seem that the reality is very different from what I was imagining.'

'We'll get the hang of it,' said Russell again. 'When it comes to it, we haven't got much choice – have we?'

'At least we're not agonising over a murder for once,' said Angie rashly.

'Hush, woman!' warned Russell. 'There'll be a knock on the door from Simmy's detective friend before you can say *sausages*.'

But there wasn't. Nobody came to the door until one-fifteen, when their daughter finally retrieved her troublesome baby.

In Threlkeld that morning, the fact of a violent death earlier in the week was gaining interest from people who had been too busy until then to pay it proper attention. Two old friends, on the final lap of their working lives and rehearsing for retirement, met at the Horse and Farrier for a late-morning beer. They noted with some surprise the altered arrangement of the furniture and a handsome display of flowers at one end of the bar.

'What's been going on here then?' wondered Neville.

'Wedding on Wednesday. Still haven't got everything back to how it was. Right old palaver it was,' said the barman.

'Oh, aye. I remember now. Went off all right then, did it?'

'Pretty well, if you don't count the murder of one of the guests' sons.'

'Is that right?' said Richard, the other drinker. 'Heard a bit about it. Not murder though, was it? My old lady says it's got to have been accidental.'

'Seems he was bashed over the head. All a proper muddle, sounds like. They thought he'd be OK, sent him home, and then he keeled over next day. By then, surprise, surprise, there's nothing left in the way of evidence where it happened. Too many feet trampling the spot. Ambulance and walkers and whatnot.'

'And there's some connection with the wedding?' Neville prompted.

'So I gather. Man who works for the bridegroom is father of the dead lad. I phoned the flower woman this morning. It was her who got married, and these are her blooms. Said she couldn't get here to take them down, and would I do it for her. Bit of a cheek, but means we've got some nice decoration for a few more days. Pretty, don't you think?' He indicated the flowers beside the bar.

'Somebody's got a good eye for colour,' Richard agreed. In his capacity as an electrical safety inspector, he visited numerous dwellings and offices and fancied himself as a connoisseur of interior décor.

'That's the girl who works for her, who did all this. They're all down in Windermere, which makes it a bit of a production to get up here, apparently. The bride's got a baby and the girl doesn't drive. You should have seen the schemozzle last week, getting it all sorted.'

'What's his name, then? The chap who was killed?' asked Neville.

'Now you're asking. Something fancy . . . Oh, I know! Bruno. That's it. The dad's name's Smythe, so I assume he must be Bruno Smythe. They live over in Penrith, if I've got the story right.'

'Not *Derek* Smythe? Works at the Keswick auction house? I knew him well at one time. He was in my team at the shop years ago now. Bit of an upstart but worked well enough. Always had a thing about car boots and flea

markets. But he's not old enough to have a grown-up son.'
Neville shook his head in bewilderment.

The barman nodded. 'I wondered about that. Could be it's his wife's boy and not his.'

'Could be. He was single when I knew him. Haven't spoken to him since he left the shop – has to be a dozen years ago now – but I've kept up with his news. Facebook and that,' he finished vaguely.

'Ah, well, there's the thing,' said the barman, suddenly energised. 'My missus says there's a whole lot about this Bruno lad on the internet. Follows it all, she does, like you'd never believe. Doesn't miss a thing. I can't keep up with her, but she did say there's a girlfriend, and that the dead chap was fixing to move here next week, with two pals. That empty bungalow up at the top was going for low rent because it's got damp problems or something.'

'It's a death trap,' said Richard knowingly. 'The wiring's a scandal.'

'Well, that was the plan, and now it'll be off, most likely.'

Richard laughed. 'If the murderer hadn't got him, the sockets might have.'

The others paused, and Neville frowned. 'That's a facer, though, when you think about it. Somebody here in our own village did a murder. What are we meant to make of that?'

'Nothing ever happens in Threlkeld,' said the barman. 'The way people are acting, it's as if they'd like to pretend it's all just a silly mistake.'

'Most likely that's what it'll turn out as, then,' said Richard, and he took a large swig of his beer.

When two more men came in, there were nods all round, but no more than that. The newcomers asked for beer and settled in a corner of the bar, having decided against going outside. 'Too many wasps,' said one.

In Windermere, Simmy was doing her best to keep busy, but the sparse scattering of customers did not make it easy. Tanya Harkness was with her, equally under-occupied, but there was only one topic of conversation that either of them could think of and Simmy had insisted from the start that they should not discuss the death of Bruno Crowther 'We really don't know anything about it,' she said. 'Which only leaves idle speculation, and that does nobody any good.'

'That's a shame,' said Tanya with a sigh.

Simmy checked that everything was present and correct in all parts of the shop, went meticulously through the computer records, balanced the books and tried to keep the few people who did come in as long as possible. A handful of orders came through on the computer, and she went through all those due during the coming week. Bonnie had marked them all as acknowledged, with a meticulous schedule set out for deliveries. None of the outstanding work was very time consuming. Simmy had duplicate computer files at home so that she could track everything that happened and nothing much had changed or gone wrong in the past week or so.

'I suppose my parents are coping all right with Robin,' said Simmy at eleven o'clock. 'They'd have phoned otherwise.'

'He'll be fine,' breezed the girl. 'He knows them, doesn't he?'

'I suppose he does. But I've never left him there before. I've always been with him. And it's his first time with a bottle.'

'They'll phone if there's a problem. Or they can bring him round if it gets really hard.'

'My mother would see that as a failure.'

'Oh.' Tanya was clearly bemused by this.

Simmy wished she had not raised the subject, since it produced an array of disagreeable feelings. Anxiety, guilt and frustration were dominant. If things went badly, her parents might refuse to undertake regular childcare and the whole scheme would collapse. Simmy would not be able to go back to work for far longer than hoped, since she had rejected any idea of using a nursery until Robin was at least eighteen months, but preferably a lot older than that. Bonnie would buckle under the strain and the business would flounder.

'I don't like to take them for granted,' she confessed to her assistant. 'But I'd be completely stuck without them.'

'My mother had a woman come to the house to mind us when we were little,' Tanya remembered. 'She kept us in the playroom and tried to organise games. Natalie was awful to her – wouldn't do anything she said.'

'How old were you?'

'Oh, tiny. Only about a year.'

'How can you remember?'

'I can't, but the others can. It's a family legend, how awful Nat was. Not just with the minder but with the whole family. It's a wonder Zoe didn't kill her. The minder had all three of us for a bit, until Zo went to school.'

Simmy struggled to envisage the Harkness household in those days. Five children, the youngest being twins, their mother working as an architect in an office at the top of the house, the father unhelpfully detached most of the time. Inevitably it reminded her of the Hendersons, a generation earlier. 'What happened to her?' she asked. 'The minder, I mean.'

'Oh, we still see her sometimes. She stayed with us for about five years altogether. She was like one of the family. Davina, she was called. She got married and had three boys.'

'Ben's never mentioned her.'

'Well, no, he wouldn't. They never understood each other. Zoe says he would never even speak to her. I think that was when they were thinking he must be autistic. Really, he just thought she was too stupid to bother with.'

'They thought he was autistic?'

'Apparently. Really, he was just terribly clever. Not much difference, when it comes to it.'

Simmy laughed uneasily. She had shied away from the prospect of talking to Tanya about Ben. If something was awry between him and Bonnie, as she suspected, it would be unwise to discuss this with his sister. It felt increasingly as if there were minefields on all sides. 'They do like to label people, don't they,' she said, non-committally.

'Yeah, well . . . I think it was mostly Davina's doing, to be honest. And you could see her point. He really was quite rude to her.'

Simmy found herself wondering where Helen Harkness had been in all this. Surely it was the mother's job to prevent such potential damage in her own nursery? The perils of parenthood felt as if they were closing in on her, as she went over Tanya's little story again. It had already occurred to her that she and Christopher might manage to afford a part-time nanny for a little while, if Robin proved too much for his grandparents. Now that felt impossibly risky. Nobody could be trusted – especially nannies, who came with more health warnings than most, thanks to the numerous books and films in which they exerted malignant influences.

A customer broke the silence, and Simmy and Tanya both rushed to be of service. When the woman had gone, Simmy noted that it was half past eleven. They could start putting things away in an hour's time, or even less. Tanya was supposed to be at home for one. If they closed at twelve-thirty, nobody was going to complain.

In the Horse and Farrier, it was still too early for lunch. The two men who had recently arrived were Eddie Henderson and Derek Smythe, united by their sons' friendship and the connection to Christopher, but almost strangers to each other. Eddie had phoned Derek on Friday, prompted by Jonty, who said he knew he ought to do it himself, but couldn't think what to say. His father was no more articulate, but accepted the commission. Eddie's head was a jumbled mass of questions, suspicions and worries. Something big had happened and he did not like it. He wanted everything smooth again, if that was even possible. He had found himself saying to Derek, 'Why don't we go for a drink tomorrow, see if we can make any sense of it?'

Derek had been instantly tempted by the suggestion, whilst knowing that his place was at his distraught wife's side. Tilly had fallen apart at the incomprehensible loss of her son. Her small daughters became suddenly immensely precious and she would not let them out of her sight. Derek had told them that Bruno had gone and their mother was very very sad, but it was all going to be all right, and they'd soon get back to normal. He understood that their much older half-brother would soon have faded out of their lives in any case, when he went to university and developed a life quite remote from the family. The girls had each other and Bruno was not in any way vital to their wellbeing. A weeping, wailing mother was a surprise and a bit of a nuisance, but they were old enough and balanced enough to weather a storm that their dad said would not last very long.

'I'm going out for a bit. I'll bring fish and chips back, OK? One o'clock or a bit after.'

Even Tilly perked up slightly at this. She was a woman who liked her food, however enormous the disaster befalling her.

'Can't stay too long,' Derek said now. 'But it's good to see you, mate.'

Eddie examined the man opposite him. Shadows under his eyes, inefficient shaving, hair limp and uncombed – all signs of distress. 'How's the family bearing up?' he asked.

'Everything's gone to pot, if you want to know the truth. It's like a bomb's hit us. The girls'll be all right, though. Selfish little things, at heart. So long as their routine's not changed they don't much care.'

'How old are they?'

'Lucy's five and Harriet's seven. Tilly says they won't remember their brother, but I think they will. We've got him on video, and there's books and things he gave them.'

'Jonty's very cut up,' Eddie offered, having waited in vain to be asked about his son.

'He would be.' Derek nodded vaguely. 'Best mates for a long time now. Funny pair.'

'Like brothers they were. Given neither one *had* a brother, it made sense, I s'pose. That Ben's got a brother, though. Not sure exactly how he fitted in.'

'He's another one like Bruno. Too clever for their own good, the both of them. Everybody says so. You should see young Harkness at work, tracking down all the obscurest painters and potters on the interweb, showing off. Making some of us look like fools when we get the values all wrong.'

Eddie sighed. 'Can't say that about our Jonty. Just a good, steady lad, knows his own place. He won't stay at the auction house for long, you know. He's just glad to have a bit of holiday cash from his uncle. Can't see much to get excited about in all those old things.'

'He's a good worker,' Derek confirmed. 'Idolises Ben, of course, same as he did Bruno. Seems as if that's his destiny, always a follower, with someone to look up to.'

'Unhealthy, that, as I see it. Never did like hero worship. Nor did George. Went the other way, if anything – always trying to bring people down.'

'George?'

'My other brother. Three Henderson brothers. I'm the middle one.'

'Did I see him at the wedding?'

'Maybe not. He was there for the ceremony, and then buggered off for some reason. Left me to make that daft speech. Don't know why I bothered.'

Derek diplomatically said nothing and Eddie went on, 'Must be funny working for our Christopher. Can't imagine him as anybody's boss – even if he is the eldest of five. Always too keen to be off and away somewhere to take a lot of notice of us. The Straws were a big influence on him – more than the rest of us. You knew about that, did you?' Derek shook his head and raised an eyebrow. 'It all started the day they were born – him and Simmy. The new mothers got friendly in the hospital and we had our summer holidays with them, every year for fifteen years or so. My earliest memory is Chris getting lost and Angie Straw yelling at him about it. Simmy was crying and George was crawling about with his face covered in sand. We didn't have the girls then, obviously.'

'They were born the same day?'

'Right. Makes them like twins. And now they're married with that kid. He looks exactly like our dad, you know. Uncanny.'

'Funny old world,' said Derek Smythe absently. 'Your brother's a good boss, though. Doesn't interfere too much and never loses his rag. I always thought auctioneers were inclined to bad temper, but he's always cool and calm.'

'That's because he doesn't really care,' said Eddie with sudden bitterness. 'People get killed, and he just carries on. Our *own father* was murdered, and Chris – well, he didn't react as most people would. And earlier this year, there was

167

a massive drama at the auction house, and what does he do – just takes over the reins as if everything was perfectly normal. And here we are again, with your Bruno.'

'I'm not sure I see it like that,' Derek Smythe demurred. 'He's strong – a strong character. Dependable. Generous as well. He's a good listener. I dare say you're still seeing him as he was twenty years ago. Families do that. From where I stand, Chris Henderson is just about the most reliable chap I know.'

'You haven't got to know him yet,' said Eddie stubbornly. 'He's anything but strong. Reliable, I'll grant you, when everything's going smoothly. But he's never been much use in a crisis.'

'Who is?' said Smythe. 'Show me a man who doesn't go to pieces when the going gets tough. Take me, for instance. This thing with Bruno – I'm never going to be the same man I was. I've got two little girls. I'm going to spend the rest of my life being terrified the same thing's going to happen to them.'

'Oh, well . . .' Eddie blustered, pink with embarrassment. 'I never was much good at judging character and seeing what's going on under the surface. Take no notice. It's all I can manage to cope with our Jonty. Eliza's off all day with her tourists and I get left trying to calm things down. If you want to know the truth, I'll be glad when I can get back to work on Monday.'

'When you can rise above it all – right?' Derek smiled. He had not forgotten that Eddie was a roofer, just as he had not forgotten his stepson's delighted enjoyment of the fact. Bruno had rhapsodised about the job, inventing metaphors and jokes about it. One of which Derek had just quoted. It gave him a momentary warmth to find himself channelling Bruno in this way. He must remember to tell Tilly about it when he got home.

'You'd better be going,' Eddie said suddenly. 'Didn't you say they'd be waiting for you at home?'

'God – I'm meant to be getting fish and chips. What time is it?'

Eddie inspected the phone sitting at his elbow. 'Five past twelve. You're not late.'

Derek relaxed. 'You had me worried there. Plenty of time yet.'

But the conversation had clearly run its course. 'Don't know if we've made any sense of it, have we?' said Derek. 'We got off the subject a bit.'

'It was good, though. Getting to know you a bit better, and that. If you ask me, we'll never know what happened to Bruno. That's what that girl Patsy says, according to Jonty. They went to see Bruno on Thursday. You were there, of course. Must have been quite a houseful.'

'You could say that. Tilly was rushing round making coffee for them all. The blessed Anthony was there as well, God help us.'

'Who?'

'Bruno's natural father, if that's the right word. They all came along to check there was no harm done.' Derek moaned gently. 'Little did anyone know they'd never see him again. I'd gone to work as normal – a bit late after fetching the boy from hospital, but there didn't seem any reason not to go in. Then I got the phone call. I still go cold when I think about it.'

Eddie grimaced in sympathy and swigged the last of his beer. 'The thing is, after all the confusion and messing about it's bound to be an unsolved murder forever.'

Derek moaned again. 'Don't say that. I'm not one for all that guff about closure and so forth, but I can't stomach the thought of someone getting away with it. Patsy would say that's unacceptable – she's never one to look on the bright side. Not that I know her, really. Never understood what Bruno saw in her. As far as I could tell, he was a lot fonder of Jonty and Ben than he was of her.'

Eddie snorted. 'Careful! You'll have the cops thinking she's the one who bashed him.'

Derek sighed. 'Never. She's too small, for one thing. And she'll have been at work on Wednesday.'

'Seems like everybody's got an alibi who knew him. Must have been a passing psychopath. I'm telling you, they'll never catch him.'

Chapter Twelve

DI Moxon knew himself to be a fool. Once the Penrith team had grasped that he had nothing pertinent to contribute to their murder inquiry, they made it clear that he was surplus to requirements. His wife had departed for Anglesey in her own car on Friday morning, and was now rather crossly settled into the holiday house they'd booked, enduring the critical remarks of her sister. 'Just get yourself here,' she told Moxon.

So at eight-thirty on Saturday morning he set out on the three-hour drive, deploring the waste of fuel, time and temper. He would be greeted by a quartet of women and not a male face in sight. Jane, Diana, Laura and Catherine – he repeated the names mindlessly as he drove down the interminable M6. He found himself reliving the years when Diana was producing babies while he and Jane were still processing the implacable truth that they would be forever childless. Jane had contracted a severe pelvic infection on a holiday in Turkey when she was nineteen, and the resulting damage made conception vanishingly unlikely. IVF was an option, urged eagerly by their GP, who pointed out the existence of countless viable eggs and a reasonably healthy uterus, with only some of the tubing dysfunctional. But when the details of the invasive procedures became clear, both Moxons recoiled. They looked at each other, and concluded that they'd settle for uncle-and-auntdom. Moxon had siblings with offspring. The name would not disappear – as if that mattered. The additional financial fluidity meant they could be generous, drive nice cars, enjoy the space and peace of a good-sized house and generally make the best of it.

Laura and Catherine had reaped some of the benefit, showing little gratitude, it had to be said. Jane's offer to pay for a nice, old-fashioned August break in North Wales had been received without rapture. But Moxon had remembered Simmy Brown's fond accounts of the family holidays she'd enjoyed there, and endorsed the idea wholeheartedly.

The M6 was busy, but everything kept moving and meditation inevitably resulted from the monotonous miles. His thoughts drifted from his own family to that of Simmy and Christopher. And thence to Ben Harkness and Bonnie Lawson. For a few years now he had been in a kind of thrall to the whole lot of them – though perhaps not Christopher so much. Bonnie was so apparently fragile, and yet possessed a resilience and good sense that Moxon admired without reservation. She was a lesson in how a person can recover from the most unpromising of starts, given the right encouragement. Her foster mother, Corinne, deserved most of the credit, of course, but Ben and Simmy had completed the job.

Now, if Moxon was reading the signs correctly, it was Ben who was in need of support. Something had gone horribly wrong during his brief spell at university, and the lad was not at all his usual self. Added to this, the death of one of his very few friends had been a serious blow. Moxon admitted to himself that his own unwanted efforts to be involved in the investigation were motivated almost entirely by concern for young Ben – who until now had been a brilliant and enthusiastic amateur detective. Now there was no sign that he was even vaguely searching for clues as to who was responsible. He had retreated into the shadows somewhere, without even Bonnie to sustain him.

The couple's frustration at being without transport had become apparent to Moxon only in the last day or two, when he had been thinking about them. How, he had suddenly asked himself, did they ever manage to see each other without a car? Such impediments could spell the death of a relationship, even in the most devoted of couples, if something were not to be done urgently. If only it could be done anonymously, he would buy them a vehicle himself.

He turned off one motorway and onto another, where the traffic was marginally lighter. Speeding through Cheshire, and down to the A55, he was still thinking about Ben, but had focused more narrowly on the events of the previous Wednesday. An attack that turned into murder had somehow been committed in a small Cumbrian village on a summer afternoon and nobody knew a thing about it. This was the summary that went round and round inside his head, making less sense with every circuit. The way the ambulance had been summoned; the rollercoaster of relief, followed by the horror of Bruno's startling collapse a day later; the very *normality* of everything that had happened around the death – it all lacked any kind of central fixative. There was no *logic*. Perhaps, he mused, it had not been murder after all. The pathologist who made the examination could have got it wrong, jumped to a false conclusion. They could be chasing a delusion, assuming the worst when it had been a simple accident. A branch could have fallen on his head. A stumbling sheep could have knocked him into the beck, where his head cracked against a stone in some sort of freak position that caught him behind his ear. It seemed to Moxon that it was all too possible.

But, deep down, the police detective with eighteen years' experience in the CID knew that pathologists did not make that sort of mistake. They made every effort to *avoid* a conclusion of murder. It had to force itself on them, evading all argument and smacking them in the face, and that seemed to have happened in this instance. From what he could gather, there had been no dissection performed on the body – simply a minute external inspection, which had been sufficiently conclusive for a murder investigation to begin.

None of these musings got him very far. No credible motive had manifested itself, and yet, a random, pointless killing was so rare as to be dismissed. Bruno had perhaps somehow provoked a sudden frenzied lashing-out in somebody he had never met before walking beside the beck for the sake of his mental health. The tall, detached figure strolling obstructively ahead of a power walker might need to be elbowed aside, rather too violently. Both relatively easy to believe – but who would then speed away, leaving an unconscious man to take his chances? Someone who ought not to have been there. Someone with enough trouble already, unable to face the recriminations. It was all entirely possible, yet none of it felt right.

Nor did it feel right for him to be swanning off to Wales and leaving the whole thing for someone else to resolve. He had a helpless, depressing feeling that Jane was going to find him disappointing. There would be too much emphasis on food in the absence of more compelling topics. Coastal walks, souvenir shops, a castle and a museum at best. He had not done any homework on the area and had little idea what it had to offer. His wife's nieces were unlikely to find much to occupy them, either. They were children of their time, fixated on smartphones and social media which Moxon had never even tried to follow. What was he going to talk to them about? Even when much younger, they had been difficult to engage. His only recourse had been to exaggerate the avuncular stereotype, taking them on birdwatching expeditions and participating in interminable games of Monopoly.

At last, after what felt like at least half the day, he arrived at Moelfre, halfway down the eastern side of the island. He spotted Jane's car tucked beside a cottage pleasingly positioned on high ground overlooking the beach, and pulled in tightly behind it. After gratifyingly warm greetings, Laura and Catherine immediately surprised him with an unforced affection.

'Tell us about your murder,' said Harriet eagerly. 'Aunt Jane wouldn't say anything.'

He laughed. 'She's trained not to.'

They were sitting around a small patio, surrounded by bright flowers in tubs, with the sea stretching away to the east, dotted with sailing boats. Gulls called, children shrilled and the sun pretended they were all in Greece. Jane and her sister had kept a portion of salmon salad for him, with a glass of cold white wine. He changed into a fitting costume which bared his arms and lower legs and worked on relaxing. It did not take long, despite the girls' insistence on hearing about events back in Cumbria.

'It was someone you knew – is that right?' said Laura.

'Not quite. I never met him. But he was a friend of a young man I know well. It's closer to home than I'd like, that's for sure.'

'I can't begin to imagine killing someone.' Catherine shivered. 'The *guilt* afterwards! It must be unbearable. How could you ever live with yourself?'

Moxon gave the girl a long fond look. She had light brown hair with a gentle wave in it. Her eyes were a clear hazel and the sun had caught her cheeks. He had always thought her silly, resistant to any serious conversation or ideas, excessively anxious about her appearance and level of popularity. Perhaps he had just wanted too much too soon, and here at last was a sign of imminent maturity emerging. 'It's the question we all struggle with,' he said. 'The evidence suggests that there are people who simply never feel guilt. It's missing from their character, for some reason.'

'Social deviants,' said Laura, as if remembering something from school.

'Pretty much,' said her uncle. 'It certainly seems that guilt is required for proper social functioning.'

At that point Diana came out of the house with a bottle in one hand and a half-full glass in the other. 'I thought

I should keep you company,' she told her brother-in-law. 'Drink up.'

He obediently accepted a top-up, and waited to see whether the girls would continue with the same topic now their mother was listening.

'We were talking about murder,' said Laura, with a hint of defiance.

'Don't mind me,' said Diana, sitting on a lounger and stretching out her legs. 'If Uncle Nolan's happy to fill your minds with blood and guts, I'm not going to try to stop him.'

'They started it,' he said mildly. 'We were getting quite philosophical, actually.'

'No mention of blood or guts so far,' Catherine reported.

'There was none of either in this instance,' said Moxon. 'As far as I know.'

'Why don't you know?' asked the girl.

'I haven't seen him – just read a handful of reports. The thing is,' he went on, aware that it was probably misguided, 'I was on the exact spot where it happened, probably only a few minutes earlier. I was very nearly a witness, I suppose.'

'Spooky!' said Laura, with a theatrical shudder.

'Doesn't that make you a suspect, though?' asked Diana, narrowing her eyes. 'Surely it means it could have been you who did it?'

'Mum!' squealed both girls in unison.

Moxon sighed. 'On the face of it, that's true. But so far nobody's had the courage to say so.'

'Trust me to tread on hallowed ground, then,' laughed his wife's uncaring sister.

Jane had been sitting with her back half-turned, watching the sea, leaving the others to catch up and for things to settle into a pattern. The original plan had been for the Moxons to spend a week here, and she was hopeful that nothing would interfere with that. Her husband's work, the weather, fallings-out or unforeseen accidents could all jeopardise the holiday. The third of these could best be avoided by her sitting back and letting her sister take centre stage for a while.

'You'll have to tell us every detail,' said Catherine, eagerly. 'Then we can solve it for you. It's amazing what a fresh set of eyes can do.'

'Ears, more like,' said Laura. 'We won't be *seeing* anything, will we?'

It was senseless quibbles like this which vexed Moxon the most. It made him fractious and impatient. 'I won't be doing that,' he said firmly. 'I came here to get away from the whole sorry business.'

'Come for a walk then,' said Jane, getting up. 'You'll need the exercise after being in the car all morning.'

'Good idea,' he said.

Eddie Henderson did not want to go home. The beer had kept any appetite for lunch at bay, and he felt restless. There was more to talk about, more to discover. He still felt the pressure of his commission from his son. Jonty would want him to do everything in his power to solve the puzzle of what had happened to Bruno. Where was the boy, Ben? He'd be the ideal person for another chat, now that Eddie had got to know the Smythe man better, and could get more of a handle on everything.

He cast his mind back to the wedding, looking for clues or explanations that had passed him by at the time. He had been sitting at a table with Simmy and Christopher and two or three others for a few minutes as they ran through their movements for the week. The impossibly brief honeymoon had raised some laughs. Then Simmy had said she was going to be in the shop on Saturday – which was today. Everybody who heard that gave an opinion, with advice on childminding options and their own experiences. Eddie had found himself strongly in favour of women staying at home when their kids were tiny, but he didn't say anything.

Simmy was now his sister-in-law, which gave him an even better claim on her than he had before, thanks to their shared childhood holidays. He also liked her a lot. She had always seemed to him to be sensible, modest, sympathetic. She didn't make him feel stupid, as a lot of people did. Suddenly she was the only person he wanted to see. He checked his watch. If he really rushed he could be in Windermere before she shut the shop for the day. He remembered her saying, 'It's only for the morning. I'll only be leaving Robin for four hours at the most.' There had been some sort of remark about Christopher not being ready to take charge, so the kid would be at the Straws'.

She'd be in a hurry, of course, wanting to get back to her baby at her parents' house. It was perfectly possible that she'd ask him to go there with her, and if so he would be more than happy to do as asked. Russell was easy, Angie unpredictable, but they would both be happy to talk, he was sure. They'd welcome him in, treating him as if he was thirteen again.

He flew down the A591, ignoring the speed limit imposed on part of the northern stretch. Threlkeld to Windermere was twenty miles, and in winter it could be done in twenty-five minutes. In summer, with all the visitors, and the clogged streets of Ambleside to negotiate, he'd be lucky to do it in thirty-five. But fate was with him, and he arrived breathlessly at Persimmon Petals at ten minutes to one.

Simmy was literally on the doorstep, her back turned as she checked that everything was securely locked.

'Sim!' Eddie called, before he was properly across the street. 'Wait!'

Her expression was not welcoming when she turned round. 'I'm already terribly late,' she said. 'What do you want?'

'The baby's with your parents, right? Can I come with you, if you're going there now?'

'I can't really stop you, can I?'

'Don't be like that. I've just had an hour with Derek Smythe. Give me a break.'

'Mum won't be too pleased to have another person to feed. It's lunchtime, you know.'

He waved that away. 'Don't worry about that. I've got some crisps in the car.'

'Which is where?'

He lifted his chin vaguely eastwards. 'Over there somewhere. It was a real rush to get here. I'm bound to get done for speeding. I've probably got it wrong about the parking as well.'

They were already walking towards Beck View, Simmy setting a punishing pace. Eddie was panting with the effort of walking and talking at the same time. 'What do you want?' she asked him again. 'Has something happened?'

'Not really. But Jonty's all over the place, and it doesn't feel as if anybody's *doing* anything, so I thought I could come and talk it over with you and your folks. Angie's sure to have some ideas. And where's Ben? Isn't he meant to be an ace detective or something? I just thought – somebody should be stirring things up, and why not me?'

Simmy threw him a swift grin. 'Same old Eddie. You always think you have to be the one to make things happen, don't you?'

'Do I?'

'Like making that speech on Wednesday. I could see you thinking, *Well, nobody else is going to do it, so here goes.* And now you're doing it again.'

'Is that wrong?'

'Not really. Irritating sometimes. But it does feel as if nothing much is happening about Bruno, I agree. And I can see you're worried about Jonty. He must be completely stunned. I'm just not sure that this is a good time. I'm bursting with milk, Robin's going to be starving, and I dread to think what the morning's been like in the house. Ben's up in Hartsop, by the way. And I'm taking Bonnie back with me later on. She's thrilled to be getting a lift, poor girl.'

'Chris didn't step up as childminder then?'

She stopped walking. 'No.'

'There might be a reason for that.'

'What do you mean?'

'Robin's four months old now – right? That's the same age George was when Christopher dropped him. I was barely three and Chris was five. I don't remember it properly, but it was a very big drama. They thought the baby was dead and my dad laid into my brother like a madman. I remember Chris screaming and stumbling up the stairs to get away, wetting himself. That's the part I really do remember. And Mum with the baby all floppy.'

Simmy was thunderstruck. 'He never told me a thing about that.'

'I'm no psychiatrist, mind – but don't you think he might have hidden it all away from himself, until he got his own baby and it all came back? Or maybe it's just a sort of echo, making him scared of hurting the kid, but not knowing why?'

'Good God, Eddie. What am I going to do about that? It's like something from Hitchcock.' She found herself full of images of a small brother landing on the iron spikes of a fence in *Spellbound*.

Eddie was bemused. 'What are you talking about?'

'Sorry. I'm channelling my father. He always finds a scene from a film or a book to match what's going on.'

'So he does. I forgot about that. Anyway, just go easy on Chris, OK? He'll be a great father when Robin's a bit older.'

They were walking on slowly, only a minute away from the Straws' house. 'I wonder if my parents know that story,' Simmy said quietly, before going in.

'Bound to,' said Eddie. 'I'm surprised you haven't heard about it.'

'There's a lot I seem to have missed,' Simmy said ruefully. She opened the front door, Eddie trailing after her. 'I'm back!' she called.

Russell appeared from the kitchen. 'Hush!' he whispered. 'You'll wake the baby.'

'He shouldn't be asleep. He must be desperate for a feed. Did he take the bottle?'

'Don't ask. He's worn himself out. It's been quite a morning.'

'Where is he?'

'On your mother's bed – with her. I suspect she's asleep as well.'

'Good God! What happened?'

Russell shook his head, and focused on Eddie. 'Hello, Ed,' he said. 'This is a surprise.'

'He wants to talk about Bruno,' said Simmy. 'And he might want some lunch.' She dumped her bag on a hall chair and headed upstairs.

Angie was lying on the big bed with Robin sprawled on her chest. Both were fast asleep. Simmy began to leak milk at the sight of her child, but she was loathe to wake him. This was so utterly different from what she had expected to find that she had no idea what to do. She went slowly downstairs again and joined the two men in the kitchen.

'What happened?' she asked again.

Russell smiled faintly. 'He didn't like it here without you. We did get a bit of that bottle into him, and in the end he fell asleep, first on me, and then on your mother, so I could cook. Angie wasn't in any fit state to manage a frying pan.'

'Why didn't you call me? I was only five minutes away.' She was wracked by images of her distraught infant being denied all his wishes by heartless grandparents.

'We thought we should stick it out. Take the rough with the smooth. There's no harm done.' But his worried face said otherwise. Russell Straw was not a man to endure suffering for long, whether his own or someone else's.

'He won't trust us – any of us,' she moaned. 'Me for abandoning him and you for letting him cry all morning.'

'It wasn't *all* morning,' Russell protested weakly. 'And everything's fine again now. I've made us a lovely paella – my speciality.'

Simmy had to admit that there were enticing smells coming from the Aga. Garlic, onions, tomatoes, chunks of chicken – and whatever random vegetables might be available. Russell believed in making the rice by far the smallest component.

'Can I have some now?' she asked.

Eddie was sitting at the table like a schoolboy, politely waiting his turn to speak. 'He won't remember,' he offered. 'We used to leave Jonty to cry himself to sleep all the time.'

'No wonder he hates you then,' said Russell lightly.

'He doesn't,' snapped Eddie. 'Don't say things like that. I'm only here because he wants me to try and get to the bottom of this mess.'

'Sorry. Have some paella. It's obviously not a very formal lunch today. I've been waiting an hour or more for some customers.'

'An hour!' Simmy's horror returned at the visions of her baby's nightmare morning. 'He never sleeps at all at this time of day. And if he's only had half a bottle, he must be *terribly* hungry.'

'They'll both wake up in a minute,' soothed Russell, while showing signs of impatience. 'Eat while you can, is my advice.' He turned to Eddie. 'What did you want to ask us about then?'

'Oh – well . . .' Eddie was flustered. 'That policeman. Detective, or whatever he is. He must have told you some of their thinking about what happened to Bruno. More than they're telling us, anyhow. We're just sitting around waiting for some sign of progress, and it's driving us mad. Me and Jonty, that is. Eliza's hardly at home these days. Christopher's no use, I don't suppose. He stays out of this sort of business if he can.'

'It really has nothing to do with him or me,' said Simmy. 'Other than the fact that we were in Threlkeld when it happened, there's no connection at all.'

'Ben's the connection, pet,' said Russell. 'And your husband's nephew being best mates with the deceased. Keeps it in the family, so to speak.'

'So long as nobody thinks a family member did the deed,' said Eddie, shaking his head. 'The way they're ignoring us makes me wonder whether they think we'll give ourselves away somehow. Give a man a length of rope and he'll hang himself, or whatever it is.'

'I think that's only on TV,' said Russell.

'I'm not so sure. If I've got the timings right, I'm about the only one without an alibi. I left the pub just after four and went home to an empty house.'

'You didn't take Jonty with you, then?' asked Russell, as he spooned quantities of paella into bowls and set them in front of his guests.

Eddie shook his head. 'He wanted to stay with Ben.'

'Oh, well. I dare say that if they suspected you, they'd keep on questioning you until you spilled the beans.'

'They can't possibly think it was you,' said Simmy. 'What would the motive be?'

'Nobody's got a motive, have they? Bruno never hurt a fly. He never said anything to offend, as far as I can see. Although he did like to argue.' Eddie subsided with a sigh and took a mouthful of paella. 'This is fabulous, Russ. I forgot you could cook. It was you who taught us how to work a barbecue on the beach – remember?'

'A barbecue isn't cooking,' said Russell.

The clarion cry of a waking baby silenced them all. Simmy ran to the bottom of the stairs and was halfway up when her mother appeared at the top. This staircase had seen one or two dramas in recent times, and the memory struck mother and daughter at the same moment.

'Go down,' said Angie. 'I'm coming.'

'Wait a minute,' said Simmy, still dazed by Eddie's revelations. 'Can we go back to the bedroom? Talk to me while I feed him. Just for a minute.'

Angie sat on the edge of the bed next to Simmy who made herself comfortable amongst her parents' pillows. The baby latched on blissfully.

'Eddie said Christopher dropped George when he was a baby about Robin's age,' Simmy said. 'Which might be affecting how he is now. He's scared to be left alone with Robin – he wouldn't let me leave him at home today.'

'Urgh,' said Angie, still not quite awake.

'Mum!' Simmy urged.

'All right. Yes. Frances phoned me a day or two after it happened and told me the whole thing. She was actually more concerned for Christopher than for George. Kit hit him, apparently. Told him he'd killed his little brother and would be cursed for life. Something like that. Hasn't he told you about it?'

'Not a word. Eddie thinks he's probably buried it.'

'Best leave it buried then. That's my advice, for what it's worth. Robin's going to sort him out, you know. Babies are clever little things. Although it doesn't help that he looks exactly like George did as a baby.'

'Does he?' Simmy peered at the little face with its small, neat features. 'I thought he was more like Kit.'

'Both of them. But Christopher's no fool. He'll get past it in another few months.'

'I'll have to say something. He might need some sort of therapy.'

'Possibly. But we've all got something like this tucked away. It's just part of normal life. My instinct is not to make a big deal of it. There's no need to let it spoil anything between you. Just give Christopher some slack, as your father would never say.'

Simmy closed her eyes. 'Thanks, Mum. I dare say you're right. Now I know about it, it's going to make everything much easier.'

'You ought to thank Eddie, not me.'

'Yes,' Simmy agreed.

Ten minutes later everyone was in the kitchen, Simmy reunited with her infant and biting back any reproaches she might be harbouring about the quality of care he had received from his grandparents.

'We were talking about Bruno,' said Eddie to Angie.

Angie was still pale from the rigours of the morning. 'How long was I asleep?' she asked.

'An hour or so,' said Russell. 'You'll be feeling a bit woozy – it's always the same after a daytime sleep. Have some paella.'

'Bruno,' said Eddie again, looking round at the faces of the Straw family, all of whom he had known all his life.

'What about him?' asked Angie. 'Why come to us? We've got nothing to do with it. As far as I can understand it, we'd all left Threlkeld well before it happened.'

'And Ben was with Jonty and Derek, so they can all vouch for each other.' Russell addressed his wife: 'We were just realising that Eddie is just about the only person without a proper alibi.'

'And Moxon,' said Simmy. 'He keeps pointing out that he was *right there* where it happened, at much the same time.'

'And nobody thinks it was him,' said Russell.

'We need Ben,' said Simmy, as she had said many times before. The baby burped and she spent a minute devoting every atom of her attention to him. 'Poor old Robin – was it a horrid morning then?' she crooned.

'Poor old us, as well,' said Russell. 'We hadn't quite anticipated such a strenuous struggle to keep him happy. We didn't make a very good job of it.'

'Better luck next time, eh?' said Eddie breezily.

There was a silence, in which Angie and Russell exchanged a long look.

Then Angie shrugged. 'It can't be much worse,' she said. 'But let's wait until he's on solids – then we can shovel mashed banana into him to keep him quiet.'

'He was noisy, then?' Simmy ventured. 'Didn't he like the bottle?'

'He did not,' said Russell. 'But it was more the unfamiliar scenery, I think. Maybe we smell funny to him.'

'I think I was a bit tense,' Angie admitted. 'And babies don't like that.'

Simmy gave her mother a closer inspection. 'Tense?' she repeated. 'Why?'

'Oh – just things. Breaking that tooth was the start of it. Then I got terrible cramp in my leg at the dentist. It was agony. I was a bit shaky after that. And we're full of guests as always. It just seemed to get out of control. You know how it is.' She smiled bravely. 'Better luck next time, as Eddie says.'

Everyone was still tucking in to the paella, Simmy on the chair beside the Aga, juggling the bowl and the baby. 'I was starving,' she said, when it was finished. 'That was lovely, Dad. Thanks. Now I need some ice cream and coffee. I can stay till about half past two, I'm taking Bonnie back with me. Ben's staying the night and going in with Christopher on Monday – or so I assume. He's lonely there in Keswick.'

'We haven't talked about Bruno properly,' said Eddie crossly. 'That's what I came for.'

'Tough luck,' said Angie. 'You've come all this way on a wasted journey.'

'Not at all,' said Eddie with a meaningful look at Simmy. 'It's always nice to see you. After all, we're family now.' Everyone looked at Robin, who embodied the irreversible link between the Straws and the Hendersons.

Chapter Thirteen

It was two forty-five when Simmy collected Bonnie from her home with Corinne, a few streets east of Beck View. The girl had been waiting for half an hour, having got back from the shopping trip in Kendal soon after two. 'We had a nice lunch there,' she said proudly. Eating out had been a major challenge for her since she was about eleven, but thanks to the patient encouragement from her foster mother and then her boyfriend, she had overcome much of her phobia.

'What did you have?' asked Simmy, who had learned that the subject must be treated casually, but not avoided.

'Salad with hard-boiled eggs and prawns, and avocado. I'm stuffed.' Bonnie's elfin figure never looked as if it could contain very much in the way of food. Simmy imagined the nutrients surging triumphantly through her body, carrying energy and health along with them.

'Lovely,' she said. 'We had one of my dad's paellas. He doesn't do them often, but they're always fantastic.'

On the drive up to Hartsop they recounted their respective experiences of the morning, before drifting inevitably into speculations about the death of Bruno Crowther.

'We need Ben if we're to have any hope of working it out,' said Simmy. 'Everyone else seems to have given up.'

'Ben has as well,' said Bonnie. 'He says it's impossible. Probably some random stranger bashed Bruno's head, maybe by mistake, and ran off up the mountain or somewhere. And because nobody thought Bruno would die, they didn't bother with much in the way of forensics. But he does want to know more of the exact findings at the post-mortem. It's all too vague as it is.'

'It makes the hospital look bad, missing a cracked skull or whatever it was.'

'Which they don't usually do. Brains are funny, though. You can have quite a small clot or blockage in a vital place and it stops your heart working, so you die.'

'Right,' said Simmy slowly, not quite convinced that Bonnie's medical knowledge was equal to the situation. 'But wouldn't they check all those vital places at the start? I presume they know which bit of the brain controls the heart and breathing and the stuff that keeps you alive. It must be routine to make sure they were all right.'

'I don't know,' Bonnie admitted.

'Nor do I,' said Simmy with a little laugh. 'But I expect Ben does.'

Ben was waiting impatiently at Simmy's house, grabbing Bonnie in a tight hug and then clinging to her like a baby. 'It's been *ages*,' he mumbled. 'I missed you.'

The girl disengaged herself and scrutinised him closely. 'What's the matter?' she asked.

'Oh – things.' He looked from Simmy to Christopher as they all stood around the big living room. 'Let's go for a walk or something. Just up and down the village. I'm all in a state. I keep having *ideas*.'

'Don't do that,' Christopher advised. 'Very unsettling, ideas can be.'

'My parents had an awful time with Robin,' Simmy told her husband. 'I thought they were going to refuse to have him ever again. As it is, they want to wait until he's on solids.'

'When will that be?'

'A few weeks. I don't want to do it too soon. He'll need less from me and I'm not ready for that.'

'Not a problem, then,' said Christopher easily. 'There's no hurry, is there?'

Simmy was not sure whether he understood female mechanics well enough to grasp that the process of weaning Robin would very likely render her fertile again. The question of a second baby would then arise. Until a few days ago, this had been taken for granted – by Simmy anyway. Now she felt she ought to give greater consideration to Christopher's feelings. She badly wanted to broach the subject of his childhood trauma, but could not find the words. There seemed too much risk of making everything worse if she did it clumsily. Far better to come at it obliquely, making it clear that she too found the responsibilities of parenthood daunting. Robin would be subjected to his parents' deficiencies, whatever anybody said or did. It seemed to her that the best way of dealing with that was to keep things light. Kindness, humour, optimism would all go a long way – and Christopher did not lack for any of them. They just sometimes disappeared from view.

'No hurry,' she agreed. 'Although Robin probably has his own ideas about it.'

Bonnie and Ben came back from a rather short walk and went straight up to the room he'd been allotted, holding on to each other and talking breathlessly.

Christopher watched them with a frown. 'Is this what they mean by "treating us like a hotel"?' he wondered.

'Be nice,' his wife ordered. 'They've got a lot of catching up to do.'

'They won't have sex up there, will they?'

'I doubt it – at least not until later. She's spending the night in there with him, you know. It wouldn't be very surprising.' For a long time the relationship between the youngsters had been chaste, Ben admitting one day to Simmy that he was afraid of somehow damaging his precious girl with clumsy lovemaking. Her dark childhood was still a factor, the details of the behaviour of a succession of men brought into the house by Bonnie's mother still murkily obscure. The girl had a lot to recover from and Ben understood that there were dangerous undercurrents that he would do well to avoid. But since Easter, when he had dropped out of university, and acquired troubles of his own, the roles had reversed to some extent and Simmy detected signs that the days of celibacy might be over. 'Bonnie has grown up a lot in the past few months,' she added.

When they had started to rekindle their ancient romance, Christopher had been presented with Ben-and-Bonnie as an ineradicable element in the package that was Simmy. He had resisted and complained as far as he'd dared, to no avail. Now, with Ben working alongside him in Keswick, he had capitulated completely. 'But I still don't understand him,' he regularly reminded Simmy.

'Where did you have lunch?' she asked him now. 'We had one of my dad's paellas.'

'We?'

'Me and Robin. Oh – and Eddie. That was pretty odd, actually. He obviously didn't want to go home, even though Jonty could probably do with his company.'

'Ben and I went to the Patterdale pub, but it was horribly full. We just had a quick beer and sandwich and came back. We've been here since two. Ben's been making notes. He wanted to explain it all to me, but I told him to wait for you.'

'That sounds promising. Bonnie and I were worried he'd lost interest in solving murders. That would make life very dull.'

'Not the same when it's your friend who's been killed,' Christopher said, evidently pleased with his own insightfulness.

'No,' Simmy agreed. 'But he obviously wants to spend some time with Bonnie before I get copied in on whatever he's concluded.'

'So tell me about your morning,' her husband invited. 'We can take some tea outside while you do it.'

Upstairs, Ben and Bonnie were cuddled together on the bed, not saying very much for the first ten minutes. The physical reassurance of each other's presence, and the quelling of any worries that something had gone cool and remote between them, took priority.

'I did miss you,' Ben kept saying. 'You seemed such a long way away.'

'So did you. I didn't know what you were thinking.'

'I *couldn't* think properly. I went numb. I mean – *Bruno*. He was such a big person, in every way. All that brainpower, just *gone*. That's what I keep coming back to. Some thug, with an IQ of about fifty, just wiping him away for no reason. It makes everything seem so pointless.'

'You don't really think that's what happened, do you?'

'I did – until about half an hour ago. Then something clicked and I developed a whole new theory.'

She rubbed his chest, through the thin summer shirt. 'That's my boy,' she applauded. 'I do love a theory.'

'So let me run it past you and you can point out all the holes. And I can write it down logically as we go.'

Which he did, and when he was finished, Bonnie rolled off the bed, and said, 'Now we have to go downstairs and say it all again to Simmy and Christopher.'

Ben's notes began with a list of known facts, each with a bullet point. It was written on a sheet of lined A4 paper, with additional words and phrases inserted in the margin.

Simmy sighed with relief. 'Just like old times,' she said.

'So let's hear it,' said Christopher.

Ben cleared his throat and began to read. 'I've started with the first phone call for an ambulance,' he said. 'None of it's very precise. I was thinking that tomorrow we might go round and try to talk to some of these people in Threlkeld.'

Christopher spluttered. 'How? You don't even know who they are.'

'I can probably find out,' said the young man confidently.

'I can't imagine how,' Christopher repeated. 'And what are you planning to say to them? What makes you think they'd even talk to you?'

'Get on with it,' Bonnie said, before Ben could defend himself.

Ben nodded and began a rapid resumé of his theory. 'So listen. From what I've managed to work out, Bruno is found unconscious at about four o'clock on Wednesday afternoon, by one or more passing strangers and they call 999. Moxon said it was a man's voice. The police are bound to think that might be his attacker showing a bit of remorse and then running off. In any case they stuck around long enough to find Bruno's phone and call the first person who came up on the contacts list, to say what was going on. That person was Mr Ackroyd, Bruno's father, and *he* puts it on Facebook, where Patsy Wilkins, who claims to have been Bruno's girlfriend, sees it within moments of it appearing. Then the ambulance came, and the do-gooder passers-by melted into the background, Bruno gets taken off to hospital, where Patsy is the first to see him there. Does that make sense so far?'

Simmy and Bonnie nodded, but Christopher said, 'From what Moxon told us when he came here, you have got some of it a bit wrong. There were a couple of women with Bruno when the ambulance arrived, but it wasn't them who called it and I don't think they saw anybody else near him. That means two lots of people found him.'

'OK. Good,' said Ben. 'I knew I'd probably got some of it wrong.'

Christopher was obviously fully engaged in theorising, as well as the others. 'Actually, the Facebook thing isn't too surprising. Lots of people can only convince themselves they're alive if the latest events of their day are broadcast for the world to see. Ludicrous but true.'

'I suppose that's right,' said Ben, looking to Bonnie for confirmation. She splayed out her hands as if to say *People do idiotic things these days*. Ben went on, 'Anyway, off they all go to the hospital in Penrith – Derek, Mrs Smythe, Jonty, the police – but not Bruno's dad, as far as I can see. And Jonty thinks Patsy might be based there at least some of the time, for her job, which would explain how she came to be on the scene first. They keep him in overnight, during which time he regains consciousness, but says he can't remember what happened. His X-rays look clear and he passes all the usual tests next morning. So they send him home. That's to Derek Smythe's house where he was only intending to stay another few days before moving to Threlkeld.

'His mother keeps him in bed and restricts visitors to close friends and family. And then, sometime that afternoon, she goes up with a cup of tea – or something – and finds him dead. Everybody takes it for granted that the hospital missed something, and a clot or bleed in his brain was slowly killing him over twenty-four hours. The post-mortem is done quickly, on that assumption and nothing is found to contradict it.' He looked up. 'Post-mortems are usually pretty superficial these days, you know. There won't have been any fancy stuff like you see on the telly. It'll have been a matter of ticking the box they already expected – death by trauma to the head, caused by blunt instrument. That's the key point, actually. Did they just examine him externally, or have they opened him up and done the whole range of tests?'

'Who would know?' Simmy asked. 'Surely they will have at least had a look inside his head and located the clot or bleed or whatever it was that actually killed him?'

'I think it's quite possible that they didn't. The bruising and probable crack in his skull – the whole story will have been enough for them to conclude the cause of death without much time-consuming probing into his brain. But when I hand all this over to them, they're going to have to start again and do it properly.' He beamed triumphantly at the three faces, sitting around a rickety garden table on the only patch of level ground in the Hendersons' garden. It was in shadow, as the sun sank behind the house.

'Go on,' Bonnie urged. 'You haven't explained properly yet.'

'Well – I think they might be surprised by what they find. I think somebody attacked him again on Thursday. I don't believe the original assault killed him. It didn't happen in Threlkeld after all. And nobody's alibi for Wednesday counts for anything.'

'It makes sense,' Bonnie told the dumbfounded Hendersons, with an earnest expression. 'But there's no proof.' She looked hopefully at Simmy. 'Will Mr Moxon listen, do you think?'

'He'll listen, but he's not likely to do anything. He's not really part of the investigation, don't forget. Would they be willing to do another post-mortem?'

'They ought to. It's not such a big deal,' said Ben, who knew more on the subject than any of the others, thanks to his two terms of study at Newcastle. 'It's only three days since he died. Less than that, in fact. Forty-eight hours. They might not have released him to the undertaker yet.'

Christopher was staring at Ben with a mixture of fascination and disbelief, having grown increasingly resistant to the last part of Ben's theory as it unfolded. 'You really are something,' he said, with more criticism than admiration in his tone. 'Why can't you just let it be?'

Simmy rounded on him. 'What are you talking about? Why aren't you *glad* he's been working on it? If Ben's right, then there's a far better chance that they'll catch whoever did it. Don't you *want* that?'

'Not if it's Derek or Jonty, or somebody we know and like. If nobody's got an alibi, then we're all under suspicion, aren't we? Even you,' he said to Ben. 'Where was everybody on Thursday? Who visited Bruno?'

'None of us,' said Bonnie, with a very forced little laugh. 'You were having your honeymoon, and Ben and I were at work.'

'She's right,' said Ben. 'You're talking rubbish.'

'Ben!' Simmy protested. The room became full of shocked offence as the enormity of Ben's attack became inescapable. Christopher was his employer, old enough to be his father and owner of the house where he was a guest. The words ballooned and echoed all the more powerfully because Ben Harkness almost never behaved in such a way.

'Bruno was our friend,' Bonnie said quietly. 'We want to know who killed him, whoever it was.'

Simmy smiled at the girl. 'It's a horrible feeling, knowing there's a murderer out there, very probably a person you've had as a friend. It skews all your assumptions about people. Let's just calm down and think sensibly about Ben's theory. Hasn't Moxon gone away this weekend? Somebody said he was planning to go on holiday right after our wedding, but had to postpone it because of Bruno.'

'That's right,' said Ben. 'He told us yesterday when he came to the saleroom.' He looked to Christopher for confirmation. The man was sitting back in his chair, his face pale, jaw clenched. Simmy remembered a similar look from decades earlier when Christopher had been fighting with his brothers. As the eldest he had claimed a superior entitlement and would take great offence if a sibling crossed a line. His dignity was important to him, even now.

'Come on,' she urged him. 'Don't get all high and mighty. We're all friends here.'

'You three might be – but somehow I always end up feeling I've been pushed out of the magic circle. It happens every bloody time.' He got up and strode to the back door. 'I'll be inside if you want me.'

Nobody made a move to stop him, and when he'd gone, there was a palpable sense of relief.

'Oh dear,' said Simmy.

The youngsters watched her carefully as she struggled to sort through her reactions. The situation was, as Christopher had said, not new. She had Ben and Bonnie on one hand and her partner on the other, ever since reigniting her relationship with Christopher. The advent of Robin had seemed, for a short time, to change all that. The Hendersons were a family, a secure unit that would take precedence over other commitments. Ben and Bonnie had understood and respected that. But there had always been a requirement from all three that Christopher should not be undermined or threatened by any hints of inadequacy or weakness. Ben had just blown all that away, with three words.

'He probably wants us to go,' worried Bonnie. 'Would it help if Ben went after him and apologised?'

'Don't go,' Simmy ordered. 'How can you, anyway?'

'We could get a bus to Penrith, and a train or something from there,' said Bonnie hesitantly. The prospect of such a journey on a Saturday afternoon would deter anybody.

Ben was frowning down at his notes. 'We still don't have any idea of what really happened on Wednesday,' he said. 'It could easily have been a complete accident. Although it does look as if the person responsible did a bunk before they could answer any questions.'

'Stop it,' Simmy told him. 'You were rude and you know it. But I'm not going to tell you what to do. You're old enough to deal with it yourself.'

'I'd probably just make it worse if I went after him. The thing is' – he gave Simmy a long challenging stare – 'the thing is, he *was* talking rubbish.'

'He was trying to join in,' said Simmy, before stopping herself. 'But it's not my place to speak for him, or try to explain him to you. He's your boss, apart from anything else.'

'I hadn't forgotten,' said Ben gloomily. 'I suppose I'll get the sack on Monday.'

'I doubt it,' said Simmy. Her own feelings were not becoming any clearer, although she was hurting for her husband. It did not seem to her that he had been talking rubbish, except for the implied inclusion of Derek in the list of suspects. He had been in Keswick on Thursday, up until the time his wife phoned him with the news that Bruno was dead, so could not have been near Bruno in the hours leading up to that moment. By storming out Christopher made himself appear childish and sulky. Worst of all, he had done just what her first husband, Tony, would have done – and that was disappointing. She smiled at Bonnie, instinctively seeking another female in a moment that felt as if the sexes were forever to be divided. 'Life can get very complicated sometimes, can't it?' she said.

For the past hour, little Robin had been sound asleep upstairs. His traumatic morning had worn him out, and the solace of his cot and the familiar voices of his parents downstairs had sent him into relaxed oblivion that might well last all afternoon.

'Don't you need to make sure the baby's all right?' asked Bonnie now. She had heard about some of the events at Beck View and agreed with Simmy that it must have been hard on the child.

'I'll hear him when he wakes up,' Simmy assured her. 'I think he needs a good long sleep.'

Ben was fidgeting. His brilliant theory was being forgotten, with nobody suggesting any action. 'I should talk to Jonty,' he said. 'See what he thinks.'

Bonnie was immediately attentive. 'You need to be careful,' she warned. 'Don't forget that if you're right, some people haven't got an alibi any more.'

Ben scowled, apparently aware that his behaviour had not been ideal. 'You mean Jonty might have killed Bruno? That's insane.'

'Maybe it is, but I don't think you should tell anybody else about your idea until we've run it past Mr Moxon.'

'He's away,' Simmy reminded her.

'He'll have his phone, won't he? We can call him.'

'Will he listen, though?' Ben worried. 'And should it be him, anyway? How about finding the SIO in Penrith and telling whoever it is what I think?'

'You should have some evidence,' said Simmy, recalling earlier episodes. 'They won't want vague theories without anything to back them up. They'll say you're wasting their time.'

'That means talking to Bruno's mum, then. She'll know who visited on Thursday.'

Bonnie pulled a face. 'You'll need to be careful, even with her,' she said.

Simmy's heart thudded. 'You don't think his *mother* killed him?' She thought of her own precious little boy upstairs and concluded that such an act was completely out the question. It could just never ever happen.

'No, I don't,' said Bonnie. 'But if we tell her what we think, she might talk to whoever did it, without realising, and spoil everything.'

Simmy tried to compile a mental list of potential suspects in the light of Ben's new ideas. 'So, who are you thinking might have done it?' she asked.

'I'm not naming names,' said Ben stiffly. 'Every single one of them loved Bruno, as far as I'm aware. He was such a brilliant guy. Never did a minute's harm to anyone. But you have to push all that aside when you're working out the possibilities. You have to ignore the emotional stuff.'

'Which is just what Christopher was trying to do,' said Simmy.

'And which means you have to keep Mrs Smythe – whatever her first name is – on the list,' Bonnie said.

'She's called Tilly. And then there's Bruno's dad – Jonty said he visited on Thursday as well. He probably wanted to write about it on Facebook.'

'He sounds like a proper plonker,' said Bonnie. 'Have you ever met him?'

Ben shook his head. 'But I've read all his postings. I'm not sure he's all there, to be honest.' He paused. 'So that means Patsy, and I suppose Jonty and his dad should be included, because they all had opportunity. At least . . .' he tapped his teeth with his pen for a moment. 'Eddie won't have gone there, will he?'

'We'll have to ask,' said Bonnie.

'Good God, you can't include Eddie,' Simmy protested. 'You'll have Christopher after you all over again if you do.'

Bonnie raised a hand, as if in a classroom. 'You said he went to see you today – in the shop,' she said. 'And then to Beck View for lunch. Did you ever figure out what he wanted?'

Ben raised his eyebrows. 'It's a long drive. He must have had a good reason.'

Simmy took a deep breath, preparing to defend a man who nobody seemed to fully like or understand. 'He was upset, mainly because of Jonty, I think. He's always been fond of my parents, in a funny sort of way. I think he just needed some sort of reassurance. But he never really said what he meant to. He was thwarted by all the baby talk, and Dad's paella.'

'Hang on,' said Ben. 'First he went to the shop – and what then?'

'We walked over to Beck View together, and my dad gave us paella. Robin was asleep upstairs with my mother. I missed quite a lot of what he said to my dad, I think. I was more concerned about Robin.'

'I need to see Jonty,' Ben announced. 'Can you drive me over there?'

Chapter Fourteen

Derek Smythe was at home, immersing himself in excessive attention to his two little daughters. His wife was in the kitchen, weeping over a mug of cold tea. There was going to be another whole day of this before he could go back to work, he thought miserably. The fish and chips had raised a few spirits for a little while, the children eating most of their mother's portion as well as their own. Tilly had done her best, bless her – picking at a bit of white meat here and there and forcing the occasional watery smile – but Derek watched her struggles to swallow with growing distress. He had never seen her go off her food before.

For himself, he was employing all his most rational skills in an effort to diminish the suffering. He was repeating lines to himself, such as *Your children leave you anyway, sooner or later* and *We'll always remember him at his best*. Bruno had been a friendly and rewarding lad at about the age of twelve, reading books from earlier times and eager to explore the land he felt lucky to call home. He had been bright-eyed and optimistic in those days. But from about sixteen he had changed into a much less attractive cynic, hooked on websites and areas of YouTube that seemed to encourage a very dour outlook on the world. Derek had been left behind, bemused by quotations from unknown characters with names like Heidegger and Kierkegaard.

Jonty Henderson had been embraced as a good influence on Bruno, even though nobody could understand what the two had in common. Derek and Tilly told themselves that Jonty was a living sign that their son was not quite as peculiar as they feared. Perhaps, after all, there was nothing much to worry about. He was growing out of his nihilistic phase and reverting to something closer to his pre-teenage self. The plan to rent the little house in Threlkeld looked to them to be something positive, a safe stepping-stone into the wider world. The advent of Ben Harkness had felt less relevant. Another clever boy, a foil for Bruno's philosophical speculations, but worrying in some ways, too. Dropping out of university, just as Bruno was preparing to start his first term as an undergraduate, struck them as ominous.

Tilly had thrown herself into the scheme for independent living with admirable zest. She had provided bedding, crockery, even a surplus chair, in an attempt to smooth the process. Bruno had smiled and thanked her, and reminded her that the bungalow came fully furnished.

'Yes, but you always want a few of your own things,' she had insisted. 'It makes it more homely.'

Derek had gone with the boys for a look at the place, before agreeing that they should rent it for a few months. He had vivid memories of a flat he had shared as a student, with its smells of socks and sour milk. It had made him nostalgic to think his stepson was embarking on a similar enterprise, despite the obvious differences. Bruno was not earning any money, for a start. His share of the rent would come from his inheritance, but Derek thought he would be much better off getting a job. Derek himself had never been without earned income since he was sixteen. Even as a student, he had worked in a cinema in the evenings and at weekends.

'But it's hardly any money,' Bruno had protested. 'I won't even notice it. And I'm going to be doing a lot of reading for the Bristol course.' This was not enough to persuade Derek – what was the wretched boy planning to *do* all day? There was a limit to the time a person could sit around reading. When Derek voiced these thoughts, the response was vague. 'Oh, I expect I'll go for walks, do a bit of writing, keep the place clean, if I need some variety.'

Derek had laughed, whilst acknowledging that Bruno was extraordinarily clean. He dusted and tidied and vacuumed his bedroom to the point where it made the rest of the house look sleazy by comparison. No unwashed socks or festering bits of pizza under Bruno Crowther's bed.

Derek had pushed away a flickering worry that the boy must be mentally unstable. 'Isn't there a term for people like him?' he said to Tilly. 'OCD or something?'

'Don't knock it,' she told him. 'Most people would be thrilled.'

Derek himself liked things to be tidy. One of his favourite tasks at the auction house was to go along the shelves on the day before a sale and set everything at the perfect angle for maximum appeal. And then the early-morning viewers would move them all about and ruin the effect when it was too late for him to do anything about it.

Tilly loved her husband's new job. She attended some of the auctions and sometimes bought the random 'job lot' boxes, full of silver plates and china and knick-knacks that had been swept off the mantelpiece in a deceased old lady's house without much attention. 'There's always at least one bit of treasure,' she insisted.

Given that such boxes mostly sold for four or five pounds, Derek made no objection. When Tilly sold the contents on eBay for impressive profits, he found himself becoming more and more supportive. But Bruno had deplored the practice, because the purchases tended to accumulate around the house and the business of packaging and despatching items to eBay customers was messy and intrusive. He had become quite unpleasant about it, more than once.

So did Derek Smythe review the life of his stepson; a process that did a lot to assuage the initial shock and grief at his death. It enabled him to proceed to the next stage – which was an attempt to understand just how the lad had actually died, and what it could possibly mean.

Eddie arrived home to find his son slumped on the sofa with the curtains drawn and the television showing some sort of fantasy series that might well have been a favourite with Jonty and Bruno. 'Did you have any lunch?' Eddie asked. 'Has your mother been home at all?'

'No and no. She phoned. Back about five, she said. I did have some cheese. Where've you been?'

'I went down to see Angie and Russell. Couldn't get much sense out of them – it's all about that baby with them these days.'

'Huh. Oh, Patsy called as well. She's coming over again.'

Jonty's gaze had not left the TV screen, but Eddie was used to that. He almost found it reassuring. 'What does *she* want?'

'Same as before, I s'pose. Wants to talk about Bruno. She'll cry, most likely.'

'Lord help us. We can give her to your mother if that's what's going to happen. They can cry together.' They both knew that Eliza was never going to shed tears for her son's best friend. Eddie had found himself making a mental list of people who would barely miss Bruno; his wife was definitely on it. 'Is she staying for supper?' he wondered.

'Dunno.'

Before Eddie could attempt any further conversation, Jonty's phone jingled. 'Ben,' he said, before responding to the call. Eddie ascertained from Jonty's half of the exchange that Ben would also be paying them a visit within the next hour, arriving by bicycle on his own. Jonty extended willing hospitality without consulting his father.

'All the way from Keswick on his bike?' Eddie queried. 'He's a braver man than I am.'

'No – he's at Simmy's. He wanted her to drive him, but she wouldn't. Nor would Uncle Chris. It sounds as if it's a bit . . . I don't know . . . what d'you call it when people can't think of anything but their baby?'

'I don't think there's a word for that,' grinned Eddie. 'I remember now. Simmy told me she'd got Ben and Bonnie there tonight, for some reason. Why's he coming here without his girlfriend?'

'She hasn't got a bike, so she can't get here.'

'Will he be staying for supper?'

'Dunno,' said Jonty again. 'At this rate, there'll be five of us. Can't see Mum being too pleased about that.'

'No,' his father agreed, with the strong sense of an impending storm. A storm that was all too likely to take place in his very own living room. Eliza Henderson was a disorganised cook, leaving her husband and son to fend for themselves a lot of the time, excusing herself by insisting that the freezer was always full of ready meals, pies, joints and sausages. Eddie muttered about fresh vegetables and interesting fruit, from time to time, to no avail.

'We'd better tidy up a bit, then,' Eddie said, looking around the room. 'How many cups of tea have you had today? Can't you reuse the same mug?'

Jonty shrugged, and his father gathered up the debris from a day spent in front of the TV. 'I thought all boys were as messy as you until I met Bruno and Ben,' he said thoughtlessly. When no answer came, he turned to see his son's face resting on his knees, his fists clenched. 'Hey! Sorry, lad. I wasn't thinking what I was saying.' He paused. 'But you'll have to toughen up a bit, you know. You can't go weeping every time Bruno's name crops up.'

'It's only two days.' Jonty sniffed. 'It keeps coming over me.'

'Well, that's how it goes, sad to say. You've just got to get through it. Maybe Ben'll be a help. Or Patsy.'

Ben cycled eastwards, the sun behind him, and sank into a reverie not unlike that which DI Moxon had experienced on the road to Anglesey. But Ben felt a more acute set of dilemmas. He wanted to reveal his new theory to someone other than Bonnie and Simmy, but didn't dare. Whoever he might choose could turn out to be the killer. Even Jonty, or Bruno's mother, or the Ackroyd man could conceivably have done it. With no way of knowing whether or not the theory was credible and with no idea how the fatal blow might have been dealt, he was treading on very delicate ground in the dark. The very least of the dangers was that he would lose Jonty's friendship.

Seeing Jonty felt like a crucial next step. He had been to visit Bruno on Thursday and had better knowledge of the family set-up. He was even vaguely acquainted with Patsy Wilkins, who was unacceptably mysterious. He resented the way Bruno had kept her separate, never mentioning her and seldom even seeing her. A dawning suspicion was arising that the whole relationship had been conducted almost entirely online. That wouldn't be unusual these days.

His thoughts moved on to the scanty facts known about the discovery of the injured Bruno on Wednesday in Threlkeld. His peculiar father had immediately put the whole thing on Facebook with the result that Patsy was at her boyfriend's bedside before pretty much anyone else. On a working day amidst the supposedly hectic schedule of a busy social worker, she had found time to check her phone and hurry to Penrith. Although she might possibly have her own office at the hospital and could have been only yards away when Bruno was brought in. That sort of information had to be obtained before he could go any further with his speculations.

There was a nightmare element to the whole business – like needing desperately to get somewhere, only to find a high brick wall in front of you that could not be scaled. Being separated from Bonnie made it all much worse. Christopher and Simmy had both flatly refused to drive him to Eddie's house, when asked. The fact that Eddie was his brother cut no ice with Christopher. Nor did appeals on behalf of Jonty – his nephew – or even a reminder that Derek Smythe would be eternally grateful for help in finding who killed Bruno.

'For all we know, it could have been Derek's own son, if what you say is right,' Christopher had growled. Ben had to admit that was theoretically possible.

'Phone me,' Bonnie said. 'Or text. I want to know *everything*.'

When he got to the house, he propped his bike against a low stone wall between the road and the garden and headed for the front door.

'Hi!' came a female voice behind him. 'You must be Ben.'

He turned to see a thin woman in her twenties of middling height and very white skin. Just behind her was a tall, thin man who was startlingly identical to Bruno, except for darker colouring.

'I am,' he said. 'Are you Patsy Wilkins, by any chance? And can this be Mr Ackroyd?'

'Correct both times. Why are you here?'

Ben wanted to return the same question, but held his tongue. He was saved by Jonty appearing in the doorway, looking from face to face in bewilderment.

'Did you all come here together?' Jonty asked.

'No, no. Just arrived at the same moment,' said Ben. 'We've introduced ourselves, that's all. It's good to meet you at last,' he said politely to the woman standing at his shoulder.

'Can we go round to the garden?' Jonty asked, looking worried. 'My mum's a bit frazzled with so many people. Lucky Bonnie couldn't come, actually.'

Ben was already wondering what he thought he was doing. He had a reputation as an amateur sleuth, known to have been of genuine help to the police on a number of occasions. If anyone gathered here in Clifton was a killer, they would have the sense to conceal and confuse, in order to evade his suspicions. And the hostility from Eliza Henderson, hinted at by Jonty, would be another complicating factor.

But Eliza was far from hostile. She came out into the garden carrying a tray on which were arranged – bizarrely – several slices of pizza. 'Call it high tea.' She smiled. 'Just like in the olden days.'

'We still have tea,' said Patsy stiffly. 'A lot of people round here do.'

At another time, Ben would have taken more interest in the eating habits of the different social classes. In his house they had a meal called 'supper' at about six o'clock or a bit later. 'Tea' was believed to be a fairly light afternoon snack, strictly at four. But Bonnie had instructed him in the matter, describing a meal halfway between the two, with something cooked followed by bread and jam and several cups of tea, taken around half past five.

'Corinne does something different again,' Bonnie had explained. 'A big first course, with fruit and cheese to finish.'

Bonnie had a difficult relationship with food, which entailed a paradoxical combination of resistance and compulsion.

One of her therapists had persuaded her that it would be beneficial to study the matter from every angle, including the anthropological. It had worked no worse than suggestions made by some of the others. In the end, Ben had made the most headway, with his patient acceptance of the girl's quirks and a steadfast determination never to criticise or try to compel.

Eliza went back for a large teapot, milk and several mugs that she distributed, and then sat down, clearly intending to participate in whatever was to happen next. There were folding garden chairs for five people, and the sixth – which was Jonty – sat on the grass.

Eddie blithely raised his mug and said, 'To Bruno!'

Nobody responded verbally, but they all lifted the tea to their lips in a silent tribute, including the fascinating Ackroyd, who had introduced himself as Anthony. Ben was impressed with the whole scene and Eddie in particular. Perhaps Christopher's brother was wiser than anyone gave him credit for. The toast was a clever move, effective in bringing the burning issue to the forefront without demanding any disclosures or triggering too much emotion.

'So,' said Eliza, fixing Ben with a terrifying smile, 'what are we all doing here?'

'Good question,' Patsy agreed loudly. 'I just wanted a few minutes with Jonty – same as yesterday. And Anthony wanted to meet you all. We're the ones with the biggest loss – the three of us. We ought to stick together.' She threw a reproachful look around the group, as if they were deliberately denying her something she felt was her right.

Ben had a sense of the two women taking control – which was a familiar feeling. Any male person of his age had long ago understood that this was the general way of things – primarily in the home, admittedly, but also in schools and quite a lot of workplaces. Indeed, the adjustment he had found himself having to make at the saleroom was because Christopher Henderson was so completely and effortlessly in charge.

'I was his friend, too,' he said loudly. 'I came because I wanted to understand more about what happened on Thursday. You two – or three—' he looked at Ackroyd with raised eyebrows, '—were there – can you tell me a bit about it?'

'Like what?' said Jonty, with a frown. 'It was OK. I mean, he seemed pretty much his usual self, just a bit pale and groggy. His head was aching, but not too badly. He said he'd be getting up later on and going downstairs for a bit.'

'Was he eating?' Ben asked, at random.

'He had a few grapes that Tilly bought for him. I had some of them as well.' Jonty seemed very young, and very much out of his depth. 'He said he thought we could still move into Threlkeld on Monday because he was sure to be all better by then.' He sniffed violently and rubbed his face. 'And all the time his brain must have been bleeding, or something, and he never knew it. That was the very last time I saw him.'

'What time was that?' asked Ben, trying hard not to sound like a policeman.

'Dunno. Before lunch. Twelve, maybe.'

'Earlier than that,' Patsy corrected him. 'I was there at twelve and you'd been gone a bit by then.'

Jonty shrugged. 'I wasn't watching the time.'

Ben turned his attention to Patsy and Ackroyd, who were sitting close together. 'Did you think he was pale and groggy as well?'

She gave him a hard look. 'More or less as you'd expect after a head injury. He looked about the same as he did on Wednesday, as far as I could see. But he was obviously getting better, because he was talking and making plans and eating his grapes.' She made it all sound obvious and unworthy of further examination, until Eddie made a surprise contribution.

'But he never said who or what hit him – did he? Did any of you ask him?'

Both shook their heads. 'His mother said he still couldn't remember and we shouldn't try to force him,' said Jonty. 'That's what she told me, anyway. "Keep it light", she said, and "focus on what comes next". So I did.' He stuck out his chin as if ready for contradiction.

'Same with me,' said Patsy.

Ben kept his focus on Ackroyd, trying to get a sense of the person and how he was taking the loss of his son. He was also inescapably comparing him to Derek Smythe. It would appear that Tilly Crowther-as-was had chosen two very different men to father her children. The one in front of him seemed to Ben to be intelligent, or perhaps quick-witted was more accurate. His black hair had a wave to it and no sign of grey. His eyes were dark and sharp, flitting from one face to another, while he said nothing. His skin was well tanned and Ben tried to guess his line of work. To his regret it was beyond his level of assertiveness to make a direct enquiry. 'You two arrived and left together, then?' he managed to ask.

'God, Ben!' groaned Jonty. 'Stop it, will you? What are you trying to do?'

To general surprise, it was Eliza who answered. 'We all know Ben's reputation, don't we?' she said with a smile. 'I've always wanted to see him in action, having heard so many stories. If it doesn't sound too tactless, I must say I'm quite enjoying it.'

Eddie gave an embarrassed snort. 'Tactless is only the half of it,' he muttered.

'Oh, you poor thing,' she flashed at him. Ben thought he could detect hurt feelings. 'Can't abide a little bit of honesty, same as always.'

'Reputation?' echoed Ackroyd, speaking for almost the first time and clearly seeking to avert a marital spat.

'Oh, yes,' said Eliza. 'This is the boy who's single-handedly solved any number of murders. Him and his girlfriend and Simmy. She's the one who's just married Eddie's brother,' she elaborated. 'Hasn't Bruno told you all this?'

'Not a word,' said the man sorrowfully. He had a face that rather suited sorrow, thought Ben. 'We didn't have much chance to talk while he was working so hard on his exams.'

'It's true, though,' said Jonty, throwing Ben a look that said he was proud to be his friend. 'Ben's a genius. If anyone here's got a guilty secret, they'd better watch out.'

Nobody responded to that, every one of them staring at the grass or the trees or the ugly teapot. Nobody looked at anybody else. Ben forced a laugh. 'Thanks, Jonty. Now nobody's going to speak to me again, are they?'

Again Eliza intervened. 'Well, we've got the picture now, haven't we, for what it's worth. Bruno seemed to

218

be recovering nicely on Thursday morning, welcomed his visitors, reassured his anxious mother, and then—'

'And then the poor woman went up at three o'clock and found him dead,' said Eddie, finishing it for her. He looked at Patsy and Ackroyd. 'You two might have been the last to see him alive.'

Ben almost laughed at the ill-judged attempt at drama. Whatever Eddie was trying to do, it was much less effective or intelligent than his earlier success in focusing everyone on Bruno.

Patsy bristled. 'Of course *I* wasn't. Those little girls were in and out of his room all day, and someone would have taken him a drink at least – probably some lunch as well. They wouldn't have left him alone for three whole hours.'

'We can ask them,' said Eliza, with a glance at her husband. From what Ben had learned from Jonty, this couple were rarely in any sort of harmony. One of the boy's main reasons for moving to Threlkeld had been to escape the sour atmosphere between his parents. 'I was thinking we ought to reach out to them, as it happens. The boys were such close friends, we ought to be showing them some support.'

Ben saw nothing helpful in this display of intended solidarity, other than a possible gleaning of more information. 'You'll want to know about the funeral and everything,' he said with a nod.

Eddie was evidently still wary of spoiling his wife's comparatively good mood. Patsy was trying to catch Jonty's eye, appearing to want to join forces with him in some way, but the boy was uncooperative, and Ben suspected an element of competition between the two. Which had been Bruno's best beloved? Which was the more shattered by his loss? Ben's money would have been firmly on Jonty, but he accepted that he had almost nothing to go on where Patsy was concerned. Even more mysterious was her relationship with Ackroyd. He had to be nearly twenty years older than her, as well as being married with children. He seemed relaxed in her company, but nothing more than that. Spotting signs of clandestine romance was not Ben's strong point, but he knew enough to understand that in such cases, the couple would often make exaggerated efforts to appear completely uninterested in each other. There was nothing of that here.

In a bid to regain the attention, he sat up straighter and said, 'I suppose they will have done the post-mortem by now.' It was a line he had found to be very effective in concentrating minds. Nobody liked the thought of the procedure. Many families did their utmost to avoid any necessity for it. Undertakers would collude with doctors in an effort to sidestep it, disliking the delay as much as the distress it caused.

It was Eddie who spoke first. 'What? Why would they need to do that? They must already know the cause of death.'

Patsy was staring at Ben, her jaw clenched. 'They won't, of course – you're right. There's no question as to how he died. He had X-rays and tests, and several doctors saw him when he was in hospital on Wednesday.' She gave a little sneer. 'Mr Clever Clogs here is getting ahead of himself. He knows as well as I do that a post-mortem isn't required if the person has seen a doctor within the past two weeks.'

Ben gave her a cool look that he hoped was perceived as superior and dignified. 'Not if there's doubt as to the cause of death. How will they know that, without having a look inside his head? There'll obviously have to be an inquest and that automatically means a full post-mortem.'

A whimper from Jonty warned Ben that he was on delicate ground. He was already uncomfortably unsure of the exact legal position.

Patsy was not deterred. 'They looked at his head when he was alive, you idiot. Look – you're upsetting everybody with this sort of talk. It's bad enough already, surely, without you showing off? Somebody bashed poor Bruno over the head in Threlkeld on Wednesday, and he died the next day. Doing a post-mortem isn't going to help find whoever it was who did it – is it?'

Ben held his tongue. His theory about Thursday was trying to force itself into the open, and he knew he must keep it back. Patsy had stated the general belief about what had happened, and all the Hendersons were nodding in agreement with her. Ackroyd was giving him thoughtfully hostile looks, as if trying to find a withering comment. Eddie looked grim; Jonty was rubbing his face again and Eliza was gathering up empty mugs. None of them appeared to approve of Ben's words. In fact, he could feel a collective withdrawal from him. He was making trouble, rocking a boat that was already on turbulent seas. But still he badly wanted to argue with Patsy. If nothing else, it would help him to discover more about her. She was a social worker, he reminded himself. She understood distress and anxiety and hopelessness. She was very probably doing her best to protect the sensitive feelings of people who had loved Bruno. She might be thinking of Tilly and Derek and the two little girls, bereft of their son, as she was bereft of a boyfriend. Not to mention the Ackroyd man, who perhaps came at the top of that list.

It hit him then that he had come to the wrong house. He should have gone to the Smythes' instead. They had been on the spot on Thursday. They knew who had visited and exactly how Bruno had been in those final hours. Whilst any reference to a post-mortem would probably have gone down even more badly there, he would probably have had Derek at his back. Derek, of the entire cast of characters, was the one who Ben could personally vouch for on both Wednesday and Thursday.

But he was not going to get any further in his efforts to dredge up precise recollections of events two days ago. For the present, he had to extricate himself from this Clifton house without doing any further damage.

'Hey, Jont,' he said gently. 'Sorry if I upset you. You know me – always wanting to get the whole picture. Bonnie's going to bollock me when I tell her. Look – I'll be off now, but if you want someone to hang out with tomorrow, I can be around. We can go for a walk or something. And we've still got to sort out the bungalow. They probably think we'll be showing up on Monday as planned.'

Jonty gave him a bleary look. 'OK,' he said vaguely.

'Thanks for the pizza, Mrs H,' said Ben, getting up. 'I'll see you soon.'

Eliza smiled. 'You mean well, Ben, I know that. It's just all very raw – you know? Patsy's right in what she says. If you ask me, we'll never know what happened on Wednesday, and that's a tragedy for Tilly and Derek. Just – have some respect for their feelings, all right?'

It made him feel about twelve. 'Right,' he mumbled. 'Sorry.'

'Long ride back,' said Eddie, looking rather pleased. 'You're staying at Chris's again, I suppose?'

'That's right,' said Ben. 'Bonnie's there as well.'

'Course she is,' said the man, with a slightly unpleasant twinkle.

Chapter Fifteen

In Hartsop, Bonnie was feeling very much surplus to requirements. Simmy was sympathetic, but Robin had a prior claim on her. Christopher was defiant, having refused outright to drive both youngsters to his brother's house in Clifton. He had begun by asserting that such an expedition was futile, or worse. 'What possible good can it do?' he had demanded, more than once. Then he shifted to a position in which such a visit would contravene normal social rules. 'Three people arriving at a mealtime is out of the question. It would be terribly rude. What would Eliza think?'

'He's your brother,' said Simmy mildly. 'And this is not an ordinary situation, is it? Nobody's going to care about things like that.'

'Why don't you take them, then?'

'Because they asked you. Because I've got Robin to feed and put to bed. Because he's *your* brother, not mine.'

Bonnie had cringed at the harsh words, blaming herself. 'Don't,' she pleaded. 'He's gone now, so there's no need to argue about it any more.'

Then a text came from Ben.

Coming back now. We'll have to ask Moxon if there's been a post-mortem on Bruno. Met the Ackroyd man. Jonty's in a bad way, it said. Bonnie showed it to Simmy, who blinked a few times.

'Hasn't Moxon already said there was a post-mortem?' Simmy asked.

'I don't know. Has he?'

Simmy did her best to review everything that had been said by Moxon since Thursday. 'I don't know, either,' she concluded. 'It might be that everybody just assumed there had to be one. Ben did, I'm sure. How could there *not* be?' Simmy was predisposed to do all she could to help, to make up for stranding Bonnie here at Hartsop. 'Maybe I should call him now and ask – save Ben the trouble,' she said. 'His mobile number's in my phone.'

'That'd be great. It'll come better from you, anyway.'

It was a matter of seconds before she was speaking to the detective. 'Ben wants me to ask you whether there's been a post-mortem on Bruno,' she said with minimal preamble.

'He does, does he?' The tone was relaxed and affable. 'Cheeky young so-and-so.'

'I know.'

'This leads me to believe that he's begun to take a more active interest in the matter – am I right? Why can't he call me himself?'

'It's a long story, but yes, he's gone to the other extreme now. He's cycled over to Clifton to talk to Jonty, and apparently there are other people there as well. He might call you later this evening if he's got anything useful to tell you. So what's the answer about the post-mortem?'

'The answer to that is not entirely straightforward. As far as I'm aware, there has been a very thorough external examination, and no doubt a review of all the test results from the hospital. I can't be certain, but I strongly suspect there hasn't been anything more than that. Technically, that qualifies as a post-mortem examination, and might be enough to satisfy the coroner. There's a push to save costs, as well as avoiding any backlogs and delays. If the docs at the hospital can convince everybody that it was a brain injury caused by a hard blow there might not be any great need to know more than that.' He was obviously thinking hard about it as he spoke. 'A close external examination might be enough.'

'How can we find out for certain?'

'I can do that from here, in theory. There'll be a file online.'

'I'm sure Ben would appreciate that.'

'There's a lot I ought to ask him first.' Moxon sighed. 'But when have I ever managed to stick to the protocols where young Mr Harkness is concerned?'

Simmy laughed, aware that the point had been made and no more need to be said. 'Is it nice there?' she asked. 'Will you be staying all week?'

'It's remarkably nice. We even had some sunshine. I'm surrounded by adoring females and eating the most succulent fish imaginable.'

'At this very moment? Isn't it a bit early?'

'It's been ordered and I am reliably assured as to the succulence. Just at this very moment I'm drinking a cold Campari, which is a rare treat.'

'I don't think I've ever had it.'

'You wouldn't like it.'

She laughed again, feeling the warmth of a solid friendship that had been there for her ever since she delivered flowers to a wedding on the banks of Lake Windermere. 'Surrounded by females?' she repeated.

'Wife. Wife's sister and two daughters. They're all being wonderfully nice to me.'

'Of course they are,' she said. 'I'm going now. Would it be all right for Ben to call you later on?'

'Would it make any difference if I said no?'

'Possibly not,' she admitted.

In Windermere, Angie Straw was still not over her failings as a grandmother. Doubts assailed her that she had never experienced before. She felt old, which was obviously ridiculous in a person not yet seventy who had never been ill in her life. She had assumed she was good for another thirty years. If anyone was going to crumble, it was her husband, not her.

'Buck up,' Russell adjured her. 'The first time was never going to be straightforward. Look on it as an experiment, or a trial run. We know what to avoid another time.'

'Do we?'

'We have to make a proper plan. Have entertainments ready, or an outing. And once he can eat real food it's bound to be much easier.'

'Yes,' Angie agreed, while knowing the true heart of the matter had not been addressed and she did not have the courage to do so. The real problem was, she had come to realise, that she did not *want* to be a regular childminder. The blithe promises that she and Russell had made before Robin was born now seemed impossible to fulfil. Hadn't they agreed to have the child two or three days a week? Or every morning? Something that now seemed impossibly burdensome. Simmy was going to have to think again about going back to the shop, unless Angie could persuade herself to do as she'd promised, whether she liked it or not.

Her thoughts flowed inevitably onto the men in the picture. The revival of the old story about Christopher dropping baby George had made her uneasy. It felt like a secret that should have died with Frances and Kit. The fact that Eddie of all people should bring it back was ironic. Christopher could be harbouring dark thoughts about the violence men were capable of, with murky fears about his own potential to damage Robin. This had implications for his role as babyminder – which would have to be resolved before much longer.

Christopher worked on a fortnightly pattern that included one or two free weekdays. If Simmy went back to the shop, he could probably manage another day or two working from home while the baby crawled about at his feet. Russell was being annoyingly passive about it all. Merely uttering bracing homilies was of little help; if anything it risked being counter-productive. If he could be relied on to take Robin out in his buggy for a morning every week, down to Bowness or somewhere, Angie would feel a lot happier. She had no illusions about her own selfish wishes, which were nothing to be ashamed of. All it meant was that both Christopher and Russell would be called on to do their share.

But again she caught herself dodging the real issue. She felt exploited and taken for granted. The fact that about a million other grannies in the country were treated in the same fashion did nothing to mollify her. If Simmy thought she could have it all – motherhood, a business and a contented married life – then she was very likely misguided. And if she had another baby – or heaven forfend, *two* more babies – things would only get more troublesome. Angie knew people who had produced whole litters of infants at Simmy's age. Twins were more likely in older mothers, and some women went on being fertile until they were forty-five or more. In a wild flight of fancy worthy of her husband, Angie could see five or six little Hendersons all spending half their time at her house.

'Buck up,' Russell said again, finding her slumped on the sofa in their private living room. 'There'll be people in a minute.'

That, of course, was another thing. The B&B guests kept on coming, with their inexorable expectations. Bedding to be changed and washed; rooms to be kept spotless; food to be fresh and perfectly cooked; and a friendly smile perpetually glued to her face. The grind of it got everyone in the business down by the end of the summer – but here they were not even halfway through the busy season and she already felt unequal to it.

The 'people' were first-timers, doing a traditional Saturday to Saturday, bringing a dog with them and two school-age children. Russell would have to click into his local-expert routine, suggesting less obvious destinations, warning of pitfalls and giving mini-lectures on the history of the region. It was becoming increasingly unusual for whole families to use bed-and-breakfast places for an entire week. It was expensive and not as flexible as self-catering would be. The children and dog would have to behave, and there was no option but to eat out every evening. Angie did not provide cooking facilities. The best she could offer was a downstairs 'rumpus room' with games and books and battered old furniture that could withstand the mud and jumping about that often occurred on rainy weeks.

'It's too much, Russ,' she burst out, regardless of how much this might alarm him. 'We can't do it all.'

'What? What can't we do?'

'Guests, babies, weather, murder, housework, garden – it's too much, I tell you.'

'Oh. Let's sell up then and move to Patterdale. Simple.'

She stared at him, as a warm wave of gratitude and affection and amusement flowed through her. 'Yes, let's,' she said. 'But I think I might prefer Keswick. Or even that sweet little Threlkeld.'

'Bingo!' he yodelled.

Still she stared. 'You've been wanting this all along and never said anything?'

'I've been dropping hints.'

'Have you? I don't remember any.'

He shrugged. 'Doesn't matter now. Listen – don't take any more bookings. It's going to be tricky cancelling those who come every year, but there's only a handful of them anyway. I'll get this place valued on Monday. We could be gone well before Christmas. Although they might say we have to redecorate the whole property.'

'Pooh to that.' Angie was characteristically scathing about the practices of estate agents. 'We can get it valued and then sell it privately. Saves the commission that way.'

Russell knew better than to argue. The exchange had taken perhaps thirty seconds and already life was completely different. It had happened before, of course; in fact it was generally the way everything happened where he and Angie were concerned. The move up to Cumbria had been decided in a similar way, twenty years earlier.

But Angie was in a sudden panic. 'What would we *do* all day?'

'Explore. Go to auctions. Help Ben solve murders. Write a book about Castlerigg.' He paused, savouring the prospects. 'Go for walks. Sell things at car boot sales. I've always wanted to do that.'

His delight filled the room and Angie could not have avoided its contagion even if she'd wanted to. 'Castlerigg?' she echoed.

'Magical place. Haven't been there for years now. Much better than Long Meg. I wonder if we could afford somewhere with a field. We could keep a few sheep. Robin could play with the lambs.'

Before Angie could decide how she felt about sheep, the doorbell rang.

'People,' said Russell.

Ben arrived back in Hartsop shortly before seven, to find that Simmy was upstairs with the baby, Bonnie was drinking herb tea in the kitchen and Christopher was on his computer in a small room that had been created at one end of the barn conversion. The atmosphere was cool, but not exactly tense.

'Moxon isn't sure whether or not there was a full post-mortem,' Bonnie reported briskly. 'That's to say they went over his whole body externally, but probably didn't cut him open.'

Ben nodded. 'That's pretty much what I expected. What else did he say?'

'You'll have to ask Simmy. I think she was quite happy to call him, and he seemed even happier. They chatted for quite a while – and he said you could phone him as well if you want.'

'Without a proper look at his brain and checking for any other cause of death, the whole thing's hopeless. They won't budge from the idea that the attack on Wednesday is what killed him. There's every chance that my theory's right and he died from some other cause entirely. I want to make them see that if I can.'

'We didn't say anything to Moxo about your new theory. Did you get anywhere with Jonty?'

'I'm not sure. I did ask a lot of questions, which annoyed Patsy. Jonty's mum was good. She seemed to like me. But Bruno's dad is pretty strange. He hardly said a word.'

'What's Patsy like?'

'Quite fierce. She seems to have had quite a thing for Bruno and it looked to me as if she knows Ackroyd quite well. That's a whole area of Bruno's life that he never talked about at all. Not to me, anyway. I still think that's weird.'

'It is,' said Bonnie. 'And hurtful, I can see.'

Ben waved this away. 'I realised I really ought to have gone to see the Smythes. But that would probably not have worked, either. They're not likely to be welcoming visitors.'

'They might – especially if it was someone keen to work out exactly what happened to Bruno. We have no idea what the mother's like, have we?'

'I've only seen her once to talk to. Judging by her choice of men, she's probably schizophrenic. Ackroyd is as different from Derek as you can imagine.'

Bonnie laughed. 'She was probably desperate to avoid making the same mistakes twice. Whatever they might have been.'

'The thing is, it's a big can of worms to be opening. What if those little girls accidentally killed Bruno – playing too roughly and smothering him or something?'

Bonnie tilted her head in a very grown-up gesture of scepticism. 'Come on. Keep it credible.'

'At least I'm trying not to put his mother on the list, even though I've hardly ever met her. She probably had the best means and opportunity, but there's no possible motive.'

'Well – there probably is, but it's horribly far-fetched and it would be cruel to even think it.'

'Exactly. What's Christopher doing? Is he still cross?'

'A bit. But I'm starting to think there's something else annoying him, nothing to do with us. He dropped some very odd hints to Simmy when we were having supper. We didn't save any for you, by the way, but there's some salad and stuff if you want it. Better wait for Simmy, though.'

'Jonty's mum gave us all pizza. She was in a remarkably good mood.'

'Tell me more about Patsy.'

He hesitated, trying to recapture the woman. 'Thin. Nervy. Got all the woes of the world on her shoulder, as somebody must have said. It sounds like a quote, don't you think? Or is it *weight* of the world?' He drifted into a brief contemplation of the phrase, thinking that Russell Straw would probably know.

'Typical social worker, then,' said Bonnie, bringing him back to the matter in hand. She spoke from a position of personal experience.

'Maybe. She seemed to want to pal up with Jonty, sharing his grief and all that. I wish we knew more about her.'

'You're sore because Bruno never told you she existed.'

'I am rather. Especially as Jonty obviously knows her. I don't even know what sort of social worker she is. She seemed quite clued up about hospital procedures and post-mortems.'

'Did you ask her about that business with Facebook on Wednesday? More to the point, did you ask Bruno's father?'

'I forgot all about that.' He tapped his teeth. 'He really didn't seem the type to do that. About as far from it as a person can get, in fact.'

She gave him one of her looks. 'You don't really think there's a type, do you? One you could recognise just by looking? He probably works for them – Facebook, I mean. Or does something that means he has to keep a good profile.'

'You're sounding nearly as silly as me,' he teased.

'I know. So tell me more about Patsy.'

'She got very prickly every time I asked her anything. Although I wasn't asking her specifically. Just throwing out general questions.'

'People do that,' said Bonnie with a sigh. 'I suppose she told it all to the police and doesn't see why she should say it all over again.'

'Eddie is a funny chap,' Ben went on. 'I'm not sure what to make of him. Most of the time he seems like a bumbling incompetent, but then he'll come across as quite sensible. He's nothing like Christopher.'

'What's his job?'

Ben frowned as he searched his memory. 'Christopher did say, a week or so ago, when we were talking about the wedding, I know – he's a roofer. Spends all his time on the top of houses. He must be quite strong, carrying those heavy slates up and down ladders all day.'

'Wow! What a job! Like something in a storybook. Looking down at people in the street and watching all their doings.'

Ben had stayed with thoughts about the wedding, something snagging his attention. 'What happened with the puppy?' he said suddenly. 'Shouldn't it be here by now?'

Simmy was at that moment coming downstairs and heard these words. Christopher was also emerging from his little den and heard them too. Through the open kitchen door, Ben and Bonnie could clearly see what happened next.

Simmy put her hand to her mouth, eyes wide. 'Oh, God!' she cried.

Christopher watched her with a dark expression. 'You forgot,' he said. 'I thought that must be it.'

'I did. I haven't given it a thought since last weekend. And there was you, probably expecting it to turn up at any minute and wondering what was going on. Is that why you've been so cross?'

'Hurt,' he mumbled, with a glance towards the kitchen. 'Come out for a little walk and we can clear the air. The kids can listen out for Robin.'

She went without another word, leaving Ben and Bonnie to babysit.

'She promised him a golden retriever puppy as a wedding present,' Ben explained. 'He was over the moon about it. Excited as a kid. Left it all to her, expecting there'd be a surprise delivery this weekend.'

Bonnie knew a lot about dogs, and had one of her own which was largely cared for by Corinne. 'Have you any idea how much they cost?' she gasped. 'How can she afford it?'

'She's got some cash left after the sale of her house in Troutbeck, I suppose.'

'How could she just *forget*? It's not a simple matter of popping out to a pet shop and coming home with a dog. There's paperwork and microchips and insurance and people checking up on you. It takes over your whole life – like having a baby.'

'Presumably it's the baby that's addled her brain. I wonder if she ever even tried to find one – a puppy, I mean.'

'I bet she didn't. No wonder poor Chris is upset. She's let him down.'

'Did he give *her* a wedding present?'

'Not as far as I know,' said Bonnie.

'Is there anything we can do about it?'

'Not if he wants a pure-bred with a pedigree. If he'd settle for something less ambitious I guess Corinne could have a chat with her pals at the rescue and have it sorted by Monday.'

'Ask her,' said Ben, tapping the phone that sat beside Bonnie on the table.

236

Chapter Sixteen

DI Moxon was experiencing a mixture of emotions after the call from Simmy. A renewed interest in the murder investigation made him restless, and less good company than he had been earlier in the day. Not knowing whether or not there had been a post-mortem was shaming. It meant he really was very peripheral to the Penrith team, who were making no attempt to keep him up-to-date.

Admittedly he had told them he was going away; why then should they bother to include him? He had some idea of how he was regarded by his colleagues. Middle-aged, plodding and a bit soft. And yet he had an excellent track record when it came to identifying the perpetrators of crime. Even before he met Simmy Brown he had been above average in his detection rate. He liked to think he was a better listener than most, and willing to sit back and let things take their own time. It was extremely rare that this carried any risk – he couldn't remember a case where the same person had committed a second murder, as they so often seemed to do in fiction. Instead they gave themselves away more often than not. Especially when harassed by

Ben Harkness, Bonnie Lawson and Simmy Brown – or Henderson as she was now.

But this business in Threlkeld was different. The fact that it had happened during Simmy's wedding was almost paralysing. It made Moxon want to avoid even thinking about it. The awful puzzling fact that he himself must have missed the attack by a few minutes and a few yards made his mind go numb. He had to be some sort of fool to allow that to happen.

So – what was the point of doing a post-mortem anyway? The man had died from a blow to the head. Doctors had seen him, even if they underestimated the severity of the damage. Resources, as always, were stretched and pathologists were expensive. Data as to what Bruno's last meal comprised and whether his liver was in good shape were really not required. Interesting, perhaps, but hard to see how they'd be relevant. This, he reminded himself, was the real world, where what you saw in front of you was almost certainly everything you needed. Let the random and unimportant secrets of Bruno Crowther's body remain undiscovered.

And yet – that was clearly not how Ben Harkness was thinking. He was of the opinion that it was sloppy policing. And Moxon supposed that in the end he was right.

His other feelings were more personal and even more unsettling. Speaking to Simmy had been a real pleasure. It had made him feel warm and happy. There had always been very few barriers between them, and now, after a few years, there were none at all. He had worried that the advent of Christopher Henderson would spoil this harmless friendship. He had watched them at the pub after the brief wedding ceremony and judged them to be a successful couple. The baby was healthy and of a naturally calm disposition – a wonderful reward to Simmy after suffering the loss of her firstborn. And yet Moxon had felt sad. He had taken himself off for that silly walk along the beck in order to give himself a talking to. It had been stern and painful, because it had occurred to him that very day that he was actually in love with her. All the platitudes and stereotypes of romantic novels were real, somewhere inside his chest and he was forced to acknowledge them and then suppress them.

If he had walked within touching distance of a murder going on, he doubted whether he would have noticed.

Bonnie did not call Corinne until she had spoken to Simmy, having no idea how far the process of acquiring a puppy might have gone. The newlyweds came back from their walk within forty minutes, looking reasonably relaxed. Christopher was even chuckling as they came into the house.

'All right?' asked Ben. 'No sound from him upstairs.'

'Thanks,' said Simmy with a smile. Somewhere far away in her memory was a reference to 'her indoors' from one of the clunky old sitcoms that her father loved so much. Ben had seen most of them too, in his teenage years when he had felt a burning need to know everything about everything.

'He's been rehearsing for University Challenge since he was twelve,' his mother had sighed.

'So?' Bonnie prompted, with no sign of awareness that she might be treading on private ground.

'So, I'm forgiven,' said Simmy, with a grin at Christopher. 'Just.'

'Well, listen,' said Bonnie and launched into her suggestion about consulting Corinne and getting a dog that had been rejected for no good reason, and saving massively on the cost of a puppy that might well have been farmed or genetically engineered or imported from China. 'They do terrible things with golden retrievers, you know,' she concluded. 'Or they did. It might not be so bad now that hybrids are all the rage.'

Simmy grimaced. 'It's a minefield, as far as I can see. One from a rescue might have bad habits. Would Robin be safe?'

Bonnie sighed. 'He'd be fine. Retrievers are the softest things in the world. Although you probably won't get a pure-bred one from a rescue. Listen – I grew up surrounded by dogs, including a couple of pit bulls. Nothing bad ever happened to me. At least – not from the dogs.' She gave a rueful grin. 'They probably saved me, actually.'

Simmy was clearly not convinced, and Christopher was looking martyred. All four of them felt at that moment that a dog was really not very likely to happen in the immediate future.

Ben firmly changed the subject, at which nobody was surprised. 'There'll have to be an inquest, of course,' he said. 'And I always thought there was automatically a post-mortem as well.' He tapped his lower lip. 'I wonder if the law insists on it.'

'If it does, then they'd have done one as a matter of routine,' said Christopher flatly. 'Obviously.'

'I hope so. But that's not what Patsy thinks, and she seems to know better than the rest of us.'

'Google it, then,' said Bonnie.

So he did, which took barely a minute. 'Possible but very unusual to hold an inquest without the results of a post-mortem,' he reported. 'Though I dare say it's a bit more common these days, with limits to what they can afford.'

'Who decides?' asked Simmy.

'That's a very good question,' said Ben. 'It can only be the coroner, but I'll check.' He tapped his phone for another minute. Meanwhile Christopher had drifted back into his little room, mumbling something about checking the provenance of a picture somebody was trying to sell.

'I didn't know that room was going to be a study,' said Bonnie. 'I thought it would be a playroom for Robin.'

'We don't call it a study,' Simmy told her. 'But it's handy for the computer. All the broadband gubbins is in there, and the signal's best if you stay close to the box.'

'How primitive,' scorned the girl, who lived in an area with blessedly comprehensive coverage.

'It works well enough for our purposes,' Simmy insisted.

Ben was evidently accessing information without undue delay. He had found a number of helpful websites, muttering phrases aloud, until he looked up. 'There definitely should have been a post-mortem,' he announced. 'But there are enough exceptions and loopholes for it to be just about legal to do without one.'

'Even when the person's been murdered?' queried Simmy, who was still not fully engaged in the conversation. Small things could distract her and she found herself questioning the fairness of Christopher adopting the small room as his own. The house had been considerably altered from its original purpose as a large stone barn for storage of hay and shelter of beasts – but it still boasted a large central room, with kitchen, utility and a downstairs lavatory at one end and the staircase and small room at the other. A chimney had been added, with some difficulty, so that a log-burner could provide much of the heat for the house. The highly efficient and massively expensive thing had been installed quite recently and barely used thus far.

'That's the point,' said Ben. 'But think about it. They know Bruno was hit on the head – and the shape and composition and size of the weapon can all be ascertained from external examination. They did all kinds of tests on him on Wednesday. All his symptoms must have been compatible with a head injury.'

'But they obviously got it wrong, because they never thought he would die of it,' said Bonnie.

'Right. But only wrong to the extent that they underestimated the damage – as they see it, at least. Nobody – not the medics or the police – have any doubt that the blow killed him – even if quite slowly.'

'So they're stupid?' said Simmy.

'Blinkered,' Ben corrected. 'And all the time conscious that they've been told to keep costs down. That's been the case for a long time now, so they probably barely even think about it. They'll question everybody, and have a look at the place in Threlkeld, and probably cast aspersions on the dozy doctors who sent him home – and leave it at that.'

'It's the coroner who decides, then?' Simmy asked.

'Looks like it. It says here an inquest has to be held for all unnatural deaths.' He frowned. 'We did all this right at the start, at Newcastle. I thought that if a doctor had seen the person within the last two weeks, and agreed that they died from the condition they'd been treated for, then there didn't have to be an inquest *or* a post-mortem. And Patsy said the same thing.'

'We're getting very bogged down,' Simmy complained. 'Why don't you call Moxon and tell him you think it's absolutely vital that a post-mortem is done – and leave him to talk to the Penrith people?'

'Maybe I will. Of course it's still possible that there will be a PM anyway, and it's just been delayed. That quite often happens.'

'That just bogs us down even further,' said Simmy. 'All this agonising might be just a lot of wasted breath.'

'I think they've given up,' said Bonnie. 'They know there's never going to be any evidence, the way it all happened and they just want the whole thing to go away. The only person making a fuss is Ben.'

Simmy sighed. 'Poor old Moxon. They're not going to thank him if he starts raising awkward questions, are they?'

'That's his job,' said Bonnie heartlessly.

Saturday ended for Angie and Russell Straw with a timely confirmation of their decision. The latest guests had turned out to be on the demanding end of the spectrum, finding fault with their rooms and the parking arrangements. Beck View had space for two vehicles off the road, and Russell generally left his car outside the gate to make things easier for the guests. But the Spencers were in possession of a large four-wheel-drive Toyota, which they said did not fit comfortably in the driveway and would have to be reversed into heavy traffic next morning. This was apparently unacceptable.

'We expected to be able to turn round,' said Mr Spencer, as if this as a universal facility in every kind of holiday accommodation.

Russell was in no mood to tolerate such nonsense. 'I can see you out in the morning, if you want,' he offered.

'If we'd realised, I would have reversed in,' said the man mulishly. Russell shrugged. 'It's very dangerous for the children in the back,' the annoying man went on.

'I really don't think there's any reason to worry,' said Russell.

'He always has refused to back onto a road,' the wife explained superfluously.

'I'm sure it'll be fine,' said Russell, deliberately bland and unsympathetic. 'Sufficient unto the day, and so forth.'

'What?' said Mr Spencer with more than a hint of belligerence. 'What does that mean?'

'It means we should worry about it in the morning, because there really is nothing we can do about it now.'

The man narrowed his eyes at a perceived challenge. 'I could go out last thing, when there's hardly any traffic, and turn it round.'

'Indeed you could!' said Russell with feigned enthusiasm. 'That's an excellent idea.'

Angie's turn arrived when the precise contents of the breakfast came under discussion. Mrs Spencer questioned the alternatives where toast was concerned because her daughter had a sensitivity to gluten, but was very fond of toast.

Where Angie might at one time have been willing to explore possibilities, on this occasion she was disinclined to care. 'We just won't risk it,' she said, brooking no further argument. 'She'll have to go without. There's plenty of food without worrying about toast.'

Any attempt to move onto the topic of eggs was aborted when Angie simply gave a vague smile and said much the same as Russell had done. 'Let's think about that in the morning,' she said. 'Your little boy looks ready for bed.'

The Spencers were left to their own devices, with no offer of further availability from the proprietors.

'We'll see you at breakfast time,' said Angie firmly. In the kitchen, she and Russell giggled like children at their wicked behaviour. All at once it no longer mattered what people thought about them. They were unafraid of reviews or complaints. They were never going to have to kowtow to unreasonable demands again. The sense of liberation was intoxicating and many silly things were said over their bedtime drinks. Angie was the first to calm down, remembering the setbacks of the past few days and how a lot was yet to be resolved. 'We should tell Persimmon,' she said. 'She'll be pleased to have us closer, even if we don't promise to be regular childminders.'

'With the equity we'll have from this place, we can pay for a nanny,' said Russell, not meaning it for a moment.

'That's a brilliant idea,' said Angie, in all seriousness.

Russell quickly sobered. 'I was joking.'

'Well I wasn't,' she countered. 'But we can talk about all that tomorrow.'

'Provided we're not kept up all night by Mr Spencer,' he said, coming back to earth with a bump. 'He'll probably knock our gatepost down when trying to turn his car round at midnight.'

'Maybe you should help him.'

'Not a chance. I'm going to indulge in glorious dreams of mornings in bed and summers in Barbados.'

'Enjoy,' she said.

Saturday ended for Moxon much as it did for most of the people involved in Bruno's death: with a sense that enough had happened for one day and it was time to put it all aside until morning. His conversation with Ben had been brief for that very reason. 'Nothing I can do about it today,' he had said. 'But I take your point. I'll put in a call to Penrith tomorrow and see what's what.'

'Thank you,' said Ben. 'It seems to me we need to go back to the start, and see if there's a motive we've missed.'

Moxon appreciated the 'we' but knew better than to think it was seriously meant. Where Ben Harkness was concerned, all the brilliant insights flowed in one direction, none of them originating with the detective inspector. 'I'm sure you're right,' he said.

His wife and all three of the other women had become irritated by his preoccupation with his phone and the suspicion that he was unlikely to remain with them for the whole of the allotted week. Laura had tried to tease out of him just what was going on, but had made little headway.

'Only a few queries,' he had told her. 'Not really my problem.'

They had just settled down to a game of Trivial Pursuit when Ben's call came. Jane was confident of winning, but Catherine had a highly competitive look in her eye. 'I'll beat you on the entertainment questions, anyway,' she had threatened. Moxon had been surprised that the girls were so content to participate in a board game at all, instead of going out to some Holyhead hot spot. 'There really aren't any,' they had told him. 'It isn't that sort of place. Besides, Holyhead's miles away, on the other side of the island. How would we get back?' Neither of the girls could drive.

The game proceeded slowly, with Moxon's dice sending him past the significant squares, time and again, so he had very little chance of accumulating the necessary coloured pieces of pie. He wasn't great at answering the questions anyway. History was his best subject, and even there he found himself wanting. Jane knew the arts and literature, science and geography, and was soon winning by two pie segments. Catherine was thwarted by almost never landing on a pink square.

But in the end Diana won, with a sudden surge that saw her flying down the central path and getting a string of easy questions. Back to the middle, she finished with a triumphant flourish.

'It's all luck, really,' said Catherine crossly.

'And with that neat summary of the meaning of life, I'm going to bed,' said Moxon. 'It's been a long day.'

In Clifton, Eddie Henderson and his family were reaching the same conclusion. 'What are we doing tomorrow?' asked Jonty, still behaving like a much younger boy.

'Not a lot if I can help it,' said his father. He looked at Eliza, trying to remember whether she was working the next day. 'How about you?' he asked her.

She shook her head. 'I'm not needed until Tuesday now. This week's group are off to Lindisfarne and the new lot don't arrive until Monday afternoon. I'm doing Castlerigg, then down to Windermere for a lake cruise. After that it's Coniston, Hawkshead and Kirkstone. All the usual guff.'

'They really get their money's worth, don't they,' said Eddie supportively.

Jonty sighed. 'What's going to happen with the house? The one in Threlkeld. Ben and I can't afford it without Bruno, can we? And there's not really much point in doing it without him, anyway. I mean – I like Ben all right, but Bruno was my proper friend. The whole thing was his idea – we were just there to help with the rent and have a go at living away from home. Bruno wanted it for the peace and quiet, so he could read and write and think all day, there by himself. I don't want to do it now,' he finished, with a bubbly sniff.

'That's OK, Jont,' said Eddie gently. 'Nobody's going to force you.'

'Do you think Mr Smythe will still give me a lift to Uncle Chris's every day the same as before? I do want to keep on working there.'

'Why wouldn't he?'

'It's out of his way. He might think I remind him too much of Bruno – or something.'

'Listen,' Eddie ordered him. 'He's not going to need *reminding*, is he? He isn't going to forget his boy unless somebody mentions his name.' He paused. 'You know – a lot of people think like that. That's why they avoid bereaved friends – because they can't think what to say that won't be upsetting. They don't understand that there's no danger of that happening. They're *already* as upset as it's possible to be. If anything, they probably like it if somebody talks about the person who's died. It's my guess that Derek'd be glad to chat to you in the car every day.'

'I'll phone him tomorrow then, and see what he says.' Jonty's shoulders were slumped, his whole body a figure of miserable defeat. Then he looked up, straight into his father's face. 'They've got to do a post-mortem, haven't they? How can they be sure of why he died, if they don't? They're not doing their job otherwise.'

'We've only got Patsy's word for it that there isn't going to be one. And we don't know her well enough to trust that she knows everything.'

'Bruno thought she was ace,' said Jonty. 'Clever and cool and stuff. Not that they saw each other much. It was all online. Ben didn't even know she existed.' He frowned. 'Bruno didn't want him to. He said it would skew the dynamic. Those were his actual words. "It'd skew the dynamic". I didn't really know what he meant.'

Eddie puffed out his cheeks. 'Well don't ask me. Unless he thought Ben might fancy her for himself.'

'No way!' Jonty was emphatic. 'Ben's going to marry Bonnie and never even look at another girl.'

'And the best of luck to them both,' said Eddie ruefully.

Chapter Seventeen

Sunday breakfast at Beck View was prolonged and discordant. Angie toasted one slice of every kind of bread she could find, and left it to the Spencer family to sort it out between them. She had never offered the option of selecting from a wide menu of choices – simply 'yes' or 'no' to a full English breakfast – a phrase Russell had struggled to replace with something more distinctive. 'It's not even accurate,' he would grumble. 'It should include porridge, for a start. And I'm not convinced that black pudding has ever been traditional. It strikes me as a bit French.'

'Porridge is Scottish,' Angie would argue.

'And are we sure that ye olde English folk actually had sausages or baked beans for breakfast? Bacon, eggs and fried bread is all I can recall from my Dickens. Possibly the upper classes indulged in kippers, kedgeree, even chops – but no baked beans. Or mushrooms, except maybe in the season. As for tomatoes . . .'

Ignoring him, as always, Angie slapped down four plates of the complete array, including mushrooms and tomatoes. She knew much of it would go to waste, and was inured to that knowledge. But today, the prospect of giving it all up and never frying another egg was making her impatient. She wanted this to be the very last day, instead of struggling through to sometime in October. Now she was packing it in, she couldn't see how she would stagger on for another two months.

The Spencers made it easier in some ways. However polite and accommodating she and Russell had tried to be, they would still have found fault. They made her forget all the lovely appreciative guests who kept coming back and wrote glowing reviews on TripAdvisor. When the family finally marched out of the dining room and up the stairs, Angie made a rude sign behind their backs. Russell saw her and did the same.

At the kitchen table with large mugs of coffee, they developed their scheme for the next phase of their lives. For the thousandth time Angie congratulated herself on her choice of husband. He was probably the only man in the world who would ever have managed to live with her. What's more, she had known how it would be, the very first time she met him. Envisaging the coming twenty years with him as they gently lost their wits and let the world go on its wicked way without them, she felt nothing but relief.

'We should have done this years ago,' she said.

But he corrected her. 'Definitely not. This is the precise right moment. We've enjoyed it, on the whole. It's been lucrative and we've had all those afternoons to ourselves. Once Simmy came up from Worcester to be near us, it got even better. We'd have had nothing to justify giving up – not until we became grandparents. Now we're allowed to stop.'

'How much money are we going to end up with?'

'Let's have a look,' he said, and blundered his way through Zoopla and Rightmove for half an hour, jotting down figures and making calculations. 'Quite a lot, if we shift down to a two-bedroom terrace house in Keswick,' he concluded.

'What about Threlkeld?'

He scratched his chin and looked again. 'Nothing for sale there except for something they call "retirement apartments". We don't want anything like that, do we?'

'We do not,' she confirmed. 'But I would like to live there. I know what – we can go and knock on the doors of places we fancy. We might happen upon somebody who's thinking of moving.'

'What is there to lose?' he agreed. 'We'll go this afternoon.'

In Hartsop the day started much more slowly. Ben and Bonnie had chastely shared a bed, neither of them particularly interested in having sex. It had happened a few times, pleasurably enough, but they both found it almost irrelevant to their real relationship. Bonnie loved the sensation of skin on skin, and Ben would often stroke her arms and back with a hypnotic delight. They talked about it in short bursts, cuddled together in the warm bed in Simmy's spare room.

'We'll have a baby one day,' Ben said. 'In eight years' time. I'm saving myself for that.'

Bonnie laughed. 'Boy or girl?'

'Either would be entirely acceptable.'

'I'll have to fatten up before that'll ever work,' she warned him.

'Plenty of time,' he said equably.

She hugged him hard and gave thanks for the blessing that was Ben. He was definitely more highly evolved than men of previous generations who seemed to exist in a gruesome thrall to their lower urges, of which Bonnie had become aware at far too young an age. Ben had been willing to listen to her accounts of predatory men brought home by a mother who was careless to the point that her child had to be removed from her by the social services. What was it about human beings, they had asked themselves, that they thought sex was so important? Other creatures saved it purely for reproduction, which Ben and Bonnie thought was a lot more sensible.

'I talked it over with Bruno,' Ben had disclosed. 'And I thought he absolutely felt the same. That was before I knew about Patsy.'

'He should have told you about her.'

'I know. It makes me feel he didn't trust me. It isn't a very nice feeling.'

'Seems to me he didn't think she was very important. He didn't want her muscling in and spoiling things.'

Ben was doubtful. 'I'm not at all sure about that,' he said. 'I think it must have been more complicated. I even wonder if it was the other way round and I was the interloper, endangering his relationship with her.'

'That isn't at all how it looked to me.'

'Oh well.' He shrugged sadly.

'What happens next, then?' she asked. 'There's got to be all kinds of stuff going on out there that nobody's telling us about. At least we're closer to everything, up here. Windermere felt like another continent.'

'I know,' he said again. 'We can't go on like this.'

She shivered. 'I hate it when people say that. It scares me.'

'Nothing's going to spoil it between us,' he promised her. 'I'll get a car somehow.'

'Maybe I should change jobs and find something in Keswick. We could rent a little flat together.'

'You can't let Simmy down like that. What about the shop?'

'I know,' she said.

Christopher seemed chastened over breakfast, despite having claimed the moral high ground the day before. He came down carrying Robin, and kept the child on his lap while he ate toast, awkwardly spreading butter and jam on it while balancing his passenger.

'Can I take him for you?' asked Bonnie, who had made the toast and was hovering in case she could be useful. Ben was at the table with a mug of tea.

'No, thanks.'

Bonnie watched as the small fist reached out to intercept every bite his father took. 'He'll be wanting solid food any day now,' she said.

'So they tell me. Simmy says there's no hurry, but my sisters don't agree. Apparently it's a contentious subject. I'm trying not to get involved.'

Bonnie and Ben exchanged glances, having already come to the conclusion that Christopher was rather too quick to avoid involvement when it came to the care of his little son.

'We don't want to get in your way today,' Ben began. 'We could take a packed lunch and go off somewhere for a long walk. There's a loop we could do – up to Grizedale, then along to Patterdale and back the same way we walked yesterday. I've never really seen Grizedale.'

'Sounds strenuous,' said Christopher lazily. 'Sim's probably planning some sort of roast for lunch.'

'I don't think she is,' said Bonnie.

Christopher looked at her accusingly. 'Oh?'

'We've already said we don't want her to go to any trouble like that. We can easily fend for ourselves. We've already been enough of a nuisance.' She wanted to remind him that she had no way of getting back to Windermere other than being driven by him or Simmy, at least to Penrith station. She would be expected to open Persimmon Petals on schedule next morning.

'It's nice to have you,' said their host, almost convincingly. Then he went on, to their amazement, 'I was thinking, actually, that you could probably borrow my car this evening. Then Ben can take you home, before going back to his digs in Keswick for the night. Or early tomorrow – makes no difference to me. Just have the car undamaged at the saleroom by nine o'clock. Simmy can drive me in.'

'Golly gosh,' said Ben. 'What about insurance?'

'It's covered for anyone driving it with my permission provided they've got a full licence.'

'In that case . . .' Ben's wide eyes met Bonnie's '. . . do you think we could have it today as well? Then we could both go and see the Smythes, and maybe have a little look at Threlkeld again. There's a whole lot we could be doing that needs a car. Is that too much to ask?'

'The Smythes won't welcome you,' Christopher warned. 'They'll be furious. Don't you go upsetting Derek any more than he is already.'

'We'll be very diplomatic.'

'Sensitive,' added Bonnie. 'But actually, I think it'll be OK. I think they'll be glad to talk to us.'

'Up to you,' said Christopher, peering into the face of his child, as Robin twisted round to stare at him. 'I've been told I should spend the whole morning enjoying quality time with my boy. Not that it'll be any hardship.' He stuck his tongue out at Robin, who chuckled. Bonnie was impressed at the infant's wisdom. Keeping on the right side of his father was obviously instinctively understood to be a sensible move.

The provision of a car made an immense difference to the whole day. It was intoxicating. 'I'll replace any fuel I use,' Ben promised. 'And I won't leave it anywhere it might get scratched or anything.'

'I trust you – I think. It takes unleaded. Don't put the wrong stuff in it, will you?' Christopher said.

Ben did not confess that he had never once refuelled a car, and that parking was still a significant challenge. The prospect of slotting it into a space in an official car park and then reversing it out while avoiding all other vehicles made him nervous. In a strange car, it would be much more difficult.

'Should we phone the Smythes first?' Bonnie wondered. 'They might have people there – relatives or something.'

Ben gave it prolonged consideration before deciding it was better to just turn up, as long as they made it clear they were quite content to be turned away. 'If we phone, they'll feel under some sort of obligation,' he said. 'It'll be pressure.'

'We'll aim to get there about eleven then,' said Bonnie. 'Then it'll be obvious they don't have to offer us any food.'

Christopher's car was parked on a moderate slope beside the house. Simmy's was next to it. Ben was already visualising the necessary manoeuvres to get it out onto the small road that ran through Hartsop, facing the right way. How long, he wondered miserably, did it take before all this was automatic?

At ten-thirty, Simmy came downstairs for the first time that day. As if it had been planned, her phone, left on the worktop in the kitchen, began to warble a few seconds after she came into the room. 'It's my mother,' she said, before answering it.

There followed a tantalising one-sided conversation which had everyone – including Robin – watching her intently. 'When did this happen?' and 'Are you sure?' and 'Of course it's entirely up to you' and 'That's not going to work, is it?' were just some of Simmy's responses. It felt like hours before she finished.

'They're selling up and moving to Threlkeld,' she summarised at last. 'They decided last night, apparently.'

Nobody spoke for fifteen long seconds. Then Christopher said, 'Good Lord. That's so typical of them.'

'Isn't it,' Simmy agreed. 'She's terribly excited. They're going to look for a house this afternoon.'

'How? I mean – have they spoken to an agent already?'

'Not quite. She thinks they should have a good look around, and then if they see something they like, they'll knock on the door and ask if there's any chance it's for sale.'

Bonnie actually clapped her hands. 'I love it!' she crowed. 'Trust Angie to do it like that.'

'They'll think she's insane,' said Christopher.

'It's worth a try,' said Ben slowly. 'But there could be an easier way. The bungalow I was going to rent with Bruno and Jonty is likely to be up for sale before long. The people are trying to decide what to do with it. If they had an offer privately, they might well accept it right away.'

'Ben,' cautioned Bonnie, 'isn't that a bit like wishful thinking? Would Mrs Straw suit a bungalow?'

Simmy had given a little squawk of excitement. 'Why wouldn't she? Have you got their number? Can Mum and Dad go to look at it?'

There followed fifteen minutes of discussion, description, flights of fancy and anxious examination of implications. Then Bonnie nudged Ben and reminded him of their plans to go to Penrith. Ben had supplied the name and phone number of the owner of the Threlkeld bungalow and was happy to leave Simmy to take things from there. Christopher had removed himself and Robin to the grass at the back of the house with a picnic blanket, and was giving the baby a lecture on the thrills and spills of starting a new garden. He saw no necessity to involve himself in the whims of Mr and Mrs Straw.

The drive from Hartsop to Penrith involved two large roundabouts, as well as a terrifying right turn onto the fast-flowing A66. 'Will you be able to find the house?' Bonnie asked. 'Is it in the middle of the town?'

Fortunately the Smythes lived on a quiet street on the eastern side of Penrith, and Ben had been there often enough to remember the way. No one-way streets popped up to confuse him once they were through the town centre, and they arrived unscathed at ten past eleven. Only the complications of finding somewhere to park remained.

'I feel so pathetic,' he moaned, once it had been accomplished. 'Nobody else seems to find the whole thing so difficult.'

'You overthink it,' Bonnie told him. 'It probably gets better with practice.' She had hardly dared to open her mouth during the drive, for fear of distracting him at a crucial moment. Whatever happened, they had to return the car to Christopher undamaged. For part of the way she had kept her eyes closed as well as her mouth.

One of Bruno's small half-sisters opened the door to them, gazing up at this pair of apparent strangers with avid interest.

'Hello,' said Ben. 'Remember me?' She shook her head. 'I'm Bruno's friend, Ben. I saw you here not very long ago.'

'Oh. Who's she?'

'I'm Bonnie, Ben's girlfriend. We thought we should come and see how you all are. Where's your mum and dad?'

'In there.' The child turned and pointed along a hallway to an open door. 'I expect it's all right.' She frowned uncertainly. It began to seem odd to Ben and Bonnie that nobody had come to check the identity of the visitors. 'People keep coming,' the little girl explained. 'Sometimes it's a policeman.'

Ben took the initiative, and gently pushed his way into the house. 'I work with your dad,' he said reassuringly. 'He knows me.'

'Bruno's daddy came.'

This piece of information was received with a gratifying if daunting response from Ben. 'Did he? When? I mean – he's not here now, is he?'

The child found herself unequal to any further conversation. 'Mummy!' she called. 'Can you come?'

Instead, Derek Smythe emerged, looking very inhospitable. 'What is it now?' he demanded. 'Can't we have *any* peace?'

'Sorry,' mumbled his little daughter.

'Not you, darling. You're all right.' He checked himself as he recognised Ben. 'Oh! How did *you* get here?'

'By car,' said Ben, with a flicker of boastfulness. 'We'll go away if it's a nuisance.'

'Well – we are a bit ravaged at the moment. The day started badly and we're still . . . well, you might imagine.' His eyes were blurry and his chin bristly, but he seemed inclined to talk. 'You wake up, the sun's shining, and for about half a second you forget there's anything to worry about. Then it hits you. And I swear it hits you harder every day. Tilly's a complete mess this morning.'

'Bruno's father was here – is that right?' Ben saw no reason to let this information drop.

'Why wouldn't he be?'

There was no easy answer to that, which Derek probably knew when he said it. It was a conversational device that Ben had noted on previous occasions, and which infuriated him. But he had reckoned without Bonnie.

'How is he?' she asked. 'Is he still putting everything on Facebook? Did he see Bruno before he died?'

Derek blinked. 'I don't know,' he mumbled. 'You'll have to ask Tilly.' Then he shook his head. 'No, don't do that. She's in no state to be interrogated by you two. Yes, he did see the boy. He was here on Thursday, apparently. I didn't see him. You don't know him, do you?' He was addressing Ben, as Bruno's friend. 'He hasn't been in evidence at all lately.'

'No. I never met him until yesterday,' said Ben. 'Jonty has, though. He and Bruno were friends for a long time before I joined up with them.' He was speaking slowly and clearly as if to a deaf person.

'Yes, yes. I know that,' snapped Derek. 'No need to use that tone.'

'Sorry,' said Ben. 'It's just . . . I don't know. It's just that everything seems to have got stuck and I can't stop wondering exactly *why* did he die like that. It must be the same for you.' He finished with a hopeful look at the man. 'Isn't it?'

Derek Smythe shook his head, as if to clear it. 'Not really, to be honest. I know what you're like, Ben. We've all seen how you can be. But not everything's a mystery to be solved, you know. Bruno's head got hurt and he died. We still can't be certain it was a deliberate attack. And quite honestly, it sounds bad, but we don't actually *care* very much. He's gone and nothing's going to change that, is it? There'll be an inquest, months from now, and that'll be bad enough. If you start getting everybody exercised about murder and alibis and witnesses and forensics, that's just going to prolong it and make it all worse. Do you see?'

'We'll go,' said Bonnie, taking Ben's arm. 'We wanted to come in person – just to see if you were OK, you know? It's what people do. At least – sometimes they don't, and you feel abandoned and rejected. Avoided. But if lots of people are coming, you don't need us, do you. Come on, Ben.'

Ben went with her, in a thoughtful mood. 'Doesn't he care about justice?' he demanded, incredulously. 'Did he really mean what he just said?'

'Probably not. It's all terribly raw still. And he's bound to be worrying about the little girls. Poor little things.' She sighed.

'So where now?' he asked, as they got back into the car. 'I'm completely out of ideas.'

She giggled. 'Carlisle? Leeds? Glasgow? Anywhere we like, now we've got wheels.'

He did not return her laugh, but instead heaved a deep sigh. 'That's not why we've got the car. We have to stay focused on Bruno. I *want* to. Let's go to Threlkeld and take it from there. That's where it all began, after all.'

'Have you still got that same theory about it?'

'What?'

'At the wedding on Wednesday, you said it couldn't be as sweet and innocent and old-fashioned as it seemed. You had some idea that there were dark forces working beneath the surface.'

'That was Bruno. I mean – he said that. I was quoting him, really.'

'So – what did he know about the place? Was it something terrible, that might explain why he was killed?'

'I doubt it. He was talking about ancient history. We often talked about that – and history in general.' Ben made no attempt to start the car, but simply sat behind the wheel, letting memories flood through him. 'He had so many ideas. He'd read such a lot. That's what he *did*, most of the time. Stuff from the eighteenth and nineteenth centuries, following all sorts of threads and connections.'

'Like we did in Hawkshead?'

'A bit. Enough for me to understand what he was on about, anyway. But he was *miles* ahead of me in understanding it all. He was a real genius, not like me.'

'Hey! Why not like you?'

He shook his head. 'It's not false modesty or anything. We were quite alike, I admit. But he was much better read than me. Biographies, politics, whole chunks of forgotten history from Africa and South America. He just *inhaled* it all, and remembered practically everything.' He sniffed back sudden tears. 'How can all that just be *lost*? That's what I can't get a handle on. Where did it all go?'

'I don't know,' said Bonnie in a small voice. 'Nobody does.'

'Does the person who killed him have any idea what they've done, though? What a hugely terrible thing it was? When I'm eighty, I'll still be trying to get over it. I'll still remember what Bruno was and how he might have been something amazing. He might even have changed the course of history somehow.'

'It was probably just a stupid bit of temper. Nothing planned or deliberate about it. That's if you're wrong about somebody getting to him on Thursday at the house.' She put a hand on his arm. 'You know, I'm starting to think that might be all wrong. It means it would have to be somebody really close to him that did it. Derek or Jonty or even his own father. And what if it was just some freak accident after all?'

'I know. I'm starting to doubt everything I've been thinking. Bruno did say he thought something fell on him.

Maybe it did. A tree branch or something dropped out of an aeroplane.' He turned to look at her. 'I'm not sure that would make it any better, though.'

'It would, Ben. There wouldn't be anybody to hate for the rest of your life, for one thing.'

'There absolutely must be a full post-mortem. It's outrageous that there should be any doubt about it. And if the family have been pleading for there not to be one, that looks suspicious in itself.' He was reviving rapidly, coming out of his grief-stricken paralysis and wanting to make something happen.

'Yes,' said Bonnie. 'If they have – are we sure about that?'

'It was a strong implication yesterday. The Ackroyd man and Patsy both seemed to be saying it would cause huge distress for no good reason.'

'I don't suppose anybody likes the idea,' said Bonnie. 'And I'm fairly sure the police take almost no notice of what the family say, when it comes to it.'

'That's true.' He started the engine. 'Let's go to Threlkeld, and see where we go from there.'

Again, Bonnie was reluctant to risk any distracting talk as they drove along the A66 at a very careful pace. Other vehicles kept overtaking them, which Bonnie found embarrassing and Ben hardly noticed.

'We ought to go and explain what's happening to Mrs Padgett,' he said, after a few miles.

'Who?'

'The woman who was renting us the bungalow. I think Jonty said he'd phone her to cancel it, but I'm not sure he did. And we should probably warn her that I've given her number to the Straws. It's all going to seem a bit chaotic to her, at this rate.'

'I thought you might have spoken to her by now. You're meant to be moving in tomorrow. She'll probably keep your deposit, because of mucking her about.'

He forced himself to concentrate. 'We paid her a month's rent in advance as well. I forgot that. Technically, I suppose that means we can use it if we want to. I'd rather be there than in my place in Keswick. I told them I was leaving tomorrow, anyway. I should have taken all my stuff away by now.'

'Where would you put it?'

'Good question. There isn't much – I should take it back to Bowness, I suppose. Although . . .'

'You don't want to do that. But you do have to decide what you're doing. Make a plan.'

'I *had* a plan,' he said forcefully. 'I was going to spend the rest of the summer with Bruno and Jonty, remember.'

'Where does Mrs Padgett live?'

'In one of those retirement flats in the village. She can't manage all the housework any more, which is why the bungalow's available. She's trying to decide what to do with it. I told you. She knows she should sell it, but I think she's scared of the wrench.'

'You did. It sounds a bit odd, though. How can she afford the flat if she hasn't sold the bungalow?'

'I didn't ask,' he said curtly. 'It's not my business.'

'If I didn't have to work at Simmy's shop, I could move in there with you and Jonty. Wouldn't that be great?'

'Yeah,' he said absently. 'But it's all just for the summer. Everything's going to change at the end of September. Somehow or other,' he finished vaguely.

'Won't you and Jonty still be working at the auction house, then? Is that definite?'

'Nothing's definite. Isn't that just what I've been saying?'

'I don't know,' she flashed back. 'Is it? Because there hasn't been very much sense coming out of you for the past ten minutes. I don't even know why we're going to Threlkeld at all. There's not really any need to see the Padgett lady in person, is there?'

Abruptly, with no warning, he slewed the car to the left into a convenient layby and switched off the engine. 'You're right,' he said. 'I'm a mess.'

Chapter Eighteen

In North Wales, DI Moxon was having a similar moment of self-criticism to Ben's. The weather had turned cloudy, and there was much less to do than first hoped. There was Beaumaris Castle, a few ruins and one or two museums he thought might warrant a visit. When he mentioned them, Diana helpfully googled them all and Moxon listed them in order of appeal. When he shared the findings with the others, there was considerable disagreement as to which they should favour.

'We don't all have to do the same thing,' said Jane, aware of her husband's resistance to being organised.

'The Swtan place looks nice,' he said, half-heartedly. 'But it won't take very long.'

This was a carefully preserved stone cottage with thatched roof, containing all the authentic artefacts of earlier times. It would be agreeable to go for a look, provided it wasn't too crowded, but he knew it would make very little impression on him. The lives of nineteenth-century Welsh peasants was not very high on his list of interests.

'The art gallery looks all right,' he suggested. On closer inspection, Anglesey was turning out to be a place well past its glory days. Apart from a few obvious advances in technology, it could be the 1950s in many of the small villages. Shops were mostly drab, with charities occupying far too many of them. Moxon liked the aura of nostalgia this induced in him, but he foresaw a rapid disaffection on the part of the girls. Everything depended on the weather, and Wales was not famous for co-operation on that front.

'I'm cooking us a big roast for lunch,' said Catherine. 'Don't forget that.' She had gone out and bought all the necessary food, before Moxon had arrived the previous day. He found himself quite looking forward to a good helping of meat and vegetables. Then perhaps a lazy afternoon somewhere looking out to sea. If the sun came out, that would be nice enough. That's what he had come for and that's what his wife expected and deserved: a relaxed husband, forgetting all about work for a few days and giving her some overdue attention.

But he still felt jangled and inescapably guilty. He should be back in Cumbria, following up Ben's question about a post-mortem, and listening to the boy's latest theories. He should confront his stupid feelings about Simmy, and deal with them firmly. It was all wrong being here with four women, doing nothing remotely constructive and forcing himself to stay cheerful.

He could at least try to settle the issue of the post-mortem. The more he thought about it, the more important it seemed.

Jane kept eyeing him, obviously checking his state of mind and finding little reassurance in his efforts to remain cheerful. 'Pity about the weather,' she said, experimentally. 'But we can just slob around with a book if you like.'

'Mm,' he said. 'That sounds nice.'

'But . . . ?' she prompted.

'But I'm ashamed to admit I can't stop thinking about things back at home. There's something I really ought to check. If I get that done, I'll be more likely to settle down into a proper holiday mood.'

'Do it, then,' she told him.

He called the police station in Penrith and asked the women who responded was in that morning. She rattled off a few names and he selected the one he thought was most senior. 'Just a quick word,' he said. There was no attempt made to frustrate him and the man who picked up sounded affable.

'Ingram here,' he said. 'What can I do for you?'

Moxon had only met the man once, at least a year earlier. He was not deceived by the welcoming tone. He prepared to tread delicately. 'It's DI Moxon, from Windermere,' he began.

'Yes, I know. Jilly told me when she put you through.'

'Oh. Right. So, the thing is, I've been wondering about the post-mortem on the Crowther boy. I never saw any report on it. I know I'm not officially copied in on everything on the case, but that seems to be a bit of an oversight. You'll have heard that I know a lot of people who were close to him. I was there on Wednesday when he was attacked.'

'Close by, I assume. Not exactly *there*, or we'd have had you brought in as a witness. Or a suspect.' The man laughed.

'Right,' said Moxon neutrally. 'So . . . ?'

'What was the question again?'

'The post-mortem. Did it throw anything up that came as a surprise?'

'You're not fooling me, you know. I'm quite sure you'll be aware that there hasn't been a full PM, and isn't likely to be without a very good reason. The body was very closely examined externally, with nothing to indicate any need for full dissection. The budget's at critical point, and everyone agreed that there'd be no sense in cutting him open just to show us what we already know.'

'Believe me when I say I did not know that. It seems a bit . . . unorthodox. Doesn't it lay us open to all kinds of accusations of incompetence, if not malpractice?'

'Strong words, old man.'

'But how can there be a sustainable prosecution brought, if there's no real evidence of what killed him?' The more he thought about it, the more disgraceful it seemed.

'Between you and me, my friend, there seems scarcely any prospect of there ever being a prosecution. The whole thing's impossible, even if we invoked every scrap of modern technology in the book. Whatever happened to the lad last Wednesday is lost and gone for ever. No witnesses, no motivation, nothing whatever to go on. We interviewed everyone we could think of, and just about all of them have rock solid alibis for that afternoon. The problem is, we can't even say for sure it was murder. It might have been an accident.'

'A post-mortem could probably settle that, at least.'

'Don't see how. He was dealt a blow to the head with a piece of stone. We can see that externally. The X-rays showed no skull fracture. Precisely how his brain took it upon itself to conk out is really not very relevant. Is it?'

'It might be,' Moxon persisted. He knew this was the real world, where corners were cut and rationalisation ruled the day. He knew there was a strong chance that a post-mortem would amply confirm everything Ingram was saying and make Moxon and Ben Harkness look foolish. But there were protocols and rules and if he had any influence, he would use it to make sure they were adhered to. 'I don't think you've given me any real justification for neglecting the normal procedures.' He was shaking, he realised. This was the closest he had ever got to outright insubordination.

'Oh God,' his superior sighed. 'You're intent on rocking the boat, then?' The tone was still perfectly friendly, as if nothing that was said concerned him very much. 'All right then. I won't fight you about it. If you feel so strongly, then I'll send him off for a complete and thoroughly comprehensive autopsy first thing tomorrow. No harm done – unless it's to your career. I warn you, Moxon, I won't be forgetting this.'

The final words were uttered calmly but coldly, and Moxon was afraid. And then he became defiant. He was not directly answerable to this man in Penrith, anyway. He was based in Windermere, where he was effectively left to his own devices, even in these times of line managers and oversight and infinite quantities of paperwork. He had achieved his goal, and Ben and Simmy would be happy with him. That was what really mattered.

Simmy and Christopher spent much of the morning reminding themselves that they had been married for less than a week and somehow that fact kept sliding away from them. Christopher was inclined to blame Ben

Harkness for this, which Simmy perfectly understood, but also deplored. 'It wasn't his fault that Bruno was killed,' she said.

'I realise that. I am trying to ride the waves and accept that I have no right to demand that life runs smoothly, but I think I'm allowed to feel a bit resentful. Anybody else would be having an idyllic honeymoon in the Seychelles, with not a cloud in the sky. I'm surrounded by grief-stricken young people, an annoying brother and a somewhat untrustworthy employee.'

She fastened on this last point. 'Who? Derek Smythe? You think he's untrustworthy?'

'There's something off about him. At first I just thought he was a bit dim. Well-intentioned and eager to learn, but essentially thick. Have you seen his handwriting? Of course you haven't. He does it all in capitals, but even then you can hardly read it.'

'Does he have to do much writing, then?'

'More than you might think. We still do a lot by hand. The initial cataloguing of the lots is done on a notepad and then Fiona puts it all on the computer after any queries or mistakes have been sorted out. We tried doing it directly, and that was hopeless. All kinds of things went through that shouldn't have done.'

'Sounds daft to me,' said Simmy, hardly even thinking about it. 'Why can't you check it and make corrections on the screen? That's got to be more efficient than writing it down first.'

'It's not,' he said crisply. 'You don't understand how it works. They do it in pairs, one with all the entry forms –

which are almost always handwritten – marrying the vendor up with the actual object and reading out the description and estimated value to the other, who writes it down and then takes it to Fiona for a good scrutiny before she logs it all in for the final catalogue.'

'Oh,' said Simmy. 'So why can't Derek be the one who reads it all out?'

'Because he's not clever enough. He still can't tell Poole from Worcester, or wool from cotton. To be brutally honest, he's turning into a bit of a liability.'

'Poor man,' said Simmy, thinking of Verity, who was employed in her flower shop to assist Bonnie, and who had proved to be a very mixed blessing. 'I suppose it's quite a common story. Nobody's allowed to be a failure these days.'

'Anyway, I didn't really mean to cast aspersions on Derek's character. It's not that I think he killed Bruno or anything. He's just rather annoying sometimes.'

'I expect he knows that, and it makes him worse.'

'Which is probably the same catch-22 that exists in every workplace,' sighed Christopher.

Then, at just before eleven o'clock, Simmy had a phone call from her father. 'I understand your mother has already given you the news?'

'If you mean the bit about selling Beck View and moving to Threlkeld – yes, she has.'

'And what do you think?'

'I think it's quite exciting, but also rather sudden.'

'Right in both instances. But we very much took to dear little Threlkeld at your wedding party. We're going there this afternoon to look at houses.'

'Yes – Mum said. Are you wanting me to go with you or something?'

'No, no. Just checking your reaction now you've had a little while to think about it.'

Simmy did not have the heart to admit that she had deferred that particular topic in favour of other more pressing matters. 'I think it will be wonderful,' she gushed. 'A whole new lease of life. Mum needs new interests, new friends. She's got into quite a rut these last few years.'

'We'd be a long way from your shop,' he reminded her. 'We're not sure how that might affect the childminding.'

Simmy had a sense of her own virtuousness at not having thought of this fairly major snag. 'Don't worry about that,' she breezed. 'We can work something out.'

'That's very noble of you.'

'Not really,' she said modestly. 'I can hardly expect you to let my child get in the way of your plans.'

'A lot of people would.'

'Anyway, I think it's fantastic news, Dad. I'm surprised how good it makes me feel. It's a relief to think you won't have to keep slogging on with all those wretched B&B guests.'

'Thanks, love. And you can come with us this afternoon if you want to.'

'I think I'll leave that to you for today. But you could come here after you've been to Threlkeld, and tell us all about it.' She had another thought. 'You might be able to take Bonnie home with you – again. She's been staying here since yesterday, and needs to be back at the shop tomorrow. Ben's got Christopher's car, so I suppose he was going to take her back tonight. It's all getting very complicated, logistically.'

'All right,' said Russell vaguely. 'Angie thought Bonnie talked too much, on Wednesday. She just wouldn't stop. It gave your mother a headache.'

'Unusual. She must have been excited about the wedding.'

'Oh, yes. She was. It's a good thing, really, that we didn't know about Bruno at that point. Your mother wouldn't have liked that.'

'None of us like it, Dad,' said Simmy, half-reproving. 'But I've got to go now. See you later. Good luck.'

Christopher had gathered snatches of the news, and waited for elucidation. When it came, he grinned. 'They're serious, then. There'll be some hefty equity on the house. Should be enough to oil a few wheels.'

'Meaning?'

'Well, for a start, they should enjoy a comfortable old age. And if there's any left over . . .'

'It won't be *that* much, you fool. They'll probably spend three-quarters of it on the next place. I doubt if Threlkeld's cheap.'

'Threlkeld's impossible,' he said flatly. 'I bet there hasn't been a house on the market there for years.'

'But Ben says that bungalow's likely to be up for sale. It could all work out easily.'

Christopher rolled his eyes. 'I missed that bit. Of course, they'd still have to sell Beck View, and turn away bookings, and uproot themselves after all these years. I can't see it "working out easily", as you put it.'

'You underestimate them,' she said. Then she changed the subject. 'So there's just us two for lunch, which is nice. What do you fancy?'

'Nothing special. You know me. I'd be very happy with one of those lovely pies we got at the supermarket, or a frozen lasagne. Quick and delicious.'

'And blessedly easy. Let's have lasagne – a big one each, because it's Sunday and we've just got married.' She was foolishly happy at the prospect of not having to do any cooking. A connection was made with her mother, who was apparently on the brink of abandoning all those infernal breakfasts she had cooked for the past twenty years.

Christopher had gone quiet. 'I had a dream,' he began slowly, when Simmy cocked her head at him in a silent question. 'The night before we got married. It's been haunting me ever since.'

'Tell me.'

'My father was there. He threw Robin down the stairs. You and my mother were just chatting in the kitchen as if nothing was happening. And then there was a baby lying in the garden, all twisted. It was Robin and George, all at the same time. It seemed to go on all night. When I woke up, I was crying.'

'Oh, darling! You poor thing!'

'I've been working out what it meant. I think there was something like that when I was small. But there's nobody I can ask, because both my parents are gone. Something to do with a baby. It seems to grab hold of me when I've got Robin.' He gave her a tragic look. 'It's scary, Sim.'

'So I see. But listen – there's my mum you can talk to. She might know what it's about. Or even Eddie.' She wanted to tell him what she had learned the previous day, but feared it would seem like a betrayal. Better, she guessed, to let Christopher retrieve the memory in his own time, and draw his own conclusions from it. 'Or you could get yourself hypnotised into remembering what happened,' she added lightly.

He frowned, and stared at the floor. 'I might just do that,' he said, to her great surprise. 'Because I need to get it sorted. I'm not going to mess things up for you and the baby – that's one thing I'm sure of.'

'You'll never do that,' she assured him, taking his head in a clumsy hug.

None of the people suffering the loss of Bruno made anything much of Sunday lunch that weekend. Tilly Smythe rallied just enough to grill a few sausages for her young daughters; Jonty Henderson failed to even put in an appearance at the makeshift meal his mother had provided. 'I don't know why it should hit me so hard,' said Eliza. 'I suppose it's because it could have been Jonty.'

'Eh?' said Eddie, who was not properly listening. 'Jonty who what?'

'Died, you idiot. What do you think?'

'Oh. Right. You mean you're too upset to cook?'

'That's it. It came over me just now. We take everything for granted, and then something like this happens and it all feels so . . . *fragile*. As if the bottom could just fall out and we're left standing on thin air.'

'Huh!' said Eddie. 'That sounds nasty. Floating around with nothing to stand on.'

'Shut up,' said his wife.

Even Patsy Wilkins was missing out on a decent meal. She was due at the hospital that afternoon, where a suicidal young client was being discharged, and Patsy was needed to help with the transition to the foster home for the teenager. Sundays were nothing special in her line of work.

Ben and Bonnie were still wondering what to do and where to go in their intoxicating freedom. For want of any better ideas, they had made their way to Threlkeld, planning to park in the area at the top of the village where walkers left their cars. But it was already full, and the stress of turning round and leaving again put Ben in a shaky mood.

Just as he was completing the manoeuvre, a couple appeared from the path leading up to Blencathra, and waved at him. 'We're going,' they said. 'Do you want our space?'

'Thanks,' he nodded, dreading the forthcoming need to reverse into the alarmingly small gap. First he had to get out of the way of the departing car. It all felt impossible. 'What if I scratch it?' he muttered.

'You won't,' Bonnie assured him. 'It's easy.'

It wasn't easy at all. How did people do it, he wondered. It was impossible to know exactly where every part of the vehicle was, even with mirrors and all the electronic beeping it did. There were still blind spots and spaces between the sensors. A shiny silver BMW was sticking out in just the wrong place, next to an old Ford of some kind.

'I must be brain damaged,' he concluded. 'None of this makes any sense to me.'

'Come on,' his girlfriend snapped. 'I'll get out and guide you. Just don't run me over.'

It went better after that. Bonnie even told him which way to turn the wheel, and how much space he had. At last they were snugly slotted into the vacated spot.

'How did you ever pass your test?' Bonnie said.

'Lots and lots of practice. I never had to do anything like this, either. Plus it was a smaller car. The sooner you get your licence, the better. You can do all the driving then.'

'I'd love to, if I could afford it,' she agreed.

'We'll have to work on that,' he said. 'Because I don't think I'm ever going to make a keen driver.'

'Cars are going to be banned soon anyway,' she consoled him.

'Bring it on, then,' he said, with a disbelieving laugh. 'Although I'm not holding my breath.' Ben Harkness was too well-informed to put very much credence in the wilder claims about climate and its implications. References to anything resembling a 'scientific consensus' made him very argumentative.

'Where are we going right now, this minute?' Bonnie asked, as she had done a few times already that morning.

'How about the pub? I'm hungry.'

She pulled a face at that. 'Not Sunday lunch. I couldn't face that. Isn't there a shop where we can get crisps and an apple or something?'

'There might be.' They hurried down the little road to the main street running through the village and located a modest shop that also offered coffee and snacks. Business was brisk and the couple did not linger once they'd bought a few rations.

279

'Mrs Padgett next,' said Ben. 'She lives along here.' They ate as they walked, admiring the view to the north and rehearsing what they would say to Ben's would-be landlady. 'She won't be very pleased,' he said.

'She'll probably understand, when she hears the whole story.'

'I'm hoping she'll have heard it already.'

The retirement flats were set back off the road, down a slope, with neat flowerbeds and everything new and well-tended.

'Oh! That's her,' said Ben suddenly. An elderly woman was sitting on a rug, laid out on a patch of grass under a tree. 'How funny.' They approached uncertainly. 'She might not recognise me,' Ben whispered. 'And she's never seen you before.'

'So what?' Bonnie replied in a normal voice. 'Are you Mrs Padgett?' she boldly asked the woman, when a few feet away.

'I am, dear. Enjoying the sunshine, as you can see.' She looked round, and beckoned Bonnie closer. 'There's no *garden*, you see. Not a proper one. So I have to come out here, where everyone can see me. Not that I care about that. Not really.' Her face told a different story, as did the heartfelt sigh.

'It doesn't look very comfortable,' said Bonnie, dropping down onto the rug. 'Isn't there a balcony or something where you can catch the sun?'

'Aren't you one of the boys taking my bungalow?' She was suddenly a lot sharper, as if Bonnie's questions had aroused suspicion. 'Have you come looking for me?'

280

'Yes, actually,' said Ben. 'I expect you heard about the trouble here last week, by the beck? My friend was attacked, we think, and he died the next day. So that means . . .'

'You won't be taking the house. Is that right?'

'Well, we can't really afford it now, with only two of us.'

The old lady beamed at him and clapped a bony hand onto his shoulder. 'That's the best news I've had for a month,' she said. 'It's been nagging at me ever since, wondering if I had the guts to tell you I've changed my mind.'

'Um . . . ?' said Ben. 'Have you?'

She got to her feet using an inelegant process of rolling onto hands and knees and raising herself bit by bit, shamelessly gripping Ben's hand for added leverage. 'Come on,' she said. 'And I'll explain it all to you.'

She took them halfway up Blease Road, where the bungalow sat on sloping ground to their left. Ben and Bonnie were drawn inevitably to the spot further up the hill, on the other side, where Bruno had been found lying on the ground with a damaged head. It was not visible from the road, being behind several houses as well as the little school and its playground. 'We'll go over there after this,' Ben murmured, as they obediently followed Mrs Padgett.

The elderly woman halted at the gateway into her property and stared at it with something akin to disapprobation. 'I've decided to sell it as soon as I can,' she said abruptly. 'I can't live in it on my own, however much I might want to. And I don't like the flat. So I need to think again.'

The youngsters eyed her uncertainly. Wasn't she too old to be 'thinking again'?

'Really?' said Ben. 'I can't say I'm surprised. I think we guessed that would happen, actually.'

'I won't weary you with the details. It's not your business, is it? But I've been wishing I hadn't agreed to let you rent it. It's my sister's doing, if you must know. She lent me the money for the rent on the flat, knowing me better than I know myself.' She chuckled at her own folly. 'She knew I wouldn't like it. Now she says we're going to live in Spain. She's worked it all out – right by the sea, plenty of other English people and a very good health service. But we need the money from the bungalow.'

'And we think we might know some people who'd buy it,' said Ben rashly. 'They're coming up here later today, I think. Can I show it to them? I've got a key.'

Mrs Padgett blinked. 'Shouldn't it be me that does that?'

'I just thought I could save you the bother.'

'Very nice of you, dear. I know you've paid me for a month already, so I can't stop you letting people in, even if I wanted to.' She gazed up at Blencathra as if for enlightenment.

Bonnie also seemed to find things rather confusing. 'Spain?' she murmured. 'Won't it be very hot?'

The old lady and Ben both laughed. 'That's most of the attraction,' said Mrs Padgett. 'My sister and I both feel we've suffered this climate long enough.'

'You're lucky to have her, then,' said Bonnie, still trying to follow the story.

'I dare say I am. And the other way around. All we need now is to find somewhere big enough that we can get away from each other. She can be very irritating, you know.'

'So . . .' prompted Ben, impatiently.

Mrs Padgett went on, as if he hadn't spoken. 'A lot of my things are here, of course. I was letting it furnished – which you know, silly me. I'm very sorry about your friend, poor young fellow, so nice and quiet and sensible he seemed. I can't let myself be glad to profit from such a tragedy, can I? But maybe it helps you to know there's not any sort of problem with the house as far as you're concerned. And if you really do know people who might want it, then I'll be very much in your debt. I was dreading having to deal with estate agents.'

'Gosh!' said Ben. 'That is a relief. I'll tell Jonty.' He slumped suddenly. 'He'll be disappointed. We were really looking forward to being here.'

'Plans go awry,' said the woman, as if quoting. 'You have to pick yourself up and be ready for something different. I've followed that motto all my life.'

Suddenly both the youngsters wanted to get away. At the same moment, each had observed a glint in Mrs Padgett's eye that worried them. The somewhat dithery old person concealed a more focused and perhaps heartless character. She had got what she wanted and could not conceal her satisfaction.

'We'll go now,' said Bonnie. 'It's been nice to meet you.'

'We'll be getting our deposit back, then,' sad Ben, looking the woman straight in the eye. 'If we don't use the house at all.'

'If I remember rightly, it was your poor dead friend who paid it. I expect I need to talk to his father about that,' she said, with another hint of steel that suggested Derek might come off badly in any argument – not that there seemed any risk of there being one. 'Just you go off and enjoy yourselves. All's well that ends well, as they say.'

Ben and Bonnie headed up the hill towards the car park, not speaking until they were sure they were out of earshot. Then Bonnie said, 'What a funny old woman! Will the Straws like the house, do you think?'

'Probably. The view's fantastic. There's a garden. What's not to like?'

'People are funny about houses.'

He took a deep breath and turned to look back to where the bungalow stood below them. 'I can't really imagine them here. What are they going to *do* all day?'

'What anybody does, I guess.'

'It was so perfect for me and Bruno and Jonty. It seems such a pity . . .'

'I know. But perhaps you should let Mrs P keep the deposit and have the house for a month. That's a lot better than nothing. It gives you time to work out what to do next.'

But Ben's thoughts had diverted to Bruno's death and the mysteries surrounding it. Mysteries that extended further back in time, to include Bruno's life and the way he lived it. 'I'm still getting to grips with all the things I've found out about Bruno,' he said. 'I hadn't properly noticed the way he never told people anything. He kept everything so secret. Like me having no idea about Patsy. That's very weird in itself. And his knowing Simmy's dad – same thing. And being so good at chess. He never said anything about any of that. And he never talked about money. Some things he told Jonty and not me. But, the thing is—' he looked at Bonnie with a complicated mix of misery, suspicion and foreboding. 'All this might explain why he was killed.'

She gave it some thought. 'I didn't think you ever got to know him very well, anyway. How much time did you really spend with him? A few evenings in your digs, or at the pub, or going for walks – what else?'

'It's true, I suppose. But he was so . . . *easy*. Everything felt natural and friendly. Relaxed. There was no friction with Jonty, either. When the three of us were together, it was just as good. I was really looking forward to knowing him better.'

'But he was definitely going to Bristol, wasn't he? So you'd only have two months in the house here, before he'd be gone. And you and Jonty would have to find somewhere else, because this place would be too big for two. Too expensive.'

Ben shrugged. 'I think we thought we might find a third person or something. It wasn't going to be all that expensive, anyway. We might have managed it. It was down to Jonty, really. His dad was pushing him to apply for a course somewhere.'

'Let's walk down by the beck,' Bonnie said, as they reached the car. There was a small gate at the lower end of the car park that led to a footpath. 'We ought to have a look while we're here.'

'Good point. We meant to do that all along, didn't we?'

They found themselves between the small beck on their left and the backs of houses on their right. Modest gardens were squeezed into gaps between the buildings.

Everything sloped gently away from Blencathra and towards the village.

'Moxon said something about this,' Ben noted, pointing to a huge pipe opening onto the little waterway. 'It must drain those fields.' There was new-looking stonework holding the pipe in place.

From the other side of a fence they could hear children arguing. Then a voice came from a higher point, and they looked up to see a boy of about ten at an open window. 'Stop it!' he shouted. 'I'll shoot you if you don't.'

'Did he say what I think he said?' wondered Bonnie.

'He's probably got a water pistol or something.'

A girl squealed. 'No, Nathan, not again! I'll tell your daddy if you do it again. You know he said you mustn't.'

'I will, though. Dad's not here, is he?'

Ben and Bonnie watched as the boy brandished a catapult. 'I made another one, after he confiscated the first one. It's easy.' He pulled back the elastic, or whatever it was, and released it without firing a missile.

'Uh-oh!' said Ben. 'Are you thinking what I'm thinking?'

Chapter Nineteen

'But we can't just walk in and challenge them,' Bonnie insisted, as they went further down the hill feverishly discussing what they'd seen and heard. 'We'll have to tell Moxon and leave it to the police.'

'And if my theory's wrong, and this *is* where Bruno was killed, those kids are going to be damaged for life. You don't have to be very old to get sent into custody these days.'

Bonnie shuddered, but then squared her shoulders. 'Older than them, I think. But whatever happened would be bad enough. But it's probably too late to worry about that. If it was them, they must already know they hit somebody, seeing that there was an ambulance and a lot of people milling about. They might even know that he died the next day. If so, they're withholding vital evidence and deserve everything they get. Even if they are kids. Although . . .' She sighed. 'I don't know *what* we ought to do. We might have jumped to a completely mad conclusion, anyway.'

'Let's think it through properly. Could be they have no idea what they did. Or only the boy. If he saw his missile hit Bruno, he might have quickly run downstairs and carried on playing in the garden as if nothing had happened. That's what I'd do. Maybe his dad confiscated his first catapult ages ago, and didn't know he'd made a new one. Nobody ever suspects a child, do they? He'd know that.'

'Not everybody's as clever and devious as you,' she said, affectionately.

'It's not especially devious. Just acting out of self-preservation.'

'And if your theory *is* right, then they just knocked him out for a bit, and the real killing was done next day. I really hope that's what did happen.'

'Except then we've got to worry about somebody else being locked up and their lives ruined. Like Jonty.'

She gazed into his face. 'Is that who you think it was?'

'It might have been, in theory. But he seems so absolutely desolate without Bruno, and is such an innocent character, it would take far more acting and downright lying than I think he could possibly manage. If it was somebody we know, they must be a lot sneakier than they seem on the surface.'

'Jonty's not sneaky,' said Bonnie with certainty.

'Let's hope not,' said Ben. 'He's Simmy's nephew now, remember.'

They had forgotten about the bungalow and its potential future as the home of the Straws. They had also forgotten about Simmy and Christopher and the dog they may or may not acquire. The chilling suspicions that surrounded Bruno's death, whether inflicted by a child or by somebody close to and trusted by the victim, had been overwhelming.

'There's no good outcome,' said Ben. 'Whichever way you look at it. Even if we say nothing, and the police never prosecute anybody, it'll hang over us forever. We'll wonder about Bruno's family, and who knew what, and if there's never a proper autopsy, we'll go on guessing about poison or lethal injections or suffocation with a pillow, until it drives us mad.'

Bonnie pulled him to her for a hug. 'It wasn't any of those things,' she said, her voice muffled against his chest. 'They'd all leave signs. Stop it now, and let's think about something else.'

Angie and Russell had also foregone the Sunday lunch as offered by the Horse and Farrier. They set themselves the task of scrutinising every house in the village, as well as inspecting the views from every angle and measuring the decibels arising from traffic on the A66. The task could have been avoided if Angie had taken her phone with her and answered the call from her daughter telling her there might well be a bungalow available. The result of their search, however, was perfectly compatible with this missed information. It didn't take them long to establish that the prime spot was somewhere along Blease Road – where Mrs Padgett's bungalow was, if they did but know it.

'This is perfect,' said Russell. 'So long as we can manage the slope.' The road did decline quite gently to the main street. Angie protested that she could not imagine herself ever unable to get up and down it. She walked to and fro, past a few houses on the same side as the school, shamelessly staring at them from every angle.

'Which one should we go for first?' she debated, eyeing the door of a house she liked the look of.

Russell was hoping that a person would spontaneously come to the door, curious to know who this nosy couple might be. But that did not happen, probably because almost every resident of the Lake District was accustomed to having strangers peer through their front windows. It was all part of living in a tourist area. When it came to the point, he was reluctant to accost an unsuspecting homeowner and suggest they sell their property to him. It seemed foolish, if not downright impertinent.

'Gosh – hello!' came a girl's voice from some yards away. 'Fancy meeting you here.'

'Bonnie!' Russell felt that rescue had arrived. 'You're the answer to a prayer.'

'Am I?'

'Is she?' demanded Angie. 'How?'

'Another viewpoint. Someone to talk things over with. And Ben,' he finished weakly.

'We'd be glad of the exact same thing,' said the boy. 'We've just had something of a revelation. Or we *think* we have. It might all be our imagination.'

'Let's find somewhere to sit,' said Angie. 'We've been walking for an hour and my legs are complaining.'

'We could have coffee or something at the village hall,' Ben suggested. 'They've got a sort of little cafe at the back. We can sit outside.'

It was readily achieved, and the foursome were soon sitting around a table behind the building, invisible to anyone walking along the main street. Quite why he felt any need to be unseen, Ben could not have explained – but he did. Between them he and Bonnie reported their theories based on the boy with the catapult. It sounded thin and improbable, even to his own ears.

'A bit circumstantial, don't you think?' said Russell, who had listened patiently. 'And wouldn't somebody have seen it happen and collared the wretched lad?'

'We should ask Moxon,' said Angie suddenly. 'He kept saying he was right there at the same time. He might have noticed the kids playing about with catapults.'

'Surely he would have made the connection with Bruno, if that was so?' said Bonnie. 'Stones whizzing over his head would have been quite a giveaway.'

'You'd think so, but he was in a funny mood,' said Angie. 'Happy to be going on holiday, mushy about the wedding and Persimmon being happy and all that. And he might have had a bit too much beer – which would be why he went for the walk – trying to be sober enough to drive. He certainly didn't seem in any hurry to go anywhere.'

'Careful,' warned Russell. 'It's an officer of the law you're slandering.'

'When he came to see us he was feeling guilty about not noticing anything,' Angie remembered. 'He didn't really have a proper reason. I think he just wanted somebody to talk to.'

'When was that?' asked Ben.

'Thursday, I suppose. Late afternoon.'

'He came to the shop as well,' said Bonnie. 'On Friday morning.'

'And he was at the auction house on Friday,' Ben contributed. 'So we all saw him within twenty-four hours of Bruno dying. He certainly got around, considering he was meant to be on holiday.'

'Someone's got to go and have a word with those kids,' Russell insisted. 'And it needs to be the police, I presume. If we can persuade them it's a viable idea.'

Nobody had any response to that. If a small boy had accidentally killed Bruno the implications were beyond terrible.

Eventually Angie voiced their common thought. 'Might be best to leave it,' she murmured. 'What good could it do?'

'It would help Derek and Bruno's mum to know the whole story,' said Bonnie. 'And the thing is – Ben and I don't believe that was what killed him anyway.'

Angie interrupted. 'Can we talk about something else now? We came here to find somewhere to live.'

'Oh, well, you don't have to worry about that,' said Bonnie. 'We've already got somewhere for you.' And she told them all about Mrs Padgett and her bungalow.

At two-thirty on Sunday afternoon, Simmy, Christopher and Robin were strewn untidily on a rug in the garden that was still more of an idea than a reality. They could see Hartsop Dodd a short distance to the north, picking out the walkers as they inched their way to the top. Christopher had binoculars and was commenting on the progress of a man with a purple shirt. The climb was steep and most people took it slowly. Neither of the Hendersons had ever tackled it.

'Must be a fantastic view from up there,' Simmy said. 'We should do it one day.'

'We'll wait till Robin can come with us. I have an idea that small children are quite good at scrambling up mountains.'

Simmy eyed her infant doubtfully. The day when he could scale something like their local peak seemed very far off. 'I wonder how the others are getting on,' she murmured.

'Which others?'

'All of them I suppose. Ben and Bonnie and Mum and Dad. And Moxon, even.'

'Why stop there? What about Eddie and Derek and Jonty and Uncle Tom Cobley?'

She detected a tone and sighed. 'Sorry. But you've got me wrong. I was only thinking about Threlkeld and whether they'd like the bungalow. Have you seen it?'

'No – why should I? It sounds quite small. Two bedrooms.'

'I did try calling my mother, but the phone was off. She's probably left it at home. I could have saved them a lot of tramping about.'

'They like tramping about.'

'Oh well.' She felt lazy and slightly too hot for comfort. Robin was lying on his back partly in the shade of a tree, but she had got herself into full sun. The tree was large, and was not on their property. Many of the surrounding fields boasted at least one tree, often in one corner. It was a pattern she had only recently noticed. She tried to imagine how it would look from the top of the Dodd.

Christopher was growing restless. The summer felt as if it was running away from him, the best of it already over. His own emotional state could only be confronted in small snatches, with the bitter taint of Bruno's death intruding itself into his thoughts about work and family. He was impatient to set it all straight, and for that to happen, the murder had first to be solved.

'Shall I get us something to drink?' he offered.

'Good idea. I could fancy some ginger beer, if there is any.'

'You should get out of the sun. Your face has gone red. Did you put suncream on?'

'Of course I didn't.' She rolled over, to join her baby in the shade. 'This is the life,' she breathed. 'Isn't it wonderful to be doing nothing!'

'There's no shame in suncream,' he told her.

'I hate all those chemicals going on my skin.'

'Luddite.'

'Guilty as charged.'

Christopher got up and went back to the house. Robin was sleepily watching flickering shadows in the leaves overhead, waving his hands at them. Simmy did her best not to think about anything, knowing the peaceful interlude could not last very much longer. Somebody would phone or visit and stir everything up. But unlike her husband she did not feel impatient. There was no immediate pressure on her to do anything, for which she largely had Robin to thank. All that anyone could reasonably expect of her was that she should raise a healthy, happy child. And the next stage of that was shortly to begin.

'We'll try you on some mashed banana this week,' she promised. That, she resolved, would be the most significant event in their lives in the coming days.

In stark contrast, at three-fifteen, Ben and Bonnie were still in Threlkeld, having shown the Straws around the bungalow and passed on Mrs Padgett's details.

'It's up to you now,' said Ben. 'Our part is done. We're going to walk up Blencathra, while we're here.'

But they never got further than the car park.

'We have to decide what to do next,' said Bonnie. 'Let's have a think.' She pointed to a tumbled old wall at the edge of the park and went to sit on it.

Ben joined her, his phone in his hand. 'Should I call Moxon?' he wondered. 'Isn't everything still pretty stuck? We can't get anywhere until we know whether or not we're guessing right. We've got absolutely no hard evidence of anything.'

Then a car came up Blease Road and began to turn into the park.

With the swiftness of an eel, Ben dived behind his girlfriend, saying, 'Hide me!'

Knowing better than to waste time asking questions, she sat up straighter and spread out her elbows, making herself as big as she could – which still was not very big.

Ben had thrown himself behind the wall and was whispering, 'What are they doing now? Have they seen me?'

'They will in a minute. You need to be on this side of the wall.'

Keeping his back to the cars, he vaulted over and knelt down by Bonnie's legs. 'It's Patsy and the Ackroyd man,' he hissed. 'They'll recognise me.'

'But not me,' she realised. 'Just stay there and I'll keep an eye on them.'

'They're sure to see me,' he worried.

'Are you going to tell me why it matters?' She spoke with her head turned casually towards the mountain, so she could watch the newcomers without seeming to look at them, and speak to Ben without it being apparent that there was anybody with her. 'If another car comes up, they'll wonder what you're playing at,' she warned.

'Can't help that. What are they doing here? It's got to be connected with Bruno. What else could it be?'

'I don't know,' said Bonnie, whose thought processes were slower than Ben's, as were most people's. 'They've parked down in the far corner, pretty close to us.'

'If I keep my back to them, it should be OK,' he decided. 'They won't be expecting me, after all.'

'They might.' She giggled. 'If they know what you're like.'

Slowly, so as not to attract attention by any sudden movements, Ben got himself onto the wall next to Bonnie. 'You'll have to follow them,' he said. 'It's got to be important that they're here.'

'They might just want to walk up the mountain as some sort of therapy. I'm not following them if they do that. Or they might want to put flowers on the spot where Bruno fell. People do stuff like that.'

'Can you see any flowers?'

'No,' she admitted. 'But maybe they want to say some words – a prayer or something. I bet that's it.'

'Possible,' he conceded. 'But seems unlikely to me.'

'They're going through the little gate. They must know where it happened.'

'Hang on,' said Ben, thinking hard. 'What if the father of that boy with the slingshot called Ackroyd as well as the ambulance – isn't that what we think happened? So he might have given his name and number, and now they've come to talk to him. He might even have said something about the catapult, and wants to make amends, or offer to go to the police.'

'Is a slingshot the same as a catapult?'

'Irrelevant,' he snapped. 'Don't interrupt.'

Bonnie went quiet with a good grace, but did not apologise.

'I wish we could hear what they say to each other. Why are they going down the path, instead of round to the front door? Perhaps they've agreed to meet outside. Or,' he added generously, 'could be you're right all along and they just want to see the place for themselves.'

'I'm going to follow them,' she announced.

'Good. Put your phone on. I might be able to hear some of what they say, if you can get close. And record it, if you can.' Ben was walking crabwise around the side of the car park, keeping his face averted.

'You look ridiculous doing that,' Bonnie observed. 'There are people coming and they'll think you're a lunatic.'

'I need to hide my face somehow.'

'That would look just as bad. You'll have to stay here while I go after them. For all we know, they're going down to the pub and it's all a massive coincidence.'

'Not a chance,' he said. 'And you know it.'

'OK – well, I've let them get far enough ahead. Get your phone connected to mine and we'll see if you can hear what happens.'

They each activated their devices and Bonnie trotted down the path after the suspicious pair. Ben knew better than to warn her to be careful. He could see little cause for concern in any case.

A minute later, Bonnie's breathy voice came through. 'They've gone into that house where the boy lives. There's a door in the fence and someone let them in. I can't hear anybody talking.'

'Bummer,' said Ben in acute frustration. 'We'll just have to wait, then, and see what happens when they come out again. I'll come and join you.'

They moved a short way further down the path, to a small bridge across the beck. A pair of walkers met them with friendly greetings, and a loose yellow dog trotted past. A stone wall separated them from a field full of sheep. It was shady, with trees lining much of the path.

'Have you got any sunglasses?' Bonnie asked. 'That might be enough of a disguise.'

Ben spread his hands, as if to say *Where would they be?* He carried no sort of bag and had nothing but a slim wallet in his pocket.

'What if they go out at the front?' Bonnie worried. 'We'd never know.'

Ben was thinking again. 'I suppose it doesn't much matter now. We've missed everything anyway. We'll never know what they're saying.'

But he spoke too soon. There were sounds of raised voices, coming closer. The door in the fence flew open and Patsy Wilkins came stumbling out, calling back over her shoulder, 'Don't be so stupid!' She shouted, 'You've got it all wrong.'

Anthony Ackroyd was close behind her, moving more slowly. 'Leave it,' he said to Patsy. Then, to an invisible person in the garden behind the fence, 'I really thought we could be of help to each other. I would never have come otherwise.' Ben and Bonnie were barely ten yards away, hearing everything plainly. Again, Ben turned his face away.

A man's voice replied to Ackroyd. 'You come here accusing my son of murder, and then say you thought you were helping. You must be insane.'

'Nobody said anything about murder. We understand that it was an accident. We hoped, as I told you already, that you might appreciate a visit, to set your mind at rest.'

'Oh, go away,' came the voice, and the door was firmly slammed shut. A bolt could be heard being shot into place.

With a glance at Bonnie, who must have looked suspiciously like an eavesdropper, Patsy began striding back towards the car park.

Ackroyd, without a similar backward glance, hurried after her, talking loudly. 'Well, that was a waste of time, wasn't it. It was a stupid idea anyway. We should have known.'

Patsy said nothing, but kept on walking while Ackroyd pressed on, talking as much to himself as her. 'I thought if we told them about Bruno's weak heart, it might make them feel better . . .' After that, Bonnie and Ben could not hear any more.

'Weak heart?' she repeated in a whisper, looking wide-eyed at Ben. He shrugged, and then waved at her to follow the pair, pointing at her phone. She once more connected it to his, and then trotted back to the car park.

Ben remained where he was, phone to his ear. After a few moments, he could hear a muffled conversation.

'You knew about his heart, didn't you? Why didn't you want me to say anything about it?' from Ackroyd.

'It has nothing to do with anything, that's why. Listen – the fact is, that man's kid killed Bruno with a stone from a catapult. We've learned that much at least. It was worth coming just for that. He found your number in Bruno's phone and called you before he called an ambulance. He was in a panic – you can see how he is, even now. He's terrified the kid's going to get into serious trouble. And we've just made it worse for him. No wonder he's pissed.'

'Patsy – this is horrible. That poor man. He was decent enough to get help, after all. You can't blame him for wanting to protect his boy. He never thought we'd follow him up like this. And he doesn't believe the stone hit Bruno hard enough to kill him. I mean – it was just a toy catapult. It's a surprise it even knocked him out.'

'Well it did.'

'I'm still not convinced.'

Bonnie was doing a magnificent job of capturing the whole thing, but now everything went silent, with the slam of a car door confirming that there would be no more to hear. Ben went slowly after the others, and met his girlfriend at the little gate.

'They're going,' she said.

'So now we have to get really brave,' he told her.

Chapter Twenty

Ben and Bonnie found the courage to go back down Blease Road and knock on the front door of the catapulter's home. The man who answered was plainly too stunned to slam the door in their faces. 'Sorry,' said Ben. 'But we were friends of the person who died – and we think we might be able to set your mind to rest about what happened.'

'That'd be nice,' said the man with a grimace. 'Go on, then.'

The youngsters gave a mostly truthful account of themselves and explained they were eager to demonstrate how they believed young Johnny – actually named Nathan – would be absolved of all suspicion.

'Although he did do a very bad thing,' said Bonnie judiciously.

'He did, and he's suffering for it,' said the father. After hearing their account of themselves, he readily produced the offending catapult and the boy to go with it. By means of careful persuasion Nathan revealed a small collection of stones that he'd been using as missiles. 'When he knocked that chap down, he was terrified,' said the father. 'We both went out to see him. I know we should have made a clean breast of the whole thing, but we didn't see how that would do any good, and I didn't want my boy with a police record, did I? So we called somebody in his phone, and then the ambulance. After that, we came back in and didn't show ourselves. Luckily my wife was out that day, as well as today – she's always out on Sundays. Goes to see her mother. She doesn't know anything about all this.'

Ben fingered the stones, which had been well chosen. Smooth, heavy and big enough to make a nasty bruise, they were worthy of a young David confronting his Goliath. But the catapult was little more than a toy, and the force could not have been very great. 'You must have a good aim,' he told the boy.

'Wrong,' said the man. 'He was trying to hit a pigeon on the other side of the beck. Your friend just got in the way.'

'Where's your sister?' asked Bonnie. 'It was her shouting at you that gave us the first clue about what happened.'

'Sister?' said the father. 'He hasn't got a sister.'

'She means Daisy,' the boy explained, and added to Ben, 'She lives down the road and comes to play sometimes.' He sighed. 'She's mostly a nuisance.'

Ben laughed. 'Don't go blaming her. Bruno's dad would still have come round today, regardless of what we heard. You might even say she's done you a favour. Without her we'd never have guessed about the catapult.'

'How's that doing us a favour?' The man frowned.

'Well, Mr Ackroyd and Patsy would still have come to find out what happened, but we don't think they're so likely to bother with reassuring you as we are.'

'This is starting to sound serious. Are you here in any sort of official capacity? Or what?'

'No – we said, we're just friends. But we are pretty sure the real cause of Bruno dying was something that happened on Thursday, not Wednesday. Your Nathan is a red herring.'

Nathan chuckled and began to appear a lot less chastened. Bonnie gave him another of her severe looks.

They finished by saying they hoped to establish beyond doubt that Bruno had died from some other cause than Nathan's unlucky strike. Phone numbers were exchanged before Bonnie gave the boy a final adjuration. 'Just don't ever do it again,' she said. 'Do you hear me?' She remembered very clearly the defiant tone with which Nathan had threatened his little friend earlier in the day, and accordingly became his harshest judge, with Ben and the boy's father both inclined to see it as a freak accident deserving no very stern punishment. *Boys will be boys* was the implied conclusion.

'I didn't like him,' she told Ben on the way home. 'I think he's a little beast.'

'He probably is, but he's not a murderer,' said Ben.

They drove back towards Hartsop full of theories and suspicions. 'We can talk it over with Simmy,' said Bonnie. 'If she's not too busy with the baby.'

'I'm not sure,' Ben said slowly. 'Let's just find somewhere to park and go through it again.' The main road was sprinkled with lay-bys for vehicles to pull off for a break, but the first few they passed were all fully occupied. Ben began to find the driving stressful, going too slowly with a procession of impatient tourists behind him.

'Turn off here,' ordered Bonnie suddenly, indicating a left turn to Greystoke. He obeyed meekly and they very soon found a convenient gateway.

For half an hour they sat and went over every detail. Throughout, they were blocked by a complete absence of discernible motive, and the means were obscure as well.

'But we're sure the child in Threlkeld didn't kill him,' Bonnie insisted. 'All he did was make it possible for the real killer to act.'

'And we've boiled it down to two,' said Ben. 'Don't you think?'

'We might be reading too much into what we heard,' she cautioned. 'And we still have no real idea of everybody's precise movements on Thursday.'

'So we'd better go and ask,' Ben decided. 'But first I need a bit more background information.' With no further delay, he phoned Jonty. 'How well do Patsy and Bruno's father know each other?' he asked his friend abruptly.

Jonty was unsure, but helpful nonetheless. 'I do know she's been around for a long time. Bruno once said something about her knowing him when he was in hospital with his heart, when he was about twelve.'

'What was the matter with his heart? I never knew anything about that.'

'One of those things you're born with,' said Jonty vaguely. 'A hole in it, I think. They fixed him up and he never had any trouble. It got him out of games, though.'

'So Patsy's always known about it.'

'Right. She used to come and meet him after school sometimes. She was a student and he was her case study. I suppose she went to the house as well.'

'So how old is she, exactly?'

'She must be twenty-five or so. Seven years older than him. That's why he would never let me call her his girlfriend. He said it sounded daft.'

Ben paused, before saying, 'Jonty, none of this is what I thought. What about the online gaming and all that stuff?'

'Oh yeah – they did that as well. If you ask me, she'd do anything to hang on to him. Whatever he was interested in, she'd have a go at to keep his attention. It worked – he didn't find it annoying or anything.'

'Did he *love* her?' Ben asked starkly.

Jonty gave an embarrassed laugh. 'Don't ask me. But he did say he supposed he would marry her in the end. When she was about thirty and he'd done his degree and got a job. He said she might have a few issues to work through first, before she'd make wife material. I was never sure whether or not he was joking about that.'

'OK. Thanks,' said Ben. 'Don't tell anyone I was asking, will you? Not for a day or two anyway.'

'No problem,' said the incurious Jonty, and Ben ended the call.

'Are we brave enough to call Derek next?' Ben wondered. 'And if so, what do we say?'

'He won't be surprised,' Bonnie judged. 'He's probably just waiting for you. Say you can't stop thinking about it, and wanted someone to talk to. He'll be flattered.'

'The trouble is, he wasn't there at the crucial time. He's

not much good as a witness. I really want to talk to Tilly and that's not going to happen, is it?'

'Not on the phone, no. We could try going there again.'

'Nothing to lose, I guess,' said Ben uneasily. 'I might let you do all the talking.'

The Smythe household was in no better state than it had been that morning. Again the little girl opened the door, but this time with the stains of tears on her cheeks. 'Oh,' she sighed, looking from one to the other. 'Hello.'

'Harriet – is that right?' said Bonnie softly. 'You look sad.'

The child nodded, and stood holding the door as if at a loss. 'They're shouting again,' she whispered. 'Like Bruno, when he shouts at Patsy.'

At that point Derek appeared behind his daughter, putting both hands on her shoulders. 'More visitors?' he said.

'Derek,' said Ben. 'Sorry . . .' He abandoned any attempt to explain himself. 'It's just . . .'

'Don't worry,' said the man. 'Let's go for a little walk. Hattie – you can come as well if you like. We need to escape for a bit, don't you think?'

The little girl smiled, her whole face suddenly brighter. Ben and Bonnie exchanged startled glances and meekly turned round to follow Derek, the child clinging to his hand. He led them to the end of the street, and towards a green area.

'Castle Park's just along here,' said Derek. 'We can see if there's any ice cream.'

Nobody said anything until Harriet pointed out an ice cream van parked close to the park gates. Derek produced some money and bought four cornets.

'That's more like it,' he said as they all began to lick the pleated white confection. 'A nice bit of normality for a change.'

'I can't walk and lick,' said Harriet.

They found a bench and sat in a row, watching two dogs tussling over a rope toy.

Ben took a deep breath. 'Bruno shouted at Patsy, then?' he said, aiming for a light conversational tone.

Harriet nodded. 'He said she had to leave me alone.'

Derek's head went up. 'Hey, Hat!' he protested. 'When did this happen?'

'When Bruno was in bed. Patsy was tickling me and picking me up. I screamed a bit because her fingers are very *hard*.' She smiled apologetically. 'I was too noisy,' she said with regret. 'And Bruno told Patsy to put me down. He said something funny, but it made her cross. And he said it again and that time *he* was cross as well. It wasn't very nice.'

There was a distinct sense of a story finally bursting out after several pent-up days. Derek went rigid, melting ice cream trickling over his fingers.

Harriet licked hers diligently, watching all three faces. 'I didn't mean to scream,' she mumbled.

'Do you remember what Bruno said?' asked Bonnie. 'The thing that was funny?'

'Oh yes. He said, "Don't be such a pervert". She put me down when he said it, and went all red and sort of *stiff*. Bruno told me to go downstairs. His daddy was there – downstairs, I mean. He came with Patsy and they brought Bruno a book and some toffee. He went to the

307

car and told her to hurry up. But she started playing with me instead.'

'You remember it all brilliantly,' said Bonnie admiringly. 'So then you went downstairs?'

Harriet nodded. 'I think they wanted to do some kissing, even though they were still cross. Well, actually, I don't really know. She told me to shut the door, so I did.'

'They stopped shouting, did they?'

Harriet nodded. 'It was only a *bit* of shouting. Bruno was too poorly to shout much. And then Patsy came downstairs, and was nice again and talked to Mummy for a little minute. Bruno's daddy was hooting the car horn outside so she had to go.'

'And you didn't go and see Bruno again afterwards?'

She shook her head. 'It was lunchtime and Lucy was making a fuss because she doesn't like mushrooms.' Derek threw his ice cream on the grass behind the bench, to his daughter's horror. 'Daddy! That's *littering!*' she accused.

'The dogs can have it,' he said. Ben and Bonnie forced themselves to finish their own before trying to say anything. Derek gently pulled Harriet to him and rubbed the top of her head with his chin. 'Such a good girl,' he crooned. 'It's going to be all right, precious. But before then, you might have to talk to some police people.'

'That's all right,' she said stoutly. 'I like police people.'

'That's good. I am so lucky to have you – you know that?'

'Don't cry, Daddy,' she said.

* * *

The inevitable call to Moxon came at around half past five.

'Don't panic,' came Simmy's voice. 'But Ben and Bonnie know who killed Bruno.'

'Evidence?' he said, trying to remain professional.

'Not much. That's going to be down to the pathologist.'

'Well, there I can give you good news. There'll be a full autopsy tomorrow. All thanks to me, though I say so myself.'

'Well done,' she applauded, and they both laughed.

She then went on to report the events of the afternoon, having been comprehensively updated by Ben and Bonnie. The youngsters were sitting at the kitchen table with her, prompting where necessary.

When she'd finished, Moxon had very few questions. 'I suppose we've got an answer to the motive,' he said slowly. 'If it's what it sounds like, there'll be trouble for the social services people.'

'Poor Bruno. He can't have had any idea how angry he'd made her.'

'I get the feeling that might just have been a final straw,' said DI Moxon.

Angie and Russell unexpectedly found themselves drawn into the climax of the investigation when they decided to visit Castlerigg on the way home. No new B&B guests were due that evening, and the existing ones could fend for themselves.

The stone circle was sprinkled with a few visitors, which the Straws ignored.

Russell spread out his arms and turned in a slow circle with his gaze on the distant peaks. 'There can be no better spot than this in the whole wide world,' he gushed. 'Just look at it! Doesn't it make you feel small!'

Angie was more quietly savouring the landscape, aware of a young woman not far off who was behaving oddly. Even more oddly than Russell, in fact. The person was sitting at the foot of one of the stones, rocking back and forth and making a low humming. A couple passing nearby gave her a startled look and hurried off. This was not something Angie Straw would do, as a matter of principle. Far from being sentimental and not especially good at empathy, she nonetheless had a strong sense of solidarity with anyone apparently pushed to the edge. Here was a refugee from society, by all appearances, with enough echoes of the 1980s to stir Angie's feminist soul. She squatted down and tried to catch the woman's eye.

'Hey!' she said. 'What's the trouble?'

It took a minute, but finally there was a reaction. There was focus and then recognition. 'I know you,' said the woman. 'Don't I?' The questioning frown, the flickering gaze, the sudden shake of the head all seemed to Angie to indicate a return to something like sanity.

'Do you?' Angie said.

'P'raps not. What's your name?'

'Angie Straw, and that's Russell over there. We've got a B&B in Windermere.'

'Oh.' Clouds fell again on the young face. 'Do you know Ben Harkness, by any chance? He lives down there somewhere.'

It took very few further questions to establish connection and identity. Angie became alert and suspicious. The conclusion felt inevitable.

'You killed Ben's friend Bruno, didn't you?' Angie said, flatly. 'That's why you're up here, trying to deal with what you've done.'

Russell had come closer, just in time to hear this sentence. Like the excellent husband he was, he instantly placed himself alongside his wife and prepared to take his lead from her. However extraordinary and unlikely it might be, he understood what was required of him.

But as it turned out, neither of the Straws had to do anything at all.

'That's right,' said Patsy, taking out her phone. 'I'll call the police now and tell them, shall I?'

The post-mortem revealed a sudden cardiac arrest, almost certainly induced by smothering with a pillow. Bruno's eyes were bloodshot – something that had initially been ascribed to his head injury. His imperfect heart had quickly succumbed to the attack, in the opinion of the pathologist. Presented with Harriet's testimony, Tilly Smythe confirmed the sequence of events, whereby Anthony Ackroyd had gone outside to sit in his car, waiting for Patsy.

'It was a good ten minutes before she joined him,' said Tilly. 'He was hooting furiously by then. I was trying to get lunch for the girls.'

A close scrutiny of Patsy Wilkins's work records revealed careful notes of concern regarding her behaviour with small girls. A recommendation was made that she be given minimal responsibility for children, erring on the side of caution. A very good worker with troubled adults, her superiors were anxious not to lose her.

Ackroyd described Patsy's relationship with his son as 'strange but harmless'. She had been good for him through much of his teenage years, but it had been evident that he was growing tired of her. 'And a bit uncomfortable at times,' the man added. 'He spent less and less real time with her, over much of the past year. My wife didn't like her in the house, to be honest. Our little girls were wary of her, which rang a few alarms. And you could tell Patsy was resentful about it. But you must admit she gave a very good impression of being horribly cut up by his death.'

'We see that a lot,' said the police officer who was interviewing him.

Moxon remained in Anglesey for the rest of the week, fully aware that he had been entirely peripheral to the case from the start. The weather remained acceptable and he set himself to walk a daily five miles along the numerous footpaths. 'Just like home,' he quipped. But Anglesey had the advantage of the Irish Sea and far fewer visitors. It became evident to him that the fashion for holidaying in North Wales had dwindled long ago. Cafes were in short supply and a lot of shops were empty. Somewhere along the line, the 'hospitality industry' as it called itself, had blinked, and carelessly let its customers drift off to the Algarve or Ibiza or even Cumbria.

When he got home, he went to see young Nathan in Threlkeld, at Bonnie's suggestion.

'Just to remind him that you know who he is, and he'd better behave himself,' she said.

'I'll do my best,' he said meekly. 'But I'm sure you know that it's just as likely to make him worse. With some boys, being the object of police attention works like a status symbol.'

'I don't think it'll be like that with this one,' she assured him.

Jonty and his parents gathered themselves into a closer unit as a result of it all. They felt betrayed somehow, not by any actual individuals, but the world itself.

'After my dad was killed, I thought it could never come near me again,' said Eddie. 'Murder, I mean. What's *wrong* with people?'

'Oh, you,' said his wife. 'The world has always been too much for you. Get back on to your rooftops and let the rest of us deal with the real stuff.' She gave him a little squeeze as she said it, and he remembered how they'd been twenty years ago.

Angie and Russell put a hand-made 'For Sale' outside their house, and within two days had an offer from a Birmingham couple who could not believe their good fortune. 'They're just like we were, all those years ago,' marvelled Russell.

Simmy and Christopher banned all discussion of murder that Sunday evening, once the call to Moxon had been made. 'You've done everything you can,' they told the exhausted youngsters. 'Now settle down and we'll find an old film to watch, before you take Bonnie home.'

It was midnight before Ben tiptoed back into Simmy's spare room, having managed to drive to Windermere and back without serious mishap until the final moment. He spent much of the night worrying about the scratch he had inflicted on Christopher's car whilst trying to fit it into its space by the house, in the dark.

REBECCA TOPE is the author of three bestselling crime series, set in the Cotswolds, Lake District and West Country. She lives on a smallholding in rural Herefordshire, where she enjoys the silence and plants a lot of trees.

rebeccatope.com

If you enjoyed *The Threlkeld Theory*, look out for more books by Rebecca Tope . . .

◀◆▶

To discover more great fiction and to place an order visit our website
www.allisonandbusby.com
or call us on
020 3950 7834

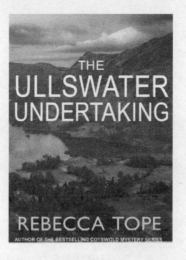

Spring has brought many new beginnings into the world of florist Persimmon 'Simmy' Brown. Not only has her baby arrived, but she and her fiancé Christopher have moved to the historic village of Hartsop in the Lake District – and they still intend to say their vows before the height of summer.

But when a former acquaintance of Christopher's reminds him of a promise he made a decade previously, their lives soon take a sinister – and deadly – turn. Yet even with a young baby to consider Simmy cannot ignore her instinct to investigate, especially with the personal link to her soon-to-be husband. Ably assisted by her would-be detective friend Ben, can Simmy puzzle out this reckoning from the past and protect her family in time for the wedding bells to chime?